MW01063157

MURDER IN THE BOOKSHOP

'THE DETECTIVE STORY CLUB is a clearing house for the best detective and mystery stories chosen for you by a select committee of experts. Only the most ingenious crime stories will be published under the THE DETECTIVE STORY CLUB imprint. A special distinguishing stamp appears on the wrapper and title page of every THE DETECTIVE STORY CLUB book—the Man with the Gun. Always look for the Man with the Gun when buying a Crime book.'

Wm. Collins Sons & Co. Ltd., 1929

Now the Man with the Gun is back in this series of COLLINS CRIME CLUB reprints, and with him the chance to experience the classic books that influenced the Golden Age of crime fiction.

THE DETECTIVE STORY CLUB

E. C. BENTLEY • TRENT'S LAST CASE • TRENT INTERVENES
E. C. BENTLEY & H. WARNER ALLEN • TRENT'S OWN CASE
ANTHONY BERKELEY • THE WYCHFORD POISONING CASE • THE
   SILK STOCKING MURDERS
ERNEST BRAMAH • THE BRAVO OF LONDON
LYNN BROCK • THE DETECTIONS OF COLONEL GORE • NIGHTMARE
BERNARD CAPES • THE MYSTERY OF THE SKELETON KEY
AGATHA CHRISTIE • THE MURDER OF ROGER ACKROYD • THE BIG
   FOUR
WILKIE COLLINS • THE MOONSTONE
HUGH CONWAY • CALLED BACK • DARK DAYS
EDMUND CRISPIN • THE CASE OF THE GILDED FLY
FREEMAN WILLS CROFTS • THE CASK • THE PONSON CASE • THE
   PIT-PROP SYNDICATE • THE GROOTE PARK MURDER
MAURICE DRAKE • THE MYSTERY OF THE MUD FLATS
FRANCIS DURBRIDGE • BEWARE OF JOHNNY WASHINGTON
J. JEFFERSON FARJEON • THE HOUSE OPPOSITE
RUDOLPH FISHER • THE CONJURE-MAN DIES
FRANK FROËST • THE GRELL MYSTERY
FRANK FROËST & GEORGE DILNOT • THE CRIME CLUB • THE
   ROGUES' SYNDICATE
ÉMILE GABORIAU • THE BLACKMAILERS
ANNA K. GREEN • THE LEAVENWORTH CASE
DONALD HENDERSON • MR BOWLING BUYS A NEWSPAPER • A VOICE
   LIKE VELVET
FERGUS HUME • THE MILLIONAIRE MYSTERY
GASTON LEROUX • THE MYSTERY OF THE YELLOW ROOM
VERNON LODER • THE MYSTERY AT STOWE • THE SHOP WINDOW
   MURDERS
PHILIP MACDONALD • THE RASP • THE NOOSE • THE RYNOX
   MYSTERY • MURDER GONE MAD • THE MAZE
NGAIO MARSH • THE NURSING HOME MURDER
G. ROY McRAE • THE PASSING OF MR QUINN
R. A. V. MORRIS • THE LYTTLETON CASE
ARTHUR B. REEVE • THE ADVENTURESS
JOHN RHODE • THE PADDINGTON MYSTERY
FRANK RICHARDSON • THE MAYFAIR MYSTERY
R. L. STEVENSON • DR JEKYLL AND MR HYDE
J. V. TURNER • BELOW THE CLOCK
EDGAR WALLACE • THE TERROR
CAROLYN WELLS • MURDER IN THE BOOKSHOP
ISRAEL ZANGWILL • THE PERFECT CRIME

MURDER IN THE BOOKSHOP

A STORY OF CRIME

BY

CAROLYN WELLS

**PLUS
'THE SHAKESPEARE
TITLE-PAGE MYSTERY'**

WITH AN INTRODUCTION BY
CURTIS EVANS

COLLINS
CRIME
CLUB

COLLINS CRIME CLUB
An imprint of HarperCollins*Publishers*
1 London Bridge Street
London SE1 9GF
www.harpercollins.co.uk

This Detective Story Club edition 2018

First published by Grosset & Dunlap 1936
'The Shakespeare Title-Page Mystery' published in *The Dolphin*
by the Limited Editions Club 1940

Introduction © Curtis Evans 2018

3

A catalogue record for this book
is available from the British Library

ISBN 978-0-00-828302-5

Typeset in Bulmer MT Std by
Palimpsest Book Production Ltd, Falkirk, Stirlingshire

Printed and bound in Great Britain by
CPI Group (UK) Ltd, Croydon CRO 4YY

MIX
Paper from
responsible sources
FSC
www.fsc.org
FSC C007454

This book is produced from independently certified FSC™ paper
to ensure responsible forest management.
For more information visit: www.harpercollins.co.uk/green

INTRODUCTION

THE resurgence of popular interest in vintage mystery fiction of the twentieth century has led to the revival of a steadily mounting number of crime writers whose works, though often extremely popular in their day, had long lain out of print and been mostly forgotten outside of occasional, cursory references in studies by genre specialists. One such renascent author is American Carolyn Wells, who once was characterized, in a 1968 magazine article by John Dickson Carr, past master of the locked-room mystery, as one of mystery fiction's 'lost ladies now well lost'. Today, a half-century after Carr penned those sad words, vintage mystery fans again are finding their way to the detective fiction of Carolyn Wells, and the former 'lost lady', now happily redeemed, is enjoying renewed popularity. This is a remarkable reversal of fortune which would, no doubt, have immensely amused the author, a woman known for her wryly humorous outlook on the myriad blows and buffets of life.

Born on 18 June 1862 in the town of Rahway, New Jersey to parents whom she termed 'the very ultramarine of Blue Presybyterians', Carolyn Wells, though comfortably circumstanced in a material sense, received at an early age some sharp slaps from the hand of Fate. Two of Carolyn's four siblings died in childhood, one from the same scarlet fever contagion that had struck her as well, leaving the future author's hearing progressively impaired over time. For the rest of her life she had to wear hearing aids to make speech partially audible. '[Deafness] doesn't bother me so much,' Wells later wrote forthrightly, 'but it is a hardship, and though I bear it smilingly it is an insincere smile.'

After graduating as valedictorian from Rahway High School, Carolyn Wells remained at the family home with her parents and her surviving sister, though she took classes with noted Shakespearean scholar William James Rolfe in Cambridge, Massachusetts and for years found a prized personal outlet in her service as head librarian at the Rahway Public Library. Wells departed the family nest for good at the age of 55 when in 1918 she wed Hadwin Houghton, a 62-year-old widower and cousin of a co-founder of the publishing firm of Houghton, Mifflin. The couple took up residence in Manhattan at the newly erected Hotel des Artistes, an elegant and exclusive apartment building overlooking Central Park that was later home for a time to such luminaries as Rudolf Valentino, Norman Rockwell and Noël Coward; but their connubial bliss was short-lived, Houghton passing away in 1919. 'I had him with me but a few years,' Wells fondly recalled of her beloved spouse, 'and those were so crammed with joyful interest that they are now my most blessed memory.' As a widow Wells remained in New York, residing with her housekeeper-companion and a cook at the same apartment at the Hotel des Artistes until her own death nearly a quarter-century later, in 1942.

Carolyn Wells made her entrée into the literary world through her interest in the nonsense literature of English authors Edward Lear and Lewis Carroll. Her earliest publications came in the form of humorous poetry which appeared in the 1890s in *Punch* and *The Lark*, a journal published and edited by her 'literary chum' Gelett Burgess (1866–1961), creator of those notorious fictional churls, the Goops, and author of a classic nonsense poem, 'The Purple Cow'. Wells was adept at word games and puzzles, a talent which served her well as an author of cleverly contrived nonsense but also came of use in her other major literary endeavour (aside from her popular children's tales about two irrepressible young girls named Marjorie and Patty): the writing of detective fiction.

Like Agatha Christie, Carolyn Wells first became smitten with detective fiction after hearing read aloud a book authored by American detective novelist Anna Katharine Green—although for Wells the inspirational text was not Green's bestselling debut mystery, *The Leavenworth Case* (1878), but rather a later, then contemporary, Green tale, *That Affair Next Door* (1897). 'To a listener entirely unversed in crime stories or detective work it was a revelation,' Wells recalled. 'I had always been fond of card games and of puzzles of all sorts, and this book, in plot and workmanship, seemed to me the apotheosis of interesting puzzle reading. The mystery to be solved, the clues to be discovered and utilized in the solution, all these appealed to my brain as a marvellous new sort of entertainment . . .'

Carolyn Wells's novice essay in crime fiction was 'The Maxwell Mystery', which appeared serially in May 1906, when Wells was 43 years old, and introduced to the world the patrician and perceptive Fleming Stone, by far the most renowned of the author's series sleuths. Wells published her first full-fledged Fleming Stone detective novel, *The Clue*, in 1909. A total of 82 Wells detective novels would appear between 1909 and 1942, of which 61 detailed the amazing investigative exploits of Fleming Stone.

During these fecund years, which also saw the publication of Wells's influential guide to writing mysteries, *The Technique of the Mystery Story* (1913), Carolyn Wells produced some of the most popular detective fiction in the United States, though admittedly she was far less well-known in the United Kingdom. (However, G. K. Chesterton, creator of Father Brown, once praised Wells as 'the author of an admirable mystery called *Vicky Van*'.) In the crime yarns, like *Vicky Van*, *The White Alley* and *The Curved Blades*, which Carolyn Wells published during the 1910s, the decade which immediately preceded the Golden Age of detective fiction, there cohered many of the elements— genteel country house settings, dastardly locked-room murders, fatally ferocious domestic squabbles—that today are commonly associated with mysteries from the bright and blindingly clever era of such insouciant yet implacable master sleuths as Hercule Poirot, Lord Peter Wimsey, Reggie Fortune, Philo Vance and Ellery Queen.

Throughout the 1920s and 1930s Carolyn Wells maintained her considerable popularity in the US, with sales of her mysteries more than quadrupling the average sales of most other crime writers. (Among her legion of fans during these years there numbered the young John Dickson Carr.) By early 1937 Fleming Stone detective novels through direct sales had grossed almost one million dollars, something on the order of seventeen million dollars today, putting her in the select company of such Golden Age American mystery writers as S. S. Van Dine and Mary Roberts Rinehart, authors who actually managed to become wealthy though mystery writing. This was a time, we should recall, when most detective fiction devotees borrowed their favoured form of reading fare at the cost of a few cents a day from rental libraries.

Contemporary newspaper interviews with Wells typically took note of her beautiful luxury apartment filled with exquisite antiques. Having been bitten, like her crime-writing countryman S. S. Van Dine, by the collecting bug (though Van Dine's passion, for a time, was tropical fish), Wells amassed a valuable hoard of nearly five hundred Walt Whitman volumes, which she bequeathed upon her death to the Library of Congress. In her pursuit of Whitman she was amply assisted by renowned bookseller Alfred F. Goldsmith, who for three decades, up to his death in 1947, did business from the Sign of the Sparrow, his basement book-shop on Lexington Avenue in Manhattan, a veritable Mecca for bibliophiles. Together in 1922 Wells and Goldsmith authored *A Concise Bibliography of the Works of Walt Whitman*.

Fourteen years after her collaboration with Alfred F. Goldsmith, Carolyn Wells fictionalized the Sign of the Sparrow as the site of the first slaying in her 43rd Fleming Stone detective novel, the bibliomystery *Murder in the Bookshop* (1936), which she also dedicated to her friend. Alfred Goldsmith has been credited with the droll remark that 'the book business is a very pleasant way of making very little money', yet in *Murder in the Bookshop* a rare book really is something to die for, with characters desperately vying for possession of a tome worth an estimated $100,000 (about $1.7 million today). The fatally contested book, an abstruse treatise on taxation, has been thrice signed and annotated by no less a personage than Button Gwinnett, one of the 56 signers of the American Declaration of Independence, whose autograph remains in especially high demand from collectors today on account of its rarity. Gwinnett was slain in a duel less than a year after he signed the Declaration and today there are only ten of his autographs held in private hands, one of which recently sold in New York for $722,500.

When avid book collector and Button Gwinnett fancier Philip Balfour is found literally skewered to death in John Sewell's rare bookshop, there are suspects aplenty in the wealthy New Yorker's death, including not only John Sewell and his smooth assistant, Preston Gill, but Balfour's charming young wife, Alli; his earnest librarian, Keith Ramsay (who has admitted to being enamoured with Alli); and his own son by a prior marriage, Guy Balfour, something of a feckless man-about-town. Though the police find themselves baffled by the murder of Balfour and the theft from Sewell's shop of the Button Gwinnett book, Fleming Stone fortunately is at hand to provide illumination. Yet even the great Fleming Stone has his hands full with crime this time, what with a second devilish murder (this one taking place in a locked bathroom), a ruthless abduction and the Great Detective's own entrapment inside a locked room! In this deadly game of *Button, button, who's got the button?*, will it be Fleming Stone or the murdering fiend who comes out the winner? You surely do not have to be another Fleming Stone or Philo Vance to deduce the answer to that question.

Appended in this volume to Carolyn Wells's *Murder in the Bookshop* is 'The Shakespeare Title-Page Mystery', a short story originally published in 1940 in *The Dolphin*, the journal of the Limited Editions Club of New York. Eleven years earlier Wells had provided an introduction for the Club's lovely edition of Walt Whitman's literary landmark, *Leaves of Grass*, and it was to *The Dolphin* in 1940 that she contributed one of her very few works of short detective fiction. This tale of literary shenanigans (with murder included) concerns the sudden appearance of a pair of putative first edition copies of Shakespeare's narrative poem *Venus and Adonis* (1593), likely the Bard's very first publication. Possibly Wells was partly influenced in the writing of this mystery by recent shocking revelations concerning the nefarious activities of British bibliophile Thomas J. Wise, who in fictionalized form figures in British mystery writer E. R. Punshon's detective novel *Comes a Stranger* (1938).

At the end of Carolyn Wells's story—one of the last pieces of detective fiction which the author, who died in 1942, ever published—we learn of a rare book that providentially survived German air raids in London and made its way over to safety in the United States. Until the war is over and the book's true owner is located, pronounces one of the characters in the story, good care must be taken of it: 'The precious little volume is also a refugee, and a refugee is ever a sacred trust.' Wells did not herself survive the war, passing away in her eightieth year, and her books shortly afterward went out of print for many decades, but today vintage mystery fans can in one volume read both 'The Shakespeare Title-Page Mystery' and *Murder in the Bookshop*, a pair of bibliomysteries that are among the rarest works in Wells's vast—and once vastly popular—corpus of crime fiction.

CURTIS EVANS
February 2018

TO MY LONG-TIME FRIENDS
MR AND MRS ALFRED F. GOLDSMITH
THIS BOOK IS DEDICATED
IN ALL GOOD-WILL

CONTENTS

CHAPTER I

THE CRIME IN THE BOOKSHOP

Mr Philip Balfour was a good man. Also, he was good-looking, good-humoured and good to his wife. That is, when he had his own way, which was practically always.

When they came to live in New York, Philip Balfour wanted to live on Park Avenue and Alli, his wife, wanted to live on Fifth Avenue. They lived on Park Avenue.

Then, Balfour wanted a duplex apartment, and Alli was all for a penthouse. So they had a duplex.

To be sure, they could have found an apartment which combined the two horns of the dilemma, but they didn't. Philip didn't favour a penthouse.

And in her three years of married life Alli had learned that compliance is the best policy. She was a darling, Alli was, with soft, short brown curls and soft, big brown eyes. Tallish, slender and carelessly graceful, she devoted her energies to the not-too-easy task of being Philip Balfour's wife. With full realization of what she was doing she had thrown over, actually jilted, a young man she was engaged to in order to become Mrs Balfour.

And had seldom regretted it. Although her husband was twenty years older than herself, she was naturally adaptable, and save for one problem that was at present engrossing her attention, she was quite happy.

She adored her home and lavished time and money on its adornment and improvement.

The main room, intended as a drawing room or living room, was enormous and was Balfour's library. He was a retired Real Estate man and an enthusiastic collector of old and rare books.

1

He had a capable and experienced young man for his librarian, but Alli did much to assist in the care of the books.

Of late, Balfour had noticed that Keith Ramsay, his valued librarian, was not quite as effective as he had been. The young man sometimes forgot to attend to an order or seemed unsure as to his collations or translations.

And when, one evening, he sat listening to his employer talk, he showed such a brooding air and such a vacant countenance that Balfour said:

'Whatever is the matter, Ramsay? Are you ill? Are you worried about something?'

'Yes, I am, Mr Balfour. Shall—shall I tell you about it?'

'If you like,' was the indifferent reply, for the speaker somehow sensed that the matter was unconnected with his books.

'Then, to put it plainly, I am giving you what is, I believe, called "notice".'

'You're not leaving me, Ramsay?' Balfour was roused now. 'That will never do! Want more salary? Anything wrong in the house?'

'That comes near it. Something wrong in the house—with me.'

'Out with it, then, and we'll soon settle it.'

The two men were alone in a small room adjoining the library. This was used as an office and also held a small specially built safe, which housed the most valuable volumes.

'I wish we could, Mr Balfour, but I doubt it. To state my case in a few words, I am in love with your wife and, therefore, I have decided to leave you as that seems to me the only honourable course.'

'You are indeed frank. You are acting nobly, I have been told angels do no more than that. And may I inquire if Mrs Balfour returns your affection?'

'I have not asked her. I am told that to run away from danger is considered a cowardly act, but that is what I propose to do. It will be best for us all.'

'Pardon me, if I disagree with that statement. It may, of course, be better for you—and possibly for Mrs Balfour—to see no more of one another, but don't undertake to say what is best for me. You are very necessary to my well-being—I cannot so readily dispense with your services. I never can find an assistant who is so perfectly fitted to look after my books, my future purchases and my collection generally. I have no intention of letting you go because of a silly flirtation between you and Alli. In fact, I think you overestimate your own charms. I doubt my wife is seriously interested in you or your attentions. So just drop the idea of leaving me. I'll speak to the lady herself concerning this, but I desire you to stay with me in any case.

'I appreciate your taking the stand you have, it is a manly thing to do. But I can't take the matter seriously, and I'd rather send her away than see you go. Now, put it out of your head until tomorrow, anyway. Tonight, later on, I want you to go over to Sewell's with me on that little marauding expedition we have planned. Good Lord, Ramsay, I couldn't possibly get along without you! Don't be silly!'

'I'll go to the bookshop with you, Mr Balfour, but don't consider the other matter settled. We'll speak of it again.'

'All right; I'll choose the time for the conversation. We'll go over to Sewell's about ten. Be ready.'

'What are the books we're after?'

'Two small Lewis Carroll books. Not stories, they are mathematical works. One is *Symbolic Logic* and one is *A New Theory of Parallels, Part I*. Not very valuable, yet hard to find and necessary to keep my collection up to the mark. Also, he may have the Button Gwinnett. If so, we'll annex it.'

Philip Balfour went into his library and was at once absorbed in his books. He was a true bibliophile. Every time he looked over his treasures it seemed to him he saw new beauties and new glories in his possessions. Pride entered into his satisfaction, but just for his own gratification he loved his books and cherished their beauty and rarity.

Keith Ramsay was entirely in sympathy with him and they had worked together happily, until the loveliness of Alli had blurred the title page or the errata of the volumes he was examining or collating.

It had been a tremendous effort for him to tell his employer, and the way Philip Balfour took the confession so amazed him that he was bewildered at the situation.

But he had no intention of changing his plans and was still fully determined to leave the next day. He went upstairs to do a little more packing and in a dimly lighted corridor met Alli.

Unable to resist, he took her in his arms and she laid her head against his shoulder as they stood in utter silence.

Then, 'You spoke to him?' she whispered.

'Yes; but he flouted my confession and wants me, for his own selfish ends, to stay on as his librarian. I can't—darling, you *know* I can't do that!'

'You must, Keith, you *must*. Think of me.'

'It's you I'm thinking of. No, sweet, it must be a complete break. I can't risk the danger for you that it would mean if I stayed here. Especially now that he *knows*!'

They drew apart suddenly as a maid came round the corner from a cross corridor.

'You two are going over to Sewell's tonight?' Alli said to Keith in a casual tone.

'Yes, very soon now—and I may not see you again.'

The maid had disappeared, and if she had not it is doubtful if Alli could have controlled herself. She reached up and kissed Ramsay on the forehead and breathed a low-voiced 'Good-bye.'

But it was not the end, a desperate embrace followed, and when at last Keith let her go, it was to turn and face Philip Balfour as he reached the top stair.

'Let's go,' Balfour said, as if he had seen nothing unusual and Ramsay went for his hat and coat.

Keith Ramsay had not at all intended to do what he had done, but there are times when human volition takes a back seat and the physical senses carry on. The occurrence made him more than ever certain that the sooner he got away from the beloved presence the better.

A few moments more and the two men were walking down Park Avenue for a few blocks and then crossing over to Lexington, on which Sewell's Secondhand Bookshop had its abode.

Its façade was not impressive, save to the lover of old bookshops. It was not of the modern building type, where one walks in on a level with the sidewalk; it was not a passé brownstone front, where one climbs twelve or fourteen steps to get in.

But it was the sort where you go down a few stone steps and find yourself in a room that has seemingly settled itself down below the street level.

A room after the own heart of E. L. Pearson, who speaks of it as a place where one feels a shyness in the presence of books.

It has not that odour of sanctity which to amateur bibliophiles means the smell of old leather.

The room discovered after descending Sewell's three stone steps was large and hospitable. The walls were book-covered up to the high ceiling, and on tables and benches and chairs were more books. And not only books, there were fascinating bits of curious crafts. Old glass, Early American as well as foreign stuff. Pretty tricks, like ships in bottles and silver teaspoons in a cherry pit.

But mostly books. Books you'd forgotten and books you wished you had forgotten. Rare books and always genuine. Queer books, holy books and poems by the Sweet Singer of Michigan.

But all these things were in the great front room. There was a smaller room back of it, where the more nearly priceless volumes were kept in safes, and where conferences were held that often proved John Sewell's right to the title awarded him as most knowledgeable of all the dealers in the city.

And it was to this back room that Philip Balfour and his librarian made their way.

They did not go round on Lexington Avenue at all. From the cross street—they were walking on the south side—they turned into an alley about midway of the block.

The dark wooden gate swung easily open and the two men stepped through, a few more paces bringing them to the rear of the shop.

It seemed inadvisable to use a flashlight, but they knew their way and Ramsay felt round for the window-sill.

'Are you going to open door or window?' Balfour whispered, and Ramsay returned:

'Window, I think. The door creaks like an old inn signboard.'

'Have you a thin-bladed knife?'

'Rather,' and Keith opened the article in question. Then he slipped it between the sashes and the window went up easily.

He stepped inside, unlocked the door and opened it carefully, to minimize the creak, and Balfour entered.

Ramsay closed the door and said, 'What about lights?'

'Of course we must have light,' Balfour told him. 'I think they'll not be noticed; it isn't very late and undoubtedly Sewell is often here of an evening. Turn on two, anyway.'

Ramsay snapped on two small side lights and they looked about the room. A little more formal than the front room, there were lockers and cupboards instead of book-shelves and a large table with several chairs around it.

The room had a scholarly air—every item was of definite interest and of distinct historic or literary value. On the walls were old prints and portraits; a panoply of savage weapons; some rare bits of textile fabrics.

Ramsay loved the room. It was one of his greatest pleasures to lounge there while John Sewell and Philip Balfour discussed bookish themes.

Sometimes there were caucuses, where six or eight connoisseurs and collectors gathered to exchange views, or more likely to get the benefit of Sewell's views.

Many experiments had proved the futility of trying to catch

him with a name he had never heard. However obscure or of however recent prominence, Sewell invariably proved to be thoroughly acquainted with the man and his works, his history and his place in the literary world.

On a side table lay some delightful old silver toys. Groups of tiny people playing games or working at ancient machinery. Sets of furniture, of silver or gold filigree, and silver boxes of bewildering and intricate charm.

There was a silver skewer, a foot long, plain, with a ring fixed in the end for utility, that might once have been used in the kitchen of some lordly manor or regal palace. Fascinating bits, everywhere.

Ramsay knew all of these by heart. Balfour knew well any of them in which he took a personal interest, and meant some day to purchase.

A silence fell, as the two men hunted sedulously for the volumes they hoped to find. Both found it hard to resist the continual temptations to pause for a dip in this or that tempting volume or brochure, but both put aside the thought and worked diligently.

At last Ramsay found a book that made him open his eyes wide. It was not a very large volume, and it was labelled *Taxation in Great Britain and America*. He glanced across the room at Balfour, and saw only his back, the book-lover being absorbed in a volume he was scanning.

Ramsay slipped the book he had discovered into the side-pocket of his topcoat, which he had not removed, as the place was chilly. After which, he went on with his search, noting that Balfour was still engrossed in reading.

Suddenly, the lights went out and the room was in black darkness. Ramsay turned and stumbled in the direction of Balfour.

It was some time later that Keith Ramsay sat down at Sewell's desk and took up the telephone.

He tried, and successfully, to control his voice as he said:
'Give me Police Headquarters.'

The response came duly, and it was swiftly arranged that Inspector Manton, with a detective from the Homicide Bureau and others would arrive as soon as possible.

Then Ramsay called Sewell at his home.

'No,' Mrs Sewell told him, 'John isn't home. Anything wrong?'

This question Ramsay ignored and said:

'Do you know where Mr Sewell is? Can I get him? It's rather important. Or do you know where Gill is?'

'No, I don't know anything about Preston. But you *may* find Mr Sewell at the Balfour home. I think he intended to go there this evening. Who is this? Where are you speaking from?'

'Thank you,' said Ramsay, briefly.

He cradled the instrument and sat back in the swivel chair, looking deeply thoughtful and carefully avoiding any glance in the direction of Philip Balfour, who lay dead on the other side of the room.

After a moment he took the telephone again, and called the Balfour home.

'Potter,' he said, as the butler responded, 'don't mention my name, understand?'

'Yes, Mr—Yes, sir.'

'That's right. Is Mr Sewell there?'

'Yes, sir, he is talking with Mrs Balfour.'

'Ask him to take a telephone message on this extension. If he wants to know who's calling, say you don't know.'

'Yes, sir.'

And in a few moments Ramsay heard John Sewell's voice inquiring as to his identity.

'Keep quiet, Mr Sewell, don't mention any name. But come down here to your shop right away. I can't tell you on the telephone, but there's serious trouble. Get here as soon as you can, but don't breathe a word to Mrs Balfour. Tell her you're called to the home of an important customer or something of that sort.'

'All right, I get you. Be there in two jumps.'

Sewell returned to the library where he had been sitting and told Mrs Balfour that he must hasten away on important business. He bade her good night in his courteous way and shook hands with Carl Swinton, another caller.

'Glad I'm not leaving you quite alone, Mrs Balfour. When your husband returns, please tell him I will see him tomorrow about the Button book. He will be pleased, I know.'

Sewell went away and strode down Park Avenue, then crossed over to Lexington.

With his key, he entered his own front door, and finding the front room dark, went quickly through it to the lighted rear room.

As he did so, the police arrived at the back door, which Ramsay opened to them.

Sewell stared at the incoming visitors, stared harder as he saw Balfour's body on the floor, and stared hardest of all at Keith Ramsay, who seemed to be going about like a man in a dream.

'Well, now, what's this all about?' asked the Inspector.

'That's what I'd like to know,' Sewell declared; 'can you explain, Ramsay? Who killed Mr Balfour? Is he dead?'

'You called Headquarters, sir?' and Inspector Manton looked at Ramsay.

'I did.'

'Will you please tell your story? Please explain the conditions we find here?'

'I'm not sure that I can, but I'll tell all I know.'

'Go to it, my boy,' Sewell urged. 'How did you get in the shop? Has Gill been here? Who jammed that skewer in Balfour's breast?'

'Just a moment, Mr Sewell. Let me conduct the inquiry.' Inspector Manton had a nice way with him, but his speech was a trifle dictatorial. 'Tell me names, please. Who is the dead man, and who are you?'

Keith began, slowly. 'The man who is dead,' he said, 'is Mr Philip Balfour, who lived on Park Avenue, several blocks farther uptown. He was a wealthy man, retired, and devoted to the hobby of collecting old and rare books. I am—was—his librarian, and I had charge of the details of the library's business affairs and kept it in order generally.'

'And I can vouch for both of them,' declared John Sewell, eager to vindicate his friends from any thought of wrong-doing. Mr Balfour was one of the finest gentlemen I have ever known and Mr Ramsay is an ideal librarian.

'Facts we're after,' put in Captain Burnet of the Homicide Squad. 'What are you two men doing here, and who killed Mr Balfour?'

'Were you here when these men arrived, Mr Sewell?' asked Manton, who thought he had heard Sewell come in just as he came in himself.

'Well, no,' Sewell returned, looking a little perplexed. 'I just came in myself, as you did. Tell your story, Keith.'

'I will,' and Ramsay's face grew stern and set, 'but I am afraid you'll find it hard to believe.'

'Out with it,' Sewell urged. 'I know neither of you two did any wrong, whatever happened.'

The Inspector nodded at Ramsay and he began.

'It was the wish of Mr Balfour to come here tonight to see about some books. He bade me telephone Mr Sewell that we were coming, but I couldn't get him on the telephone, so Mr Balfour said he was probably here at the shop and we would come along, anyhow.'

'H'mm,' observed Sewell, not with any seeming doubt, but expressing a mite of surprise.

'So we came over soon after dinner and, as Mr Balfour wanted to find a couple of books, we both looked for them.'

'What were the names of these books?' asked Burnet.

'They were two of Lewis Carroll's less well-known volumes. One was *Symbolic Logic* and the other *A Theory of Parallels*. You know them, Mr Sewell?'

'Yes, yes; oh, yes,' he replied, but Captain Burnet shrewdly declared to himself that though the sagacious book-dealer doubtless knew the books, he did not know why Mr Balfour was over in his shop hunting for them.

But he said nothing and Ramsay went on.

'You may find this hard to believe,' he hesitated a little, 'but I swear I am speaking only the exact truth. I was looking along those shelves opposite the outside door and Mr Balfour was on the other side of the room, near the door. I heard no unusual sound, saw nothing unusual, when suddenly the lights went out and the room was in total darkness.

'Then I heard a thud as if Mr Balfour might have fallen to the floor, and I tried to grope my way over toward him, when I was chloroformed. Don't tell me I don't know what I'm talking about, for I do. Someone grasped me, held a saturated cloth against my nostrils and held me so firmly that I couldn't move, until I became unconscious. The swivel chair, the desk chair, was nearest, and I assume my assailant seated me in that after I was entirely oblivious.'

'Who was your assailant?' asked John Sewell, gravely.

'I've no idea. I can only assume the intruder was a swift worker, that he put me out of commission, then took that long silver skewer from the table there, drove it into Mr Balfour's heart and departed.'

'You think Mr Balfour put up no fight?'

'I can't say. But it's quite possible that the killer chloroformed his victim and then stabbed him when he was helpless.'

'Go on.'

'I've little more to tell. After a time, I've no means of knowing how long, I began to come out of the stupor and even then it took some time to regain my full senses. When I was able to do so I went over and looked at Mr Balfour and saw him as you see him now. I looked hastily round, saw no intruder present, saw no definite or striking evidence that anyone had been here, yet there was the dead body of my employer and friend. I did the only possible thing, I called the police. Then I tried to get Mr Sewell. He was not at home, but Mrs Sewell told me he was probably even then at Mr Balfour's house, and I called up and he was there. I asked him to come here without telling Mrs Balfour anything about it, and I assume he did so.'

'I did,' said Sewell, 'and of course I believe your story, Keith. In fact, it's the only thing that could have happened. How else could Philip Balfour have been killed?'

'For my part,' said the detective, 'I don't believe one single word of Mr Ramsay's recital. We will investigate it, of course, but it doesn't ring true to me.'

CHAPTER II

DOCTOR JAMISON, the Medical Examiner, was what the novelists call a strong, silent man. Two not indispensable traits for one of his calling, for his strength was seldom needed and his silence was frequently exceedingly annoying.

On his arrival, he gave a brief nod that seemed intended as a general greeting, and went straight to the body of Philip Balfour.

The situation seemed to him quite apparent. Beyond doubt, Philip Balfour had been killed by the vigorous stab which had also felled him to the floor.

'What's this thing?' the Examiner demanded, carefully drawing the long weapon out of the wound.

'It's an old silver skewer,' Sewell told him. 'Early English, Georgian, most likely. It is my property and was lying on that table beside you when last I saw it.'

'Then it was handy for the murder,' exclaimed the Inspector. 'They often pick up a weapon on the spot. Eh, Jamison?'

The doctor made no verbal reply nor did he look toward the speaker. Manton held out his hand for the skewer and took it gingerly on a sheet of cardboard he held ready.

It was a beautiful piece. Twelve inches long, exactly, it tapered from the point to the ring at the top, which measured an inch across.

The ring and the blade were all in one piece, the ring being not unlike a plain wedding ring.

'There's a hallmark on it,' Manton observed, 'you know, four little bits of squares under one another with designs in them. A lion and a sort of crown and a letter H and something I can't make out. And above it all, some letters—'

'Give it to me,' said Burnet, 'you'll spoil the fingerprints—if any.' The Captain took the skewer and laid it carefully aside.

The finger-print man, who with the camera men had come at the time Jamison did, turned his attention to the weapon.

'It served its purpose,' he remarked; 'in all the detective stories, the killer uses a dagger from foreign parts, masquerading as a paper-cutter. I'll bet there's no prints on it. The killer was too cute.'

'He knew his way about,' vouchsafed John Sewell. 'He took his ready-made weapon from the table and he lifted it with a cloth that belongs here. See that piece of flannel on the floor beside Mr Balfour's shoulder? That's a duster I keep to flirt around now and then. And I keep it in this desk drawer, which, as you see, is now empty. So you're looking for a chap who knows this place familiarly.'

Sewell stopped suddenly, for he realized this could be made to apply to Keith Ramsay, who sat staring at him but saying no word.

'Oh, yeah,' said Detective Burnet. 'You been here before, Mr Ramsay?'

'Many times,' said Keith, speaking indifferently.

'I have a couple of dozen friends who come here ten times as often as Mr Ramsay,' Sewell declared, 'and they all know where I keep that dust-cloth. That's no clue. But I'll give you a pointer. A new development in finger-printing allows prints to be secured from fabrics—a trick only lately used. Save that duster, Inspector, you may bring in your man with its help. And you needn't look toward Mr Ramsay; I wouldn't have mentioned it if it were possible to imagine him implicated.'

The Examiner rose from his stooping posture and said, succinctly: 'Stabbed straight through the heart with that skewer. A strong, hard blow. Died practically instantly. Stabbed by a man who used his right hand. Took the blow without resistance, so probably unconscious at the moment.'

'Was he chloroformed, too?' asked Burnet.

'I think not. More likely knocked out by a blow. Here's a lump on his jaw made by a blow that would have smashed an ox.'

'How long's he been dead?' Manton asked.

'Dunno. Not long. Half an hour more or less.'

'The blow on his jaw didn't kill him?'

'No. Guess I'll be gettin' on, now. You can send the body to the morgue. Any notion who killed him?'

'No,' said John Sewell, before anyone else could speak.

'I have,' said Keith Ramsay, slowly. 'It comes back to me now that a man came in at the back door—it must have been the back door, because I heard a slight creak—and I heard a noise like someone falling, and when I looked round, I saw a man with a black satin mask on coming toward me, and as I looked past him, toward Mr Balfour, I saw he was crumpled up on the floor.'

Detective Burnet regarded the speaker with unconcealed derision.

'Just made that up?' he inquired, sarcastically. 'An important fact like that, and you forgot it in your first account!'

'Exactly,' returned Keith; 'and you'd forget things, too, if you were given a knock-out dose of chloroform.'

'Tell me a little more about the man in the iron mask,' said Manton as the Medical Examiner went away.

'It wasn't iron,' said Keith, seriously. 'But it was black satin. Not just a piece of stuff with eyeholes cut in it, but a regular, well-made mask, like you'd buy for a party.'

'You looked at it very carefully, Mr Ramsay,' and Manton shook his head a little.

'Not consciously. For a few seconds I saw the man coming toward me and, as I stared, the mental picture of that mask fixed itself in my brain permanently. I think I should know it if I saw it again. It was stitched round the edges and had a sort of ruffle that covered his mouth and chin.'

Burnet looked at him with mock admiration.

'You certainly succeeded in getting a mental photograph of the thing, didn't you?'

'Couldn't help it,' Keith said, carelessly. 'You see, when the lights went out it was dark, but always, in a few seconds, one's eyes adjust themselves to the change and you sort of see things dimly. I did, anyway. I heard Mr Balfour fall and then I discerned this figure coming toward me. I could see a large white handkerchief, or cloth, in his hand, but my attention was caught by that mask and I stared at it. I could see his eyes glittering through the eyeholes and then, in a moment, the sickening whiff of chloroform came to me and though I struggled for a few seconds, I lost consciousness. When I came to the lights were on and Mr Balfour lay on the floor with that skewer sticking in his heart. The man was not here.'

'How long were you under the influence of the anaesthetic?' asked Manton, looking at him curiously.

'I've no idea,' returned Ramsay; 'how could I have? One doesn't time one's actions in such circumstances.'

'Yet you seem to have a pretty clear idea of what went on.'

'Not at all. When I regained consciousness, which came slowly, I saw Mr Balfour dead—'

'How did you know he was dead?' interrupted Burnet.

Keith Ramsay looked at him, calmly. He did not seem to resent the Captain's questions, but he seemed to think him ignorant or impertinent.

'It doesn't require a very vivid imagination to assume a man is dead when he lies motionless, in a distorted position, with a dagger in his heart.'

'What did you do?' asked Manton.

'I started to cross the room, to go to him, but I found myself wobbly and had to wait a few moments to get steady enough to walk.'

'And then you walked?'

'I did. My brain cleared more rapidly than my muscles co-ordinated, and when I found myself at Mr Balfour's side I sat down in that chair and thought out what to do.'

'And you decided to call Headquarters?'

'I did. That is the duty of any citizen who discovers a crime. I was, of course, aware that you would at once conclude that I was the criminal. That is for you to prove, if you can. I did not kill Mr Balfour, I would have no reason for doing so. He was a splendid man. I admired and respected him. I used my best efforts to be a satisfactory librarian to him and he said I was one. I have learned much about rare books, both from him and from Mr Sewell, and I am deeply interested in collecting them.'

'Yes, yes, Mr Ramsay,' the Inspector said, 'but let us get to the facts of what happened here this evening. At what time did you and Mr Balfour come here?'

'I think soon after ten o'clock. Mr Balfour said we would start at ten, but we were delayed a little.'

'I'm not quite clear about the details of your visit. If Mr Sewell was not here when you arrived, how did you get in?'

John Sewell looked at Ramsay. He had every confidence in the young man, but he very much wanted to hear the answer to that question.

The witness hesitated. Implicit as Sewell's confidence was, he had to admit to himself that Keith Ramsay looked like a man with something to conceal.

Detective Burnet spoke.

'I'll tell how you got in, Mr Ramsay; you forced an entrance through that back window.'

He pointed to a window in the rear wall next the door.

It was closed now, but the detective had examined it. He went on: 'You shoved back the catch with a jack-knife or something like that, pushed up the window, climbed in—'

'And then opened the door to Mr Balfour,' said Keith, calmly. 'Yes, Inspector, that was the way of it. I think, Mr Sewell, if I tell you it was all right, you will believe me.'

'Well, yes,' Sewell returned, 'but it seemed a little odd at first.'

'Seems odd to me yet,' declared Burnet. 'Why the breaking and entering act, Mr Ramsay?'

'I can give you no answer to that except the truth. Mr Balfour was exceedingly anxious to come here tonight. He wanted to find two certain books that are missing from his library, and he thought they might be down here—by—by accident.'

John Sewell showed amazement in every line of his countenance.

'What's that, Ramsay? What books are you talking about?'

'Please leave the witness to me, Mr Sewell. The titles of the books are of no interest, we want to get at the facts of the murder. Go on, Mr Ramsay. Did Mr Balfour, then, come here on a secret errand? Did he know Mr Sewell would not be here and he would have opportunity to hunt for his books by himself?'

'That I can't say. It was Mr Balfour's habit to keep his plans or motives to himself. Many a time I would start off with him having no idea of our errand or our destination.'

'Did you go to the front door first?'

Sewell began to look more and more amazed; Keith Ramsay became more and more hesitant and embarrassed.

'We did not,' he said, after a pause. 'Mr Balfour stopped at a narrow alley that runs part way through the block, and we came along that until we reached the rear of this house, and Mr Balfour asked me if I had a pocket-knife and if I could force the window catch with it. I could and did, but I do not look upon it as a felonious entrance for we had no wrong intent. If Mr Sewell had been here, Mr Balfour would have knocked at the door and been admitted.'

'Are you often here of an evening, Mr Sewell?'

'Oh, yes, frequently.'

'And does Mr Balfour, when he visits you, always come to the back door?'

'Why, I don't remember. No, not always.'

'Sometimes?'

'Y-Yes.'

'I think, Mr Sewell, that you must admit that this is the first time the gentleman ever came here and arrived at the rear entrance. Isn't that right?'

'Oh, I don't know. I don't remember. What has that to do with it, anyway?'

'Only that, unless it was his habit, it seems very strange for Mr Balfour to make the entrance he made this evening.'

'Oh, very well, we'll agree it was strange. But of no consequence as I can see.'

A heavy tread was heard, as of someone coming through the big front room. In a moment a shock-headed youth appeared in the doorway.

'Hello,' he said, cordially. 'What's going on?'

'How did you get in?' asked Burnet, gruffly.

'Through the front door with my latch-key. My God! What's that?'

He stared at the still form, now covered with a spread from the police equipment.

'Who—who is it?' he stammered.

Sewell spoke gently. 'Sit down, Gill. Inspector, this is Mr Gill, my assistant. He has a key and comes and goes at will.'

'Is it somebody dead?' Gill persisted, looking now at Manton.

'Yes, Gill,' said the Inspector, 'it is Mr Philip Balfour. As you are here, will you give an account of your own doings this evening? Where have you been since, say, nine o'clock?'

'Well, no, Inspector; I don't care to give an account of myself, unless you have reason to demand it. Was Mr Balfour murdered? Or why the Criminal authorities?'

'Yes, Mr Balfour was stabbed by an unknown assailant.'

'Gee! Can you find out who did it?'

'We hope to, and we fully expect to. You are not helping us by your refusal to answer my question.'

'It wouldn't help you any if I did answer it. And I haven't

been in this vicinity until just now. I was passing, I saw a light, so I came in. Your henchmen in the front room didn't want me to pass, but I rather insisted and they gave in. What about it all, Mr Sewell?'

'Do you know anything about two small mathematical books that are missing from Mr Balfour's Lewis Carroll collection?' Sewell said.

'Sure I do. Want 'em? Here they are.' He took from his overcoat pocket two small books and handed them to Ramsay.

'Yes, these are the right ones,' and Ramsay laid them on the table beside him. 'Thank you.'

'What are you doing with them, Gill?' and John Sewell looked a bit accusing.

'It's all right, Guv'nor. Tell you all about it some other time. Of no interest to these uninterested onlookers. Get down to cases. Who killed poor old Balfour?'

'We'll find out,' Burnet told him. 'Let's hope it wasn't you.'

'Don't try to get me fussed,' Gill said; 'I'd hate to kill anybody. I never have, as yet, and I doubt I ever shall. Did some person or persons unknown kill Mr Balfour? I've a right to know about things, haven't I, Mr Sewell?'

'Yes, so far as I am concerned. In my opinion, a marauder came here, masked, and stabbed Mr Balfour with our old English skewer. The long silver one. There it is on the table.'

'I see it,' and Gill rose and went to the table. 'Don't be alarmed, Inspector, I shan't touch it. What's going to happen next?'

'This, for one thing.' Sewell looked anxious. 'I want you to look, Gill, and see if that little book that came today is all right.'

Gill went round the room, taking books from the shelves, here and there diving into well-filled chests, opening certain drawers, and camouflaging his real place of search, turned back to his employer, and said:

'No, Mr Sewell, it is not in the place I left it.'

'No? That's bad. Inspector, I am fairly positive that a very valuable book has been stolen from this room. A volume worth, to a collector, perhaps a hundred thousand dollars.'

'Now, now, Mr Sewell, I've heard collectors tell big yarns, but that's a whale this Jonah finds hard to swallow.'

'Value it at less, if you choose, but call it one of the most eagerly desired books in America. And now can you bring this session to an end? Or can you excuse me? I am deeply saddened at the tragic death of my friend, but this loss is not unconnected with the case. The book in question was destined for Mr Balfour and it is not impossible that the intruder who stabbed him also stole the book. There you have a motive. But in any case, I want to get busy about finding the volume. If you want to stay here—'

'On the contrary, I do not want to stay,' but the Inspector looked perplexed. 'I think I will let them take Mr Balfour's body to the morgue, and I myself will go to the Balfour home, and acquaint the family with the facts of the case, in so far as we know them. Mr Ramsay will go with me and, of course, Captain Burnet. What is the family?'

Sewell answered. 'Only his wife, I think. No one staying there, is there, Ramsay?'

'No, not just now; they have lots of guests, coming and going, but nobody at present.'

'There was a chap calling when I was there just now,' Sewell said, 'but he'll most likely be gone.'

'If not, we'll chuck him out. Come on, Inspector, let's go. I want to get some dope on this case. Sergeant Glass, here, will see to the morgue arrangements and he'll make the report, *res gestae* evidence and all.'

Captain Burnet's energy overcame Inspector Manton's natural inclination toward delay and they were in the elevator, going up to the Balfour apartment, before any word had been said as to who should tell Mrs Balfour of the tragedy.

'I'd better do it,' Sewell said, as they walked along the hall. 'You're too nervous, Ramsay.'

Keith nodded his head without speaking.

He had his key with him but he preferred to let Burnet ring the bell, which Potter answered.

Sewell stepped forward.

'We must see Mrs Balfour, Potter,' he said; 'give us a room where we can have a conference. The matter is important.'

The butler showed them into a formal reception room and went away.

In a moment Alli was with them.

In a black velvet hostess gown, her only ornament a rope of pearls, she came into the room with a calm composure that only those who knew her best could see was achieved by a desperate effort.

'What is it?' she said; 'I know it is tragedy of some sort. Where is Mr Balfour? Why are the police here? Tell me—'

She moved a step toward Ramsay, but John Sewell stayed her.

'Sit down, Mrs Balfour,' he said. 'It is a tragedy of which we must tell you. And I think it kinder to tell you the frank truth at once. Your husband was at my shop this evening, while I was here, and some mysterious intruder attacked him with a—a sort of dagger—'

'And killed him—'

She spoke in a low tone, her great dark eyes gazing at him as if she were hypnotized. She sat motionless save for a quiver that shook her slender figure now and then.

'Yes,' said the Inspector, who felt this was his scene. 'We have to bring you this sad news, and I trust you will be willing to answer a few questions that will help us in our search for the criminal.'

'Of course,' and her voice suddenly became tense. 'I know you have to investigate the case at once. I am quite willing to tell you anything I can. Do not be afraid, I shall not break down.'

Sewell looked at her pityingly. He saw she was straining her nerves to retain her composure and he marvelled at her success.

'You knew where Mr Balfour was this evening?' asked Manton.

'Yes, certainly. He and Mr Ramsay went down to Mr Sewell's shop to see about some rare books.'

'What books, Mrs Balfour, and what did they want to see about them?'

'I haven't the least idea. I am interested in my husband's collection as a whole, but I know nothing of details or transactions.'

'You knew that Mr Ramsay went with him?'

'Oh, yes; I saw them go.'

'Will you tell me the happenings here the rest of the evening?'

'Why, yes. I sat in the library and read a magazine. A telephone call came from a friend and I talked quite a long time with her. A friend who lives in this building dropped in for a little call and Mr Sewell also called. Mr Sewell seemed anxious to see Mr Balfour and I asked him to wait as I expected my husband home soon.'

'And Mr Sewell waited?'

'Yes, until called away by telephone. Then he left the house, seeming a little preoccupied, I thought.'

'And this was about what time?'

'Why, I don't know. Somewhere around eleven, I should say. But I'm not at all certain, I never know the time.'

'Your other caller was still here?'

'When Mr Sewell left? Yes. He went away shortly after.'

'He lives in this house, you say? What is his name?'

'Yes, he has an apartment on the second floor, I think. His name is Mr Swinton and he is a long time friend of Mr Balfour and myself.'

'Well, now, Mrs Balfour, this may sound a hard question, but I must ask it. Do you know of anyone, anyone at all, who would have any wish to kill Mr Balfour?'

'Certainly not!' The brown eyes blazed. 'He was a man friendly to all. He had few intimate friends, but he had a very wide circle of acquaintances and I am perfectly sure no one of them would wish him the slightest harm.'

'He was on friendly terms with Mr Ramsay, his librarian?'

She smiled faintly. 'Indeed, yes. I often told him he spent more time with Mr Ramsay than he did with me.'

'You helped him with his books?'

'I couldn't really help him, but I often sat in the library while they discussed the books and I learned more or less about them.'

'Did you know that Mr Balfour had bought or was about to buy a book from Mr Sewell that would cost something like a hundred thousand dollars?'

'Oh, yes, I know all about that. Did you get it, Mr Sewell?'

'The deal is still hanging fire. I can't yet give a final report.'

'It is probable, Mrs Balfour,' Burnet put in, 'that your husband's death is due to his possession of that book, and—he was possibly killed by a member of this household.'

CHAPTER III

GUY DEMANDS HIS RIGHTS

IF Captain Burnet expected to shock Alli Balfour, he must have
been disappointed.

She sat up straight, resting her hands on the arms of the
high-backed chair, and said in a gentle voice:

'Don't talk in riddles, Captain. What do you mean by household? We are only three here. My husband, myself and Mr
Ramsay. Do I understand you suspect Mr Ramsay—or me?'

'Not you, madam, certainly not.' This from Manton. 'But
there are circumstances that make us feel that your husband's
librarian must be asked a few questions.'

'Ask him, then, by all means. He was a great favourite with
my husband. Mr Balfour depended on him for all matters
connected with the library. The slightest suspicion of Mr
Ramsay's guilt is too absurd. But I hope you will prove this to
your own satisfaction.'

'We sure will,' Burnet told her. 'Now, Mr Ramsay, where is
this very valuable book that has been spoken of?'

'I've no idea,' Ramsay declared. 'It was Mr Balfour's errand
tonight to get the volume from Mr Sewell, who, Mr Balfour
supposed, had it ready for him.'

'Where was this marvellous volume to come from?' and the
Captain turned his inquiring glance on Sewell.

'That information is entirely unnecessary to your work,
Captain Burnet, and I don't care to give it. Transactions in the
more valuable rare books are, as a rule, confidential among the
parties concerned. However, the book has disappeared and if
you can find it in the course of your investigation, I shall be
glad indeed to see it again.'

'How large is the book? Could Mr Balfour have found it and put it in his pocket?'

'In an overcoat pocket, yes. Not easily in a coat pocket.'

'You don't care to tell me the name of the book?'

'I don't, and I'll tell you why. The book itself is not the treasure. It is the fact of the owner's signature on the fly-leaf and some other points, not of any meaning to the man in the street, but significant to collectors. It is quite possible that Mr Balfour found it on my shelves. If so, he had every right to take it, for I bought it for him and should have given it to him at the first opportunity. If there's a chance that it was in his over-coat pocket, will you not telephone the morgue and find out? His clothing will be cared for there.'

'I'll do that,' and Burnet rose and left the room.

'I don't see what all the fuss is about,' said Gill, who had been listening with a perplexed air. 'If a bad man came in and killed Mr Balfour and knocked out Ramsay, why consider any other possible criminal, and why not assume he has the rare book and set to work to get it back?'

'It is not so easy as that, Mr Gill,' and Manton looked at him closely. 'There are many angles to be considered. For instance, you will probably be asked to give a more definite report of how you spent this evening than you have yet done.'

'Rubbish! I was miles away at the time the killing took place.'

'At what time did the killing take place?'

'Lordy! don't you know that? And you an Inspector! I thought you nailed down the time the very first thing.'

'I'd be glad to. But nobody seems to know anything about it. When did you leave the shop?'

'About eight. And as I was back there something like half-past eleven, I'm assuming Mr Balfour was attacked between those hours. Now who did it? For if it was someone who wanted that book, it is conceivable that was the motive for the crime; but if the murderer was someone who knew nothing of rare books, then we have two criminals to look for.'

'Where was the book?'

'Like Mr Sewell, I can't consider that question relevant. I will only say that it was in the shop when I left there, and when I returned it was not there.'

At this moment, Captain Burnet came back. He looked a little excited.

'I called the morgue,' he said, 'and they will look for the book. It hasn't been noticed so far. But I learned some more vital evidence. May I ask, Mr Ramsay, why your belongings are all packed up? Your clothes in trunks and suitcases, your books in boxes and your rooms partly dismantled?'

'Yes,' and Ramsay spoke indifferently. 'I planned to go away—on a trip.'

'A longish trip, I take it, from the amount of luggage made ready. I fear we cannot let you go tomorrow, Mr Ramsay. What was to be your destination?'

'I planned a short stay in Boston where I have some business, and then I expected to go abroad.'

'On a book-buying trip for Mr Balfour?'

'No, on business of my own.'

'Then, you were leaving Mr Balfour's employ?'

'I had intended that, yes.'

'Did Mr Balfour know of this move?'

'He did.'

'And approve of it?'

'No, he did not approve of it,' Alli broke in; 'Philip didn't want him to go at all. In fact, he wouldn't agree that Mr Ramsay was going. He just said, "Oh, nonsense," whenever it was spoken of.'

'Will you explain this situation, Mr Ramsay?' Inspector Manton asked. 'Your belongings all packed to go away, yet your employer did not want you to leave him. What was luring you away from this position, which seems ideal for a man of your tastes and ability?'

Keith Ramsay hesitated. Then he said, slowly, 'I had the offer of a more advantageous position.'

'More lucrative?'

'No, not that. But more desirable for other reasons. I cannot feel, however, that these queries have anything to do with the crimes we are considering. Mr Balfour wanted me to stay on here because I can be of help to him in his library. But that has nothing to do with the matter of his murder or with the disappearance of his rare book.'

'We are not entirely sure of that.' Manton looked grave. 'A book that is worth anything like a hundred thousand dollars is as much a motive for crime as a great diamond or emerald.'

'That is true, Inspector, but as I am innocent of murder or theft, I cannot see why I am, or seem to be, under suspicion.'

'I do not say you are under suspicion, Mr Ramsay, but I do want you to defend your actions. The question, at present, centres round your visit with Mr Balfour to the Sewell bookshop this evening. I still feel you have not made clear the reasons for your getting in by the window.'

'That's nothing,' Sewell declared, 'my customers are welcome to come in by the window if they like. I wish I had been there when Mr Balfour came.'

'Where was this wonderful book you are talking about? Was it hidden in your shop?'

'Now, Inspector, don't talk like that. What's the use of my having a snug hidy-hole, if I tell where it is? I have several rather clever places of concealment for books that I want to conceal. But if I tell of them, they are secret no longer. But the book was hidden in my shop and now it is missing. And it must be found. I am sure it was stolen by the murderer of Mr Balfour, so I think the two mysteries may be treated as one.'

'How many people knew of this rare volume?'

'Not many,' Sewell returned. 'I heard about it and had to have a long correspondence with its owner, before I could induce him to part with it.'

'My good Heavens!' exclaimed Alli Balfour, 'we must notify Guy.'

'Who is Guy?' Manton inquired.

'He is Mr Balfour's son, the child of his first wife.'

'Where is he?'

'In the city. He lives down in Greenwich Village somewhere. We must let him know about his father. Keith, will you see to it?'

'It will be attended to,' said Manton. 'Captain, you telephone, will you? What is the address, Mrs Balfour?'

She told him, and he asked a few questions about the young man.

'No, he doesn't live with us,' Alli told him. 'Oh, yes, we are all friendly, perfectly so. But Guy belongs to the younger set— not exactly Bohemian, but modern and—er—informal. The sort of people Mr Balfour didn't enjoy. So it was arranged that Guy should live by himself. His father gave him a liberal allowance.'

'And is young Mr Balfour interested in rare books?'

'More or less. It is difficult to be in the house with an enthu- siastic collector and not fall under the spell of the old volumes. I knew almost nothing about it when I married Mr Balfour, but I have learned a little, and now that the library is mine, I want to keep it up and care for it and add to it, as my husband would have done had he lived. I sincerely hope Mr Ramsay will stay for a time and advise me about the collection.'

'You know then the conditions of Mr Balfour's will? The great library will be yours?'

'Yes; with the exception of his son, and some charities and minor bequests, I am the sole legatee.'

'Mr Guy Balfour is in the habit of coming here often?'

'Yes, he is frequently here for dinner or to spend the night. He and his father were congenial in many ways.'

'How old is the young man?'

'About thirty-five.'

'You are not as old as that yourself?'

'No, I am twenty-five. Mr Balfour, my husband, was nearly fifty-six. But the difference in our ages seemed negligible, we

were so at one in our interests and in our tastes and temperament.'

In response to Burnet's call, Guy Balfour came.

Of medium height and graceful carriage, he entered the room
and, seeing no vacant seat near Alli, fetched a chair from the
other side of the room and placed it beside her.

Then he sat down, took her hand in his, and said, 'Tell me
all about it.'

He took no notice of the others and leaned toward his stepmother, awaiting her response.

A handsome chap, with fair hair that curled and dark blue
eyes that seemed both wise and mysterious. Yet his aplomb
bordered on insolence and did not at all please Inspector
Manton.

'I will give you the details, Mr Balfour,' he stated firmly. 'You
must realize that this is an official inquiry, not an informal
gathering. When did you see your father last?'

'Why, I don't know—a few days ago, I guess. When was I
up here last, Alli?'

'Wednesday night, I think. Or maybe Tuesday.'

'Tuesday it was. And now it's Friday. I think that's the way
of it, Inspector.'

'You were here, then, last Tuesday evening?'

'To the best of my memory and belief, yes.'

Guy's tone was not really sarcastic, but it gave an impression
of superiority and sounded as if he were patronizing his ques-
tioner.

Manton realized this but imperturbably forged ahead.

'You've not seen him this evening, then?'

'Certainly not. What has happened? Has Dad committed
some crime? Or why are the police present?'

He still showed no serious concern, but when Manton said,
gravely, 'Your father is dead, Mr Balfour,' he voiced an explosive
'No!' and became eagerly inquisitive.

'Tell me about it,' he cried. 'Somebody called up and ordered me to come here at once. Gave no reason. Now you tell me this! Where is he? Who did it? What happened?'

'Hold on there, Mr Balfour,' Burnet said, sharply; 'if you didn't know your father was dead, why do you say, "Who did it?" implying that your father was killed—?'

'Killed? Of course, that is plain on the face of things. My father has not been ill. I come here on an order that gives me no reason for the call. I get here and find my father absent, the police here, and my father's wife pretty much all gone to pieces, what else can I think but that my father was done in by some-body?'

'Can you not think that your father may have been the aggressor and may have been—say, arrested?'

'No! I can't think anything like that of Philip Balfour! But you've no right to bait me. Tell me the truth.'

'I think you should know the truth, Guy,' and John Sewell's voice was stern and positive. 'Your father was killed this evening down at my shop. The criminal was some unknown person who came in, masked, and stabbed him.'

'Who was he? Who did such an awful thing? You must find out, you police fellows; if you don't, I'll find out myself!'

'I wish you could, Mr Balfour. But ranting and railing are to no effect. Can you tell us anything helpful about the circum-stances? Had your father a fear of anyone? Any thought that he might be molested or attacked?'

'Why no, of course not. Father was afraid of nobody! How ridiculous! He took the greatest precautions about the safety of his books but I never heard him express any fears for his life.'

'You live down in the Village?'

'Yes; Washington Square, South. But I shall move up here at once. You've no objections, have you, Alli? I am now, of course, head of the family, I shall take my father's place in the house and look after the library.'

'You are familiar with the contents of your father's will?'

'N-no, not exactly. But I am his only son, and naturally I inherit the estate.'

'Don't bank on that, Guy,' Alli advised him; 'you know that your father was very fond of me.'

'Yes, and I suppose you wheedled him into leaving you a lot of property that should by right be mine? Oh, I'm not complaining, but though you are Dad's present wife, I am his only child and I must have my rights.'

'If you please, Mr Balfour, keep your attention on the subjects in hand. We have no knowledge, as yet, of Mr Balfour's disposition of his estate. Who are his lawyers—or his trustees?'

'I don't know; you must get all that from his wife.'

'I shall do so. And now, will you give me an account of how you spent this evening, before you came here?'

'Well, no, I'd rather not.'

'And I'd rather you would. Besides it will save you trouble to do so. For otherwise we shall have to find out for ourselves, and though we can easily do that, it would mean more or less unpleasantness for you as we should have to inquire among your friends and that would look as if you were an object of suspicion.'

'Suspicion! Of killing my father?'

'Not necessarily that, but there was a very valuable book stolen tonight from Mr Sewell's shop and—I understand you are a collector.'

'Collector? Bah! I have a few odd volumes that my father gave me now and then. He said I'd better save them up for a rainy day, as they would always sell for a goodish bit. But I say, Mr Sewell, did you get the Taxation book?'

'What is the Taxation book, Mr Sewell?' asked the Inspector, quickly, before Guy could be answered.

'Please don't discuss that this evening,' Sewell said; 'I don't want to divulge its title at this moment. You shall learn all about it in due time, Inspector Manton. Meanwhile, if I can be of no further use, may I be allowed to go home? My wife will be getting anxious.'

'Yes, you may go, Mr Sewell, also Mr Gill. Since Mr Balfour plans to stay at this house, I shall adjourn this inquiry until tomorrow morning, when we will resume it. I shall then want to see the lawyer and also the servants of the house as well as the principals. Mrs Balfour, what are your wishes concerning the immediate disposal of your husband's body?'

Alli raised imploring eyes to him, as if this brutal question were the last straw.

'I—I—'

Keith Ramsay spoke for her. 'I think, Inspector, Mrs Balfour can better decide that in the morning. Can it not be left where it is until then, when arrangements can be made for the funeral?'

'I'll see to those things,' Guy volunteered. 'Mrs Balfour and I will look after the family details. I'm your right-hand man, Alli, and you can safely trust everything to me.'

She said, 'Yes, Guy,' and gave him a small smile that might mean anything at all and that did mean nothing.

She looked relieved as Guy seemed about to leave them.

'I can be excused, I suppose?' he said; 'I want to get settled in my new quarters. I'll send for my duffel in the morning. Alli, I'm going to adopt Dad's suite. It can be shut off entirely from yours, you know, and I feel it is my right to have it.'

'Very well, Guy, go ahead.' She looked at him a little distantly but made no objection to his plan.

'You're fond of that young man?' Manton said, casually, after Guy had gone.

'Not quite that,' Alli returned, 'but, after all, he is his father's son, and unless the will forbids it he has certain rights, ethically, if not legally. All those things will straighten themselves out.'

'What character do you give your stepson?' Burnet asked.

'Guy is a fine fellow. He is like his father in many ways. He has his faults, of course, but they will pass with the years. He has a splendid sense of family honour and loyalty.'

'Devoted to his father, eh?' Burnet looked dubious. 'Yet they couldn't live in the same house.'

'Don't be silly!' and Alli looked at him scornfully. 'I explained that. Guy is hospitable by nature, though his father was not. The boy would have gay parties and late parties, and my husband was disturbed of his rest. But now Guy may come home if he likes. I don't mind his frolics.'

'You are none of you definitely held on suspicion,' Manton said as he rose to go. 'But you are all held as material witnesses. I shall expect you here tomorrow morning, Mr Sewell, and Mr Gill—at about ten o'clock.'

The policemen went away leaving a strong guard on the place, which might have disturbed Alli had she known it.

John Sewell advised his assistant to go home, saying he would remain a little longer.

Left alone with Alli and Keith Ramsay, Sewell declared his intention of instituting a search for his missing book on his own account.

'The police are all right,' he said, 'on a murder case, or most other crimes, but a rare book, especially this particular one, is a matter outside their technical knowledge. So I am going to engage a friend of mine, Fleming Stone, to take up the matter of the book. And I'm wondering, Mrs Balfour, if you'd care to have him look into the mystery of your husband's death?'

'What do you think, Keith?' Alli said, in a puzzled way. 'I know so little about these things, but perhaps Mr Stone might be a great help to us.'

'Don't think I'm disparaging the police,' Sewell went on, 'for I am not. They know their business, and they do it, but this Stone chap is a wizard for getting at the heart of a mystery. And to my mind, the death of Philip Balfour is more of a mystery than the theft of the book. They may be the work of the same criminal and they may not. I can't help thinking there is some connection.'

'So far as I am concerned,' Ramsay said, 'I'd welcome the

help of Fleming Stone. I've heard a lot about him and he seems to me a wonder-man.'

'Oh, he isn't one of those story-book detectives, who startle you with their marvellous and often useless discoveries. But he is a deep thinker and a quick reasoner and, since I know his worth, I mean to ask his help. Of course, that means I should have to acquaint him with the details of this evening's tragedy and he will, I'm sure, be interested. But nothing need be said about his coming in on it unless you want him, Mrs Balfour. Perhaps you prefer to talk it over with Mr Guy Balfour—'

'No,' said Alli, quickly. 'I do want him, and there's no reason why I should discuss it with Guy. I positively want to engage Mr Stone to investigate the murder of my husband and I ask you, Mr Sewell, to make arrangements with him, if possible. You've no objections, Keith?'

'No, I haven't. He will probably suspect me—as the police do, but if he is as clear-headed as Mr Sewell says, he can't know the truth and still think I killed my employer and benefactor. I certainly approve of the plan and hope he can take up the case. Will the police mind?'

'No,' said Sewell, 'they like him and he often works more or less with them.'

'Call him up now,' Alli suggested, 'and ask him about it.'

'Pretty late,' said Keith.

'Not for him,' Sewell returned. 'He's up till all hours and it's only a bit after midnight.'

Alli urged it and so Sewell called the detective.

He was at home and agreed to take any case at the request of his friend Sewell. He proposed that he come to the Balfour apartment at once and talk it over.

'That's the sort of man I like,' Alli exclaimed, as Sewell relayed the conversation, 'tell him to come right along, we're all glad to see him.'

'I think and I hope, Alli,' Ramsay said, 'that this man can help us. I haven't yet told all I know, but I hesitated to do so

until the inquiries have gone further. I suppose, Sewell, I must
be entirely frank with Mr Stone?'

'Oh, yes, you can trust him as you would yourself. I am sure
you know more about the Taxation book than you've told, but
that's your own business. Just be utterly frank with Fleming
Stone and I'm sure both crimes will be driven home. I would
advise that we three see him alone, for though Mr Guy Balfour
is one of the family, I don't want to tell him about the missing
book at this juncture. And if Stone is to be with us, I'm glad
to talk to him before the police go further with their work.'

'Is he a formidable man?' asked Alli; 'shall I be afraid of
him?'

'No; he is charming. You can't help liking him.'

CHAPTER IV

FLEMING STONE TAKES THE CASE

FLEMING STONE arrived at half-past twelve.

Alli was somewhat surprised at his appearance. She saw a quiet, rather scholarly looking man, with a sympathetic face and correct manners.

He spoke first to Sewell, shaking his hand and saying, 'Hello, old chap,' and then, as Sewell presented him to Alli, he expressed so courteously his appreciation of her tragic sorrow that she liked him at once.

Keith Ramsay, too, felt quick confidence in the newcomer and after a few preliminary words Stone turned to the business in hand.

'Am I to understand,' he began, 'that my activities are to include two crimes, or only one?'

'I couldn't make it very clear over the telephone,' Sewell told him, 'but there are two distinct matters to come to your attention which may be interdependent or may not. My part in the matter is of an exceedingly confidential nature, involving, as it does, the disappearance of a rare and valuable book. Mrs Balfour's case concerns a much more serious crime, the killing of her husband.'

'Let me make a suggestion,' Alli offered, 'there is a room to which I think we might better adjourn. It is a small room, one that Mr Balfour had made sound-proof in order that he might negotiate for valuable books without fear of being overheard.'

'Yes,' said Sewell, 'let us go there. I know that room.'

So they went to the little room in question and found it comfortable and pleasant, with the added advantage of sound-proof walls.

'We are keeping nothing back from the police,' Ramsay said, 'but we don't want their men who are still here to get information ahead of time.'

The room they were now in was simply furnished with a table and writing materials, a small safe and a few chairs.

They told their stories in turn, Ramsay first, as he was with Philip Balfour during his last hours; Sewell next, as coming in later, and Alli last, as knowing nothing of it all until they brought her the awful news.

Fleming Stone listened attentively, making a few notes now and then.

Finally he said: 'I want to know all about this valuable book. It looks as if that might have brought about the murder, though I don't, as yet, see just how. What is the book, Sewell?'

'I'll tell you. Remember it must not be mentioned in any way, or to anybody, without my knowledge and sanction. You've heard of Button Gwinnett?'

'Yes,' Stone said. 'He was one of the signers of the Declaration of Independence.'

'Exactly that. And he is one of two whose autographs are the most difficult to find. Many collectors, you know, strive to get a full set of autographs of the signers, but nearly all of them are unable to achieve the rare one of Gwinnett. His simple signature has sold for more than fifty thousand dollars, and a book that he had owned and had autographed and had annotated would easily be worth twice that. Now, I have obtained such a book. I got it through one of my London agents. Gwinnett was an Englishman who came over here to live, entered into our politics and became a signer of the Declaration. The next year he was killed in a duel—he was a hot-headed chap—and lived in Georgia.'

'And what is the book?' Stone asked.

'It's a small book, a pamphlet, but in fine condition. It is entitled *Taxation Laws of Great Britain and U.S.A.* Gwinnett was a student of Government and Politics and this was his book.

He had not only autographed it on the fly-leaf but had signed it two other times and, moreover, had made annotations in his own hand on various pages. So you can grasp the importance of the book. Such finds do occur, but very seldom. Mr Balfour was prepared to pay a large price, although he and I hadn't entirely agreed yet as to exact terms.'

'And this book, worth a fortune in itself, is now your property, Mrs Balfour?'

'If the purchase is completed,' Alli said, looking uncertain. 'Mr Balfour's will is in his lawyer's keeping, and I only know that he told me the library would be mine at his death. So I assume that is the case. The question of my buying that expensive book, now, is between Mr Sewell and myself; of course I cannot decide right away.'

'Of course not,' Stone agreed. 'But, now, Sewell, where is the book?'

'I'll answer that question,' Ramsay announced. 'I have it.'

'You have it?' Sewell exclaimed, in amazement. 'Are you sure?'

'I am. You see, it was this way. Mr Balfour and I went to the bookshop to hunt for two small volumes belonging to Mr Balfour that were unaccountably missing. Sewell wasn't there and Mr Balfour didn't want him to be, for he feared the books had been stolen by Mr Gill. He decided on a still hunt so we went in by the window. As we were searching, I came across the Gwinnett book inside another book. This is a common dodge. We all have apparent books on our shelves, which are really only book covers and into which we tuck a rare or a precious book, as a hiding-place. Now, when I spied the Gwinnett book, inside the cover of a detective story, I slipped it in my pocket for the simple reason that I knew if Mr Balfour saw it, he would immediately forget all about the books he was looking for and lose himself in the new treasure. I wanted him to continue his search, and, when he was ready, to go home and show him the Gwinnett book there, where he could examine

it and enjoy it at his leisure and in safety. I felt a little afraid of
opening it down there, for the light might attract a policeman,
or an intruder of another sort. It is a smallish book and I slipped
it in my overcoat pocket.'

'And where is it, now?' Sewell asked, looking at Ramsay in
an odd way.

'Since I came home, I went in the library and placed it in
one of Mr Balfour's trick books. It is concealed in the fourth
volume of Gibbon's *Rome*, a book which looks just like the
other volumes, but is hollow.'

'Go and get it, Ramsay,' and Sewell looked disturbed.

'No, you go; or Mr Stone. If this must be told to the police,
they will probably suspect me of something—I don't know
what, but they're just crazy to make me out a villain.'

'I'll go,' Sewell said, and left the room.

'You both must be rather familiar with rare books,' Stone
said, looking at Balfour's wife and librarian.

'Mr Ramsay is,' Alli said, 'but I have only a smattering. My
husband told me a lot about them but I forget most of it. It is
imperative, Keith, that you stay here long enough to get the
library sold; I can't have the responsibility of such a valuable
affair. As to this new book, I shall probably buy it as Mr Balfour
really ordered it. And it will add just that much to the value of
the lot.'

Sewell returned with a small book, carefully wrapped in
paper, sealed, and labelled, with a pen, *Taxation Laws of Great
Britain and U.S.A.*

He closed the door carefully, and locked it.

'Lucky we have this safe room,' he said, sitting down at the
table—to which they all drew up their chairs. 'A book like this
must be handled as privately as a Kohinoor. Here is the little
volume that Keith brought home, and hid in a volume of the
Decline and Fall of the Roman Empire. Now, Mr Ramsay, as it
happens, this is not the book Mr Balfour wanted at all.'

'What nonsense are you talking?' Keith asked. 'It's labelled.'

'I know, but it's a fake package. I made it up myself.'

Sewell took off the paper wrapping, disclosing an inner one of cellophane. It was his habit to do up rare books this way.

But as he removed the wrappings and came to the little book itself, it proved to be a small but thick catalogue of rare books from a London firm.

Ramsay stared and so did the others.

'I did this up like this,' Sewell went on, 'to fool anybody who might endeavour to annex this big find of mine. It's all very well to say no one knows of it, but there is a grapevine telegraph among dealers that sometimes works havoc with secrets. Anyway, as you see, that is a dummy parcel, and most naturally fooled Ramsay, when he saw it.'

'Of course,' Stone assented. 'Now, Sewell, where is your real book?'

'That's the trouble. I had that hidden in a pile of old junk, in a closet. It was in among a lot of old newspapers and magazines, for I thought it was better to conceal it thus than to put it in my safe. But it is gone, and unless Ramsay brought that along, too, I don't know where it is.'

'I did not find that,' Ramsay declared, 'but I'll prophesy this: when Captain Burnet hears of this, he'll say I'm the thief. You see, as I was found on the spot, and as I have no way to prove my innocence, they're ready to nab me for anything.'

'They shan't do it, Keith!' and Alli looked militant. 'Mr Stone, you will straighten it all out, won't you? Mr Ramsay was in the full confidence of my husband, he was also Mr Balfour's friend and advisor. He is incapable of crime—as your friend, Mr Sewell, will tell you!'

'I stand by Ramsay,' Sewell said, seriously. 'I, too, feel that he is incapable of the grave crimes that have been committed tonight. But the book is still missing and though of minor importance when we think of Mr Balfour's death, yet I hope, Stone, you can solve both mysteries.'

'Now, for the usual questions,' Stone said. 'Had Mr Balfour any known enemies?'

'No,' said Balfour's wife. 'Unless they were some of his book-collecting friends or acquaintances. Otherwise, he was a most affable and genial man, making friends rather than enemies.'

'That is true in the main,' said Ramsay, hesitatingly; 'but it should be recognized that there were men who could not be definitely called enemies, but who were most certainly not good friends. Mr Balfour was a just man but a very positive one; if he formed an opinion, he would stick to it, even in the face of proof to the contrary. This caused ructions sometimes, and though I can't think he had an enemy who would go so far as to kill him, he certainly did have antagonists. And I can understand a man murdering him to get possession of the Gwinnett book. You see, often a hobby will so possess a man, that he loses all sense of right and wrong in the pursuit of his craze. Do you not think, Mr Stone, that a desperate desire for that book could lead a rabid collector to theft, and—perhaps to murder?'

'It might be so, Mr Ramsay. I say, Sewell, what's the thief going to do with that book? If he offers it for sale he'll have to tell the history of it, won't he? And once you hear of it, or the man who sold it to you hears of it, the thief must be caught. Or are there "fences" who buy rare books same as they buy pearls or precious stones?'

'No,' Sewell said, 'it can't be sold; all the book dealers on earth would be up in arms to know all about it. And the thief would be discovered pronto.'

'Then this is how it stands, it seems to me,' and Stone looked positive, 'it is a kidnapped book. Whoever took it will soon ask ransom money. It is not quite like kidnapping a human being, but it would be similar. The thief will doubtless ask you to deal with him directly and not through the police. He will dictate how to send him the money. Then, if you don't comply, he will send you a leaf torn out to prove that he really has it. He will tell you that unless you come across he will tear out the signatures and send you a few odd scraps of them, saying he has destroyed the other fragments. For unless he can sell it, and preserve his own safety, he can do nothing with it. Unless he could sell the autographs singly and without context.'

'He might do that,' said Sewell, thoughtfully; 'but you frighten me with your suggestions. I would pay a good round sum to get the book back, but not its full value, of course.'

'It seems as if you'll have to wait to hear from your kidnappers,' Stone said; 'and I'll not be surprised, now, to learn that the two crimes are connected.'

'But,' Ramsay objected, 'the criminal, whoever he was, came to Mr Sewell's shop tonight either to kill Mr Balfour or to steal that book. It isn't likely he came to do both—if he did do both. When he came in I had already put what I thought was the real book in my pocket. It is my opinion that the intruder knocked Mr Balfour down first, because Mr Balfour recognized him. He then chloroformed me in order to kill Mr Balfour and make his getaway unseen, knowing I would stay unconscious for ten to twenty minutes. That argues he wanted to kill Mr Balfour, but had no wish to kill me.'

'All true, Mr Ramsay,' Stone agreed, 'but it would be a lot better if you had a witness for all this.'

'Don't I know that?' exclaimed Keith. 'Don't I know no one will believe my story, because it is such an easy one to make up? But look at it this way, Mr Stone. If I wanted to kill Mr Balfour, would it be reasonable for me to get him over to Mr Sewell's shop, and kill him there? With the light on, with the policeman on the beat liable to look in at any minute, with Mr Sewell or Mr Gill likely to come in—I'd be a fool to arrange such a setting! And why would I kill him? I expected to leave him and I had told him so several times, but my going had nothing whatever to do with him. He has always been most kind and considerate in his manner to me. He liked my work and told me so, repeatedly. He offered me increased salary and tried every way he could think of to induce me to stay. What motive could I have to kill a man like that? I did not kill him and I did not steal the book. This dummy I brought home was an innocent gesture and I did it only because I thought it wiser for Mr Balfour to be at home before he began to examine it. The acquisition of that book was an event, and it was better it should occur here than over at Mr Sewell's.'

'Please tell me a little more definitely, Mr Ramsay,' Stone said, 'just why you were planning to leave Mr Balfour?'

'I have told you—on business of my own. It has no reference to Mr Balfour in any way. It is an enterprise of my own, that I may put over in London, and I may not. From the very nature of the business, it must be kept secret and confidential until preliminary terms are arranged. This cannot be done without my presence in London, and cannot be made public at this time. If I am held on suspicion of being instrumental in the death of my employer, I shall have to stay here, of course. Also, if Mrs Balfour wishes to engage my services in the matter of settling up some library business, in which several important purchases are in process of adjustment, I will stay for a time, until such matters can be looked over and put in proper form for my successor.'

'I do want you to stay, Mr Ramsay, at least for a time, until I find a satisfactory successor—if you feel you must go.' Alli spoke in a casual tone, but Fleming Stone's trained vision caught the merest glance of understanding that flashed between her and the librarian.

He sensed at once that there were undercurrents and side issues to this case that he had not looked for. If Ramsay and Mrs Balfour were in love with one another, that altered the whole situation.

'I am quite willing to pay a higher salary than Mr Balfour was paying, but I cannot carry on the library without expert assistance,' Alli went on. 'I do not want Guy Balfour to take it in charge, for with the best intentions he would, in his ignorance, make grave errors. I hope Mr Ramsay will consent to remain and that he can take up his London business later.'

'I fear I cannot decide that question tonight,' Ramsay said, thoughtfully.

'Nor do I want to,' Alli said. 'It may be that the library is not to be mine, after all. Perhaps it is left entirely to Guy. And, now he is one of the household, he will doubtless take over such duties and privileges as he is entitled to. I am not sure I shall remain in this large apartment, nor do I think Guy would want to run it alone. But all those questions are unimportant. The thing is, Mr Stone, to discover who killed my husband and where is his valuable book.'

'Quite right, Mrs Balfour. And those matters cannot be taken up until morning. I shall have to ask some routine questions, of course. Will you detail briefly what you did during the early evening?'

'Surely. After dinner, Mr Balfour said he and Mr Ramsay were going out on an errand, but would be back early. They left here about ten.'

'Did you know where they were going?'

'I knew they were going to Mr Sewell's shop, but I did not know they meant to go in by the window.'

'Then, were you here alone?'

'Mr Sewell came, and Mr Swinton came, he is a man who lives in this house—oh, yes, and Mr Wiley came—he lives in this house too. They all came to see Mr Balfour, of course, and each stayed a few moments to talk to me.'

'Now, Mrs Balfour,' and Stone gave her one of his pleasing smiles, 'this is the first I have heard of any definite time or times regarding the events of the evening. Please straighten out these callers, won't you? Which came first?'

'Mr Swinton came first. He came very soon after Mr Balfour left. He is a man who lives down on the second floor, a book-collector in a small way. He is everlastingly bringing a book for

Mr Balfour or Mr Ramsay to pass judgment on. Tonight, he had a copy of Omar Khayyám, which he thought was a great find. He was vexed to find Mr Balfour not at home, and he stayed a few moments, looking at some of the books in the library.'

'At what time did he come?'

'It was quarter past ten when I came into the reception room, where he was waiting for me. I was tempted not to see him, for he is a bore, but Mr Balfour was always courteous to him and liked to have me nice to his friends. Well, then Mr Sewell came in—he, too, wanted to see Mr Balfour.'

'I sure did,' Sewell declared. 'I didn't bring the book with me as I didn't come direct from the shop. But I wanted to tell him I had it and see his pleasure at the information.'

'What time was this?'

'I don't know, Stone, I never know the time.'

'It must have been less than half-past ten,' Alli said, 'for it was very soon after Mr Swinton arrived. I had just time to tell him Mr Balfour was not at home. I gave him permission to go in the library to look at the Omar Khayyáms in our collection and then Mr Sewell came. He was here maybe ten minutes or less, when there was a telephone call for him and he went away.'

'The telephone from your place, Sewell?'

'Yes, Ramsay calling. I left at once, and went right down to my shop. You can check up times by the police. They came in just as I did.'

'Yes,' Stone agreed, 'that will be all right. Mrs Balfour, I think you said you had another caller, also a tenant of this house?'

'I did. Pretty soon after Mr Sewell went away Mr Swinton left. He said he would come again to see Mr Balfour about his book. As I thought likely Mr Balfour and Mr Ramsay would stay at Mr Sewell's, talking over books in general, and as it was about eleven, I concluded to go to bed. I was just about to ring for my maid when Potter announced Mr Wiley.'

'Pete Wiley?' asked Sewell, seeming astonished.

'Yes; he, too, lives in this house and he sometimes consults Mr Balfour. But he is of the know-it-all type. I've heard him tell my husband that he was wrong on subjects to which he had given years of research!'

'This annoyed Mr Balfour?'

'Not at all. Had the man been his equal in booklore, he would have resented it, but he never would deign to argue with an ignoramus.'

'Better steer clear of Pete Wiley, Stone,' John Sewell informed him. 'He's one of those men who will build up a quarrel on the merest difference of opinion. He bothered the life out of Mr Balfour and Ramsay here. He pestered me until I told him what I thought of him. He doesn't know a holograph from a hole in the wall but he sets up as an expert. If you have the pleasure of talking to him don't mention the Gwinnett book. In fact, don't mention it to anyone until we know where we stand. Mrs Balfour, please don't tell of it, either. Ramsay, I know, will keep the secret. I don't want it talked about until I have talked with Mr Balfour's lawyer and his executors.'

'Of course,' Stone told him, 'we'll all agree to that. What about young Balfour?'

'I think we can't tell you that,' Ramsay said, 'until we know clearly how matters stand. He may be my employer, you know. And, if so, he may dismiss me.'

'This conference must draw to a close,' Stone said, emphatically. 'Mrs Balfour has had quite enough nervous excitement for one evening. And tomorrow, Mrs Balfour, I suppose it will be difficult for me to see you. You will be occupied with plans and arrangements and conferences with your lawyers and other advisors, to say nothing of the demands the police may make on your time.'

'Yes, Mr Stone, but if you will take this case in hand, I will make it a point to be ready to see you whenever you desire. Whatever the exact terms of Mr Balfour's will, I shall have large responsibilities and much necessary conference with lawyers, also many questions to take up with my stepson.'

'Is Mr Guy Balfour interested in rare books?' Stone asked.

'Only in so far as they have a money value. His father often gave him important volumes. Some he sold at once, some he has kept. I foresee no trouble with him for he is an amiable sort and I am quite willing to cede him all his legal rights.'

'You are generous, Mrs Balfour. I shall see you again after I have learned more of the police reports. I shall devote my time alternately to the question of the theft of the book and the killing of Mr Balfour. At this moment they seem to me to be more or less connected, but I may be mistaken about that. Rest assured, I shall do my best in every particular and report to you whenever it seems advisable.'

'Thank you, Mr Stone,' and Alli spoke appreciatively, but she showed a seeming despondency that had not before been noticeable. 'You may, of course, go in and out of this apartment as you wish. You may have a key, if you like; indeed, if it would better suit your work, you may have a room here. We have innumerable empty rooms.'

'Thank you very much, but I prefer to stay in my own home when possible. I live down in the East Thirties, and if I need a key, I will ask for it. Tell me, Mrs Balfour, did your husband attend auctions of rare books?'

'Never. Such purchases as he wanted to make from an auction sale, he instructed Mr Ramsay to look after, or put them in charge of Mr Sewell. He had no liking to mingle with humanity and almost never went into a shop.'

'Yes, he was queer that way,' Sewell agreed. 'He often came to my shop, but more as a club than a shop. Several of our mutual friends would drop in there of an evening, and we would have talks that wouldn't disgrace the old Mermaid Tavern. Well, Stone, shall we get along? I suppose we'll all be expected here in the morning. Good night, Mrs Balfour, good night, Ramsay.'

Stone drew his hostess a little aside, and whispered, 'Watch your step with young Guy. Don't cede him anything without legal advice.'

And then, with kindly good nights, he went away.

In the safety of the sound-proof room, Keith Ramsay took Alli in his arms.

CHAPTER V

INQUIRIES

AFTER a few moments' silence, he led her to a chair and sat down beside her.

'It is all so dreadful, dear, I hate to say what I must say. But I must warn you that we have to be very careful. We must never come into this room to talk, as we are here now. We will be watched every moment of our lives from now on. There is danger, bad danger lurking about, and we must use our best weapons of skill and cleverness to elude it. First, darling, I did not kill your husband and I did not steal his book. These two things you must believe only because I tell you—I have no other proof.'

'You need no proof, my Keith. I would know, without a word from you. And to you, I want to say, just for once—there is no one else I can say it to—I am glad Philip is gone. This sounds heathenish, I know, but he made my life so utterly miserable, he treated me so abominably, he hurt me so cruelly, I cannot grieve for him. You've no idea of the ways he made me suffer. I know you had no hand in his death, but—I shouldn't care if you had.'

'Hush, Alli, such things must not be in your heart. Try to put them out. And get this. We must never, either of us, by word or look betray our affection. Burnet suspects it already, and perhaps Manton. If they feel sure of it, they will begin to suspect not only me—but you, my precious. They will say that we connived at the murder, that we fixed up the plan in collusion, that we schemed to get rid of Philip so that we might belong to one another. It is so palpable, so clear on the face of things, that we wanted him out of the way and managed to accomplish that fact. Once they suspect us of guilty partnership they will believe the worst of us. So, realize this, we must not give them one iota of reason to suppose we are more than merely friendly. We must act as if I was just staying for a time to settle up the unfinished business in the library affairs. And now we must go. The servants, prowling, must never find us alone—'

'Can I never see you alone? Oh, Keith—'

'Not in the house; at least, not for a time. We can go for a drive sometimes, out into the country, but it must be on some apparent, definite business connected with the books. You must see the danger; you must realize what it would mean to have you suspected, either with me or alone, of any connection with Balfour's death. In the morning the police will come, and you must be discreet and careful of what you say. But don't *appear* to be careful of what you say. Treat the whole affair, not lightly, of course, but as if you had no connection with the murder, as if you really took little interest in the deed itself, but wanted to find the murderer and find the book. I know nothing of the book, Alli. I feel sure it was stolen by that man who came in, or—never mind that, we must go now. I will go first—Potter may be lingering about. Then you follow soon.'

Ramsay opened the door and left the room, saying as he went out, 'Good night, Mrs Balfour,' in gentle but dignified tones.

Potter was in the hall and Ramsay stopped to speak to him for a moment, then went on upstairs to his rooms.

He had left the door ajar and in a few moments, Alli came out. She, too, stopped to speak to Potter, saying:

'For the next few days, Potter, your duties will include many new responsibilities. I want to feel that I can trust your loyalty to Mr Balfour and to myself, and feel that you will be discreet and helpful, as I have always found you in an emergency.'

'Yes, madam, I will do my best, and may I ask if there is anything special you want me to do, to command me, no matter what it may be.'

Alli looked at the man sharply, for he seemed to imply some secret or mysterious duty to be demanded.

But she said only, 'Thank you, Potter,' and went on upstairs.

Fleming Stone arrived early the next morning. He wanted to get there before the police came.

He found Ramsay alone at the breakfast table. He took a seat near the librarian and, though he had breakfasted, he asked for a cup of coffee.

'More sociable,' he said to Ramsay. 'You expect the police?'

'Yes, at ten, I believe. Mrs Balfour breakfasts in her own rooms and young Balfour comes down late.'

'Then we have a few moments to ourselves. I want to tell you that while I have full faith in your innocence and I believe implicitly in your account of last evening's doings, there are some plain questions I must ask of you before we go much further. Can we go into the safe room—the room we were in last night?'

'Yes, let us go at once.'

Leaving his unfinished breakfast, Ramsay led Stone to the sound-proof room and they shut themselves in.

'Now, Mr Ramsay,' Stone began, 'I think your feelings toward Mrs Balfour are deeper than mere friendliness. Am I right?'

'You are, Mr Stone. We discovered, only recently, an affection between us that threatened the peace of this household and the wreck of three lives. To me, the only honourable course seemed to be to tell Mr Balfour frankly as to the state of things, resign my position with him and go away.'

'You told him?'

'I did, last night before we went over to Sewell's shop.'

'How did he take it?'

'Unfortunately, he refused to take it at all seriously. He only laughed and said he wasn't bothered by his wife's silly flirtation, as he expressed it. He said I must not think of leaving, that he couldn't get along without my work in his library. He said I overestimated my attractions and he didn't believe Mrs Balfour gave me a thought beyond simple friendliness. He said to drop the subject as we were to go over to the bookshop to see about some books. I told him we would have to resume the question later on and he merely said he would choose the time. We went to Mr Sewell's shop and the rest you know.'

'Of course, Ramsay, if this situation becomes known you will be definitely suspected of Mr Balfour's death.'

'I know that. I want you to advise me as to my wisest course. It goes without saying that since the understanding between Mrs Balfour and myself is not a silly flirtation we will wait in patience until the proprieties are complied with. I would like to go away now, because I feel I would be more of an embarrassment to her than a help if I stay here. But I can't shirk the inquiry of the police and I am willing to face it. Also, if the truth is known about Mrs Balfour and myself, it may bring about suspicion of her collusion with me. Again, she really needs me to look after the library. It is a great collection and must have someone who knows about it to settle up its business. I can leave the house, of course, but it may be that would rouse suspicion, too. And so I am asking your advice. That is, if you can believe in my innocence regarding the murder. And the theft of the book. You have a perfect right to believe me guilty on both counts.'

'That is true, Ramsay,' and Fleming Stone looked very grave. 'You have no proof of any sort. You have every reason to be suspected. The fact that I believe in your complete innocence is merely the result of my taking a liking to you and feeling confidence in you. This, if you are clever enough to hoodwink me, may be misplaced confidence. If so, I shall probably find it out. I am talking to you very frankly because your situation is so closely connected with that of Mrs Balfour that suspicion of one would implicate the other. We must find proof of all you say. But, as you know, your relations with her must not become known. The merest hint of your mutual interest would be a desperate menace to you both. You have talked with Mrs Balfour since the death of her husband?'

'Yes; after you left last night, we had a few words in the safe room. But I told her that must not occur again and that we must be most discreet and watchful lest the servants or others discover it.'

'It must be hidden—always, unless, of course, I come to have definite suspicion of either of you. I make no apology for my plain speaking, this is a matter of life and death and I warn you, if this matter becomes known, you will find you are both in serious trouble.'

'I realize that. And rest assured I shall do my best to have the secret remain undiscovered. The danger lies in Mrs Balfour's present state of loneliness, fear and general distress. She is not fond of her stepson and she has few friends. Mr Balfour allowed her no freedom in social matters. She was kept immured and he made her life a burden. I say these things because they are true. He was always kind and courteous to me, because I gave him the help he had to have with his books. But other librarians can be found, fully as capable as I am, except for my extensive knowledge of the books. So, if you advise it, I will just go away and stay away as long as necessary.'

'I doubt very much, Ramsay, if the police would let you go. Quite aside from this motive you tell of, they do suspect you, though without any real evidence. Reserve your decision and planning until after this morning's session. Await developments. We can confer at any time, if not here, then down at my place.'

Then they went out to attend the inquiry and found the Inspector and Captain Burnet awaiting them.

Manton and Fleming Stone exchanged greetings, as they were old friends, and Manton never looked upon Stone as an intruder.

Also present was Henry Scofield, the lawyer of Philip Balfour.

Sewell and Gill were there and Guy Balfour, sitting beside his stepmother.

After some preliminaries, Inspector Manton asked the lawyer to read the will of the late Philip Balfour.

From the reading it was learned that Guy Balfour, son of the testator, received one hundred thousand dollars.

Other legacies included a few relatives, all of his employees, his Club staff, a generous bequest to John Sewell, a moderate sum to Keith Ramsay, gifts to a number of charitable organizations and the rest of his estate was left entirely to his beloved wife, Alli Balfour.

No one was greatly surprised, though Guy stormed inwardly, thinking that from an estate of millions he fared poorly. He well knew it was his own fault, but that didn't help matters.

The library was left unrestrictedly to Alli with the suggestion that she should eventually present it to some institution and that she engage some competent librarian to keep it in running order. The apartment, which he owned, was also left to his widow and she was in all respects residuary legatee.

All of which, listened to most eagerly by Inspector Manton, gave him no new suspect. Unless Guy, impatient for his legacy—but a parricide, no, there was no slightest evidence to point to that.

Fleming Stone, too, listened intently. And he, also, found no new direction in which to look. He realized, more than ever, were the truth known about the affair of the librarian and his employer's wife, they would be put through an ordeal. An ordeal that would, he felt sure, lead straight to accusation and trial.

But his close scrutiny and his careful listening to the Inspector and the Captain of the Homicide Division made him feel positive that up to the present, at any rate, they had no inkling of the matter. No word, no expression on their faces, showed the least idea of such a suspicion.

That they did suspect Ramsay was clear enough, but that it implicated Alli was not at all evident.

'And so, Mrs Balfour,' Manton said, 'you are heir to this great estate, library and all, and it is to you we must address our inquiries and state our plans. We have had considerable information from those present at or near the time of Mr Balfour's death and I want some further details from you. But first, will you tell me if there was any ill-feeling or estrangement between your husband and yourself?'

Alli Balfour looked at him steadily.

'No, Inspector,' she said, 'there was not. We were devoted to one another and I think I can say we never had a real quarrel, though naturally, we differed in opinion now and then. Mr Balfour was generous and kind, and I appreciated his sterling worth. In spite of the difference in our ages we were congenial and lived happily together. Is this what you wanted to know?'

'Yes, in a general way. Your husband must have been devoted to you to leave you this large estate and also his famous library.'

'He was,' Guy Balfour declared in dissatisfied tones. 'Mrs Balfour hynotized him, that's what she did! Alli, you know Dad should have left me more of his estate than he did. Will you supplement his bequest?'

'We'll talk that over by ourselves, Guy,' she returned with a kindly smile. 'Pay attention now to the Inspector's questions.'

'You and your father were on friendly terms?' Manton asked.

'Oh, yes,' and Guy looked bored. 'I thought I told you that before. Dad and I were really fond of one another. I lived out because I wanted to throw a party now and then and the parties I liked best were not in accordance with the ideas of Philip Balfour. So we went our own ways. But when I came here, my father always welcomed me and so did Mrs Balfour.' He looked at Alli and smiled in comradely fashion.

'Are you surprised that your father did not leave you his library?'

'Oh, no; I didn't really think he would. I should probably have made ducks and drakes of it, selling the choicest books, like as not, for a fraction of their value. It's better Alli should have it, but of course she'll need help with it. I can give her some help, but she'll need a regular bibliographer, too. Ramsay's the one for that, but I hear he is leaving.'

'Is that right, Mr Ramsay?' Manton inquired. 'Are you going away?'

'Depends on circumstances, Inspector. If you've no objections to my departure, and if Mrs Balfour can find a suitable librarian, I shall go. But I would like to see the missing book found before I leave.'

'I think you'd better not plan to go quite yet,' Manton said, unsmilingly. 'I think you know we have a desire to question you further before we dismiss your case entirely. You were closely allied with Mr Balfour in the consideration of the purchase of that expensive volume and now that it is missing we want your help in our efforts to find it.'

Ramsay's face grew stern.

'If that is your attitude, Inspector,' he said, 'I am more than willing to help in your search. But if you are using that as camouflage for your wish to keep me near you for other reasons, I would rather be told frankly that you suspect me of one or both of the crimes you are investigating.'

'That's right,' and Captain Burnet spoke with emphasis. 'We do suspect you, Mr Ramsay, of implication in the disappearance of the book and possibly of being in some way connected with the death of your employer. If you can tell us anything that will turn our suspicions in another direction, we shall be glad to listen.'

'I can't do that,' and Keith Ramsay seemed to collapse like a burst balloon. 'I have no way to prove my innocence. In fact, I can think of no way to prove it except by finding the real criminal. This, I cannot do alone, but I am hoping, by the help of Mr Stone, to find the man who stabbed Philip Balfour and deliver him over to justice.'

'No one can blame you, Mr Ramsay, for the hope of that, and I should be glad to see it come about. But meantime our work must go on and we have to follow up our own suspicions by our own methods. And for these reasons, we are advising you that you cannot leave the city at present. Developments may come quickly or they may be delayed, but it is too soon yet to accuse anyone definitely. If it suits your convenience and that of Mrs Balfour, I advise that you remain here for a time and work in the library, if so inclined. Unless you agree to something of this sort, I must detain you as a material witness or perhaps even go further.'

'Arrest me, you mean,' and Ramsay spoke bitterly. 'I give you my word not to run away, and as you have no direct evidence against me, I trust I may remain unmolested.'

'For the present, yes. I feel sure further developments will soon occur that will give us a way to look. If you had any sort of witness or verifier of your story of what happened last evening, we could check up; but your masked man is untraceable and may be imaginary.'

'Why untraceable?' Ramsay spoke in deep anger. 'Many masked murderers have been run down and the fact that I have no one to corroborate my story does not lessen the necessity of investigating it.'

'That's true enough,' Fleming Stone observed; 'I think Mr Ramsay is entitled to a full and complete investigation of his story and I feel that such a course might bring out unexpected evidence.'

'I've no wish to be unjust, Mr Stone,' and Manton shook his head, 'but it is hard to set about proving a story that I can't believe myself. I know of no other potential criminals than those we now have before us.'

'But your not knowing them is far from proving that there aren't any,' said Stone, seriously. 'Granting an intruder, masked and desperate, who kills one man and stuns another, it is not to be supposed that he is an individual who would at once occur to any of us. Not likely that the vague description given would cause us to say, "Oh, that must be John Doe, he always wears a mask when he commits a crime." No, the man in the mask may not be quickly found, but he must be found. If he is imaginary, as you suggest, then that fact must be proved; if he is real, he must be discovered. It won't do to say, "I don't believe there was any masked man," and let it go at that. I want to find out more definitely just where all this present audience spent last evening. It's a strange thing that so often when a man is asked to tell where he was at a given time, he refuses—often insisting that it has nothing to do with the case, is of no importance, but—he doesn't want to tell. Mr Balfour and Mr Gill have already taken this stand and I, for one, would like to insist that they tell us. If irrelevant, we will, of course, keep it confidential, but it is really to their own interests to be frank about it.'

'Yes,' Manton agreed, 'it is advisable to know these things whether they prove helpful or not. Mr Gill, where were you last evening?'

'Well, as you'll doubtless find out, anyway, and as I've nothing to conceal, I'll tell you that I went to see Hemingway, a dealer in rare books who lives in Washington Square, and then I came up here to this house to make a call on Pete Wiley.'

'For what purpose?'

'The racket I'm always on, I wanted to sell him a book or two.'

'Did you do so?'

'Oh, Lord, no! We assistants don't sell books, you know, we only try to. But I stayed there for a while and we had a good time.'

'What time was this?'

'Dunno. I went from Pete's place right down to Mr Sewell's shop, and I got there about half-past eleven. I walked fairly fast so I reckon I left this house about eleven-fifteen or so.'

Manton turned to Alli Balfour.

'Is this Mr Wiley the man who called on you last night?'

'Yes. He came after Mr Sewell and Mr Swinton had gone. Something after eleven, I think it was. He stayed, I suppose, about ten minutes.'

'He wanted to see Mr Balfour about a book?'

'Yes.'

'What book?'

'He didn't mention it to me by name. When he found Mr Balfour was not here, he just made a little polite conversation and then went away.'

'What did he talk about?'

'Books, mostly. He said he contemplated a visit to England soon, where he expected to achieve some rare finds. I answered him politely, but I was not very sociable and he soon left.'

'He was a friend of your husband's?'

'Oh, yes, but always begging for information, even though he assumed great knowledge of his own.'

'Yes, that's Wiley all over,' Gill said.

'And what books did you try to sell this man?' Manton asked Gill.

'Not very important ones; a couple of unimportant Lewis Carroll items.'

Ramsay looked up quickly, remembering the two books Gill had brought to the shop when he was there. But he said nothing, nor did Sewell.

Manton turned to Guy Balfour, who sat moodily looking out of a window.

'Now, Mr Balfour, you will please tell us where you were last evening. You refused to answer when I asked you before.'

'My reason for refusing was simply because I was at a place where I am ashamed of having been. I was at The Medicine Cabinet, a resort that doesn't bear the best of characters. I didn't want to tell because it is not my custom to go to such places, but last night was made an exception because of the urgent request of a friend.'

'Who is the friend? Name and address, please.'

'Oh, come now, Inspector, I don't want to drag in a rank outsider!'

'Name and address, please.'

'Oh, well, then—Jack Rollinson—' and he added the address.

'Of course, we shall check up on these statements,' Manton told them, and he then asked to have the servants of the house brought in.

Fleming Stone rose, and saying he must go on one or two short errands, bade the Inspector to have careful notes of his further inquiry kept for him against his return.

Leaving the Balfour apartment, Stone went down in an elevator but got off at the fourteenth floor.

Asking the elevator attendant for Mr Wiley's number, he received it because of his air of authority.

He rang the bell and was admitted by a canny-looking Chinaman.

He asked for Wiley and soon that personage appeared. Personage describes Pete Wiley better than any other word. Of medium height and unimportant face, he strutted into the room where Stone awaited him and assumed what he meant to be a majestic air, which was a bit suggestive of a little king in a series of popular pictures.

He held in his hand the card Stone had given the man and, glancing at it, said, 'Mr Stone?' in a tone of condescension.

'Yes,' said Stone, cheerfully. 'Mr Wiley?'

The other nodded, offered a chair, and they sat down.

'I am here in the interests of Law and Order, Mr Wiley,' and Stone's inflection now sounded the note of authority. 'I will detain you but a moment but I must ask you a few questions. About last evening. Did you call at Mr Balfour's apartment?'

'May I ask why I am obliged to recount to you my comings and goings?'

'I represent the police,' Stone said, carelessly, 'but I am myself a private investigator. Unless you care to talk to me, an Inspector will call. I don't propose to ask you anything troublesome.'

CHAPTER VI

STONE AND HIS SUSPECTS

'Oh, well, go ahead. I've nothing to conceal. Yes, I called at Mr Balfour's apartment. It was a bit late, well after eleven. Mr Balfour was not at home, so I chatted with Mrs Balfour, maybe about five minutes, and then I came away.'

'What was the purpose of your call?'

'I wanted to ask Mr Balfour a question concerning a rare book. I assure you I know quite as much about old books as he did, but there was one point I wanted corroborated.'

'Not finding him at home, you came directly back here to your own apartment?'

'Yes.'

'Had you been out, during the evening, before you went to Mr Balfour's?'

'Let me see—had I? No, Mr Stone—I recollect now. I was right here all the evening, looking over my books. You know we collectors can always find something to do, some absorbing bit of collating or comparing.'

'Comparing what? Books?'

'Well, in this case, I was comparing signatures.'

'Whose signatures?'

'The author of the book. You know a volume inscribed by its author is much more valuable than one without his autograph.'

'Yes,' Stone agreed. 'And what book were you considering?'

'Oh, various ones. Just looking them over.'

'Mr Gill had been here to see you, and wanted to sell you a book.'

'Now, how did you ever know that? Yes, you're right; Mr

Gill had an autographed book of Lewis Carroll's that I wanted. I have it here, on approval. It's called *The Hunting of the Snark*.'

'I see. And why was Mr Gill coming to see you about it when you have the book here?'

'Well,' Pete Wiley looked a bit embarrassed, 'I was afraid the signature was not genuine—maybe forged, you know. I'm pretty cute about these booksellers and their tricks.'

'Surely you didn't think that a shop like Sewell's would sponsor a fake inscription?'

'Not knowingly, of course, but they might have been cheated. Anyway, I'm on to those things! They have to get up early to get ahead of me. So I asked Mr Gill to bring me some more books signed by Lewis Carroll and let me collate the names. And he did.'

'And then you were satisfied?'

'Yes—that is, practically so. Here, you look at the book, I'd rather have the opinion of a detective than a bibliophile.'

Stone studied the inscription.

'Looks all right,' he said. 'But I can't decide a matter of that kind. Now come back to cases. You were always friendly with Mr Balfour?'

'Yes, indeed. He often consulted me—'

'Why, when he had Mr Sewell's wide knowledge at his disposal?'

'Oh, well—in a multitude of counsellors, you know.'

'Yes, I know. Then you didn't go out at all last evening, except for that short call at the Balfour apartment?'

'No, not at all.'

'The elevator boy says you did. He must be mistaken.'

'Oh, wait a minute—yes, I did step out once before I went up to the Balfours'.'

'Be careful what you're saying, Mr Wiley. Where did you go?'

'Well, I stepped around to the Sewell shop—thought I'd ask Sewell himself about it. Though Gill knows such things.'

'What time did you go on this forgotten errand?'

'I haven't the least idea. I never know the time. But it was something like nine, I'd say.'

'Before you went to see the Balfours?'

'Oh, my, yes.'

'Did you see Mr Sewell at his shop?'

'No; the place was all dark and shut up.'

'Did you go anywhere else?'

'No, came right back here. What's all this about, Mr Stone? Do you think I had anything to do with Mr Balfour's death?'

'I'm not thinking, I'm just asking questions.'

'You sure are doing that! Any more? I'm getting restless.'

'Nothing more just now. But you'd better get over your restlessness, for something tells me the police may feel enough interest in you to call on you.'

'You going to put 'em up to that?'

'Oh, they don't have to be put up. They're a keen pair on this case. But you're not afraid of them?'

'Hell, no! Let 'em come when they like.'

Stone's keen eyes noticed a slight quiver of Wiley's lips, but he realized that an innocent man might be unnerved at the thought of police inquiries. Yet he felt certain that when Burnet heard that Wiley had been near the scene of the crime, he would promptly interview him.

'Well, Mr Wiley,' Stone said, 'may I have your assurance that you won't attempt to run away?'

'Of course I shan't run away! Why the devil should I?'

'I don't know, I'm sure. It would be a very foolish thing for you to do. If Inspector Manton quizzes you, just put up the same story you've just told me. Probably it will go over.'

'Why do you say that? Do you doubt me?'

'I just said it to note how you responded. You seem a little anxious.'

'Nothing of the sort. But an innocent man always dislikes being baited.'

'Lord, man, I'm not baiting you! My bait is worse than my bark. You wouldn't like it at all.'

'Huh, you needn't think I'm afraid. I'm afraid of nothing!'

'The wise man fears when fear is called for,' and with this somewhat cryptic statement, the detective went away.

He took the down elevator again, this time as far as the second floor.

Then he rang the bell at Carl Swinton's apartment.

A trim maid opened the door and showed him into a pleasant living room.

In a moment Swinton appeared, looking a bit inquisitive but courteous.

'How do you do, Mr Stone. Sit down, won't you? I know you, of course, by reputation and I wonder if you are here in connection with the sad affair of Mr Philip Balfour? If there's anything I can do to help I'll be only too glad to do it.'

'I'm not sure there is, Mr Swinton, but as you were there last night when Mr Sewell was there, I thought perhaps you might remember some little detail that could prove helpful.'

'I wish I could but I feel a little at sea as to what you want. When I went up to the Balfour apartment last evening, Mr Balfour and Mr Ramsay were both out and Mrs Balfour received me. I chatted with her a few moments and then, as I was about to leave, Mr Sewell came. I had never met him, and I stayed a few moments longer.'

'Are you interested in rare books?'

'No, not in any active way. I like to see them, but I know nothing of their value. However, Mr Sewell was called to the telephone. In answer to a summons, he said, he must leave at once. So he went away, and I very soon left also.'

'When did you hear of Mr Balfour's death?'

'This morning. My man brought me word of it when he came.'

'I see. Now, Mr Swinton, are you one of those people who never know anything about time? Or can you tell me about what time you went upstairs to the Balfour apartment last night?'

'I confess I don't keep tabs on the time usually, but I know that I was admitted by the butler and shown into a reception room to await Mrs Balfour's coming. And as I sat there a few minutes waiting, I noticed it was twenty past ten. I shouldn't have noticed, probably, but there was a little clock on the table that had a quick, saucy little tick. I felt sure it was a French clock and I looked at it with admiration, it was such a pretty little piece of property. Then Mrs Balfour came in, and I never gave the clock another thought. So I've no idea what time it was when I came home, but I was there, I suppose, nearly half an hour. That's as near as I can tell you.'

'You know the Balfours well?'

'Oh, yes; I knew them both before they were married. They've been married only three years or so.'

'What was your errand? Merely a social call?'

'A little more than that. I am a portrait painter and I had hopes of putting both of them on canvas. But I suppose there'll be nothing doing now. Just my luck! However, perhaps Mrs Balfour will let me paint her after the excitement is over. She may be glad of something to divert her mind.'

'Quite likely. Have you known her long?'

'Five or six years. We lived in the same home town, a village in Connecticut. Our acquaintance was slight, for I was not a society chap, and she was in the smart circles. But we were friendly and her father half promised to let me paint her. But the girl refused, saying she didn't care about it. And, recently, since I have known Mr Balfour, he agreed to let me do them both. I asked him a pretty stiff price, but he agreed to it and we were going to begin sittings very soon. So you see, aside from a natural sympathy for the poor girl, I am regretting my own disappointment.'

'Yes, hard lines. But, as you say, Mrs Balfour may keep to the plan. Most women like a portrait of themselves.'

'Yes, and they were good enough to praise my work. Have you any clue to the murderer?'

'Not the least hint of one. That's why I dropped in to see you. You and Mr Wiley seem to be the only people in the house who know the Balfours well.'

'He doesn't know them as well as I do. But that's not saying much. I seldom saw them. I hoped to see more of him if I did the portraits. He has a marvellous lot of books.'

'Yes, he has. Shall you call on the widow?'

'Oh, no. I don't know her well enough for that. But as I said, I wish I could help you in your work. This may sound presumptuous, but I've a natural taste for detective work and sometimes I'm right ingenious.'

'You sound helpful. But of course the police have it in charge. I'm just a private detective, retained by Mrs Balfour to assist the police.'

'I guess they're glad to have you. Who advised Mrs Balfour, or did you know her before?'

'No, it was Mr Sewell who advised her. You know Sewell?'

'Not personally. I only know he's a first-class dealer in rare books. He and Balfour were great friends.'

'Yes; and he's a great friend of mine. John Sewell is a fine man, as well as a learned one.'

'Yes, I've heard so. Well, Mr Stone, can't you think of some way I can be of use? If not, perhaps something will crop up. I'm no genius or spectacular detective but if you want me to track down anything or anybody just give me a try at it.'

Stone promised to remember this request, and rose to go.

'Wait a minute,' Swinton said, rising also. 'Perhaps I ought to tell you a bit of rumour I heard about the Balfours. I am not ordinarily a gossip, but you know there is always more or less speculation among the servants about the tenants of a house like this. Especially about the marital relations. It is the generally accepted situation that Mrs Balfour was not in love with her husband, but had given her affections to the handsome librarian.'

'Ramsay?' said Stone. 'He isn't handsome.'

'Oh, well, beauty is in the eye of the beholder. Anyway, I don't call this gossip—telling you—for it may be a help to you.'

'I understand and appreciate your motive. In the same spirit of legitimate inquiry, I'll ask you if the secretary returns the lady's affection?'

'That I don't know. But you can discover, I'm sure. What is their seeming attitude?'

'I've noticed nothing beyond courteous acquaintance on either side.'

'Well, it's only a hint, but it may be of use to you.'

Stone went away, regretting Swinton's suspicion.

He returned to the Balfour apartment just as the Inspector and Captain Burnet were concluding their inquiries of the servants.

No facts of any importance had come to light through a quiz of the staff, but the police thought that Potter might know more than he told.

Stone reported all he had learned from the two men in the house, with the single exception of Swinton's hint about Mrs Balfour and her husband's librarian.

'Guess we'll have to ask Gill about those books,' Burnet said. 'Do you know there are moments when I feel that Friend Gill is not entirely a law-abiding citizen.'

'Reasons?' demanded Manton, laconically.

The two, with Stone, sat in a room in the Balfour apartment which had been given over to the detectives.

'Can't say, exactly, only he's 'most too smart. Very glib, always ready with an answer to a question, always provided with an explanation of an odd incident and always in the right.'

'Hardly enough to prove him a criminal,' Stone said; 'yet he has seemed to me an uncertain proposition. Would he be benefited in any way by Balfour's death?'

'Only if he has that missing book,' the Inspector returned. 'To my mind the hand that held the skewer is the hand that stole the book.'

'I agree to that,' Stone told him. 'And I agree that young Gill is a right smart chap. But Sewell trusts him like a brother and Sewell is a keen observer.'

'Sewell likes him so much that he has no thought of any infidelity. But I've heard rumours of Gill's sharp dealings and it may be that he puts over some rare book deals that Sewell doesn't know about.'

'He couldn't do anything with this missing book, could he?' put in Burnet.

'He could do what anyone else could do,' Stone said, musingly. 'In fact he would have better facilities for disposing of it than Ramsay would. Ramsay is already suspected, Gill isn't. Then, too, Gill has the knowledge of various dealers and their wants and ways. He might know that one dealer would scorn to have anything to do with a book illegitimately, while another might jump at the chance. All that's the same in any business. The fact that the rare book trade is largely confined to scholars and literary men doesn't necessarily make it immune to the tricks of the trade known to other lines of business. Indeed, it's one of the easiest fields in which to practise fraud. Often the buyer knows nothing of the fine points of a rare book save what the dealer tells him. Sewell, in every way, stands for honour and fair dealing but that doesn't argue that his hirelings all do the same.'

'Of course, it would be easy for Gill to annex that valuable book,' the Inspector declared, 'but it would be hard for him to dispose of it, being with Sewell, as he is.'

'As to that,' Stone shook his head, 'he could pursue the course I have suggested. And whether taken by Gill or another I believe the Button book, as we seem to call it, has been kidnapped and is being held for ransom. If so, we can do nothing until we hear from the kidnappers. Any suspicions of young Balfour?'

'Not by me,' and Manton spoke positively. 'The old man gave him a fine allowance, and he didn't want to live here anyway, so why kill the goose that laid his golden eggs?'

'He came here to live pretty quick when the chance arrived,' Stone reminded them. 'And, of course, his inheritance means far more to him financially than his allowance did. If he continues to stay here, and if Mrs Balfour allows him to have his own way, he'll have a fine home and freedom to do as he likes in it.'

'It is possible, too,' Manton said, 'that he knows something about the affair between his stepmother and the librarian. Don't blind your eyes to that affair. It didn't begin yesterday.'

'But Ramsay was planning to leave. He had given notice.'

'Notice, my eye!' and Burnet grinned. 'When he left, the lady would have left with him. I know what happens when December and May join up.'

'I'm going to see Guy Balfour,' Stone told them then. 'He asked me to give him a session, and I'm glad to do it. You'll be talking to him, I suppose?'

'Yes,' the Inspector agreed. 'I'll wait till you report your interview.'

Stone nodded and went away. It was not often he conferred quite so intimately with the police, though he was always friendly with them. But in this case he felt that much depended on his getting information from all possible sources and through all possible channels.

He went in search of Guy, and was bidden upstairs to the young man's suite.

This set of rooms, having been Philip Balfour's, was done up in elaborate style with every known modern fitting and convenience—not modernistic decoration—that didn't please the owner—but furnishings of quiet and harmonious beauty.

'Come along in,' Guy said, as Potter brought Stone to the door.

'Glad to see you,' the young man went on, pleasantly; 'sit down, do. I'm going to rearrange matters here but it's good material to work on. Big rooms, good light and splendid fixtures. Here, just look at this bathroom place before you settle.

Bathroom! It's half a dozen bathrooms! Tub, shower, vapour—each with a room to itself. And the steam room—perfectly appointed, all of them. And the sunken pool—oh, Dad knew how to do himself, all right. I confess I like luxury, and when I get his writing room turned into a smoke room and his office here made over into a bar, I'll be just about all right.'

'You're not disconsolate over your father's death then?'

Guy had the grace to look ashamed of himself. 'Well, you see, Mr Stone, we never saw much of each other. He gave me my allowance, but that's all he did do for me. I hate to think of his taking off and I put it out of my mind all I can. I can't do anything about it and there's no use grieving over something you can't help.'

'At least, you feel sorry for Mrs Balfour?'

Guy looked up with a smile and a wink.

'Sorry for Alli? Well, not so that I'd hire a ghost to write it up. My beautiful stepmother has not, for a long time, had an eye single to her husband's affection for her, she had—well—a straying glance.'

'Yet she engaged me to track down the murderer.'

'Oh, of course. I don't mean Alli had a hand in the tragedy—nor Keith either—maybe, eh? But she has to find out, if she can, where the blame rests and hunt down the criminal if possible.'

'Have you any suspicion of anyone?'

'Sure I have; lots of people. Ramsay first, of course. He had—how does the lingo run?—motive, opportunity and weapon, all right there, crying out to be used.'

'But if your statement as to the affection existing between him and Mrs Balfour is true, it would be a mistaken thing for him to do. Surely she could not continue to care for a murderer!'

'That's so! I never thought of that. Alli's pretty high-strung. No, she wouldn't hook up with her husband's slayer!'

'Then, who's your next suspect? You've evidently given some thought to the subject.'

'Sure, I've given it thought. My next choice would be Preston Gill.'

'Oh, come now, he'd have no motive but the theft of the book. And surely, in his position, he could get the valuable volume without staging a murder?'

'Yeah, but he isn't overly fond of our Ramsay and he might have carried out his little masquerade to involve Keith in the meshes of the police net.'

'Ingenious but not very convincing. How about yourself as a suspect?'

'I've been wondering when you'd get around to that. That's what you came up here for, isn't it?'

'Partly. You must admit you're a pretty fair target for suspicion.'

'Except that a man doesn't often kill his own father. Parricide isn't done much now, is it?'

'It's not what you'd call prevalent, no. But we detectives have to look into every hole and corner.'

'I suppose so. Are those arms of the law downstairs now planning to haul me over the coals?'

'They are. But of course you knew it must come. Can I be of any help?'

'Why—I don't know. What could you do?'

'I don't know of anything. Unless you had some proof of your innocence that I could use to convince the Inspector. He's a bit determined that you are more or less implicated.'

'Why, I was at that rotten joint when the tragedy occurred.'

'Can you prove that?'

'Only by the affirmation of my friends who were there with me.'

'Not good enough, I'm afraid. Such alibis have to be quiz-proof. Can your friends put it over?'

Guy Balfour looked suddenly dismayed.

He stared at Fleming Stone, and said, 'They can—unless they don't choose to do so.'

'Just what do you mean by that? Look here, Balfour, you are not so well versed in these matters—if an alibi slips up, it's worse for you than if you'd never used it. And are any of your friends on the outs with you? Would any of them be glad to see you in trouble with the police?'

'There is one—Jack Rollinson. He'd be cheering to see me accused of theft. I'm sure he'd never think I killed Dad. Nobody could believe that! But I might be accused of stealing the Button book.'

CHAPTER VII

A LIST OF SUSPECTS

FLEMING STONE went home and sat down at his own desk in his own library to take up the case by himself. He had plenty of facts to work upon, plenty of theories, lots of evidence both true and false, a few clues and some opinions and decisions of his own.

All of these he must reduce to some sort of order before he could feel that he had his case well in hand.

Balfour had been killed Friday night and it was now Saturday noon.

Stone realized to the full the unusual features of the case, the conflicting bits of evidence, and the fairly large number of possible suspects.

He was not so much given to making lists as were other detectives whom he knew, but at times he felt that a sort of schedule was helpful.

He thought first of the more likely killers among the acquaintances of Philip Balfour, and met squarely the fact that Keith Ramsay had strong motive, ample opportunity and a most conveniently available weapon.

He was not altogether ready to suspect Ramsay, for the attitude of the young man as he related the tale of his unconquerable love for his employer's wife and his consequent determination to flee from the dangers this love might bring about, also the honourable confession of all this to Balfour himself, indicated a fineness of character incompatible with the soul of a murderer.

Yet, again, when he remembered that Balfour scoffed at this confession, and made light of what he called a silly flirtation, there was certainly a possibility that given the unexpected opportunity to remove the obstacle to his happiness, Ramsay might have acted on a sudden fierce impulse and committed the deed that cleared the way.

After all, they had only Keith Ramsay's word as to the masked intruder. There was no one to corroborate the story Ramsay told so glibly.

To be sure, everything Stone had seen or known about the librarian he had liked. He considered Ramsay a square-dealing, honourable man.

But there again, there was no one to witness his alleged confession to Balfour, no one to agree that Balfour had scoffed at the 'flirtation'.

And Ramsay was exceedingly clever. Had he been the killer, Stone was positive that he would have made up some such plausible story, and doubtless could have put it over.

To the best of Fleming Stone's knowledge and belief, cleverness made the successful criminals. He believed brain, not brawn, was the necessary element in all great crimes.

If there was any doubt about Ramsay, there was grave doubt. So grave that Stone put him at the head of his list of perhapses.

And next, with regret, he put down the name of Preston Gill.

He liked Gill and he felt sure that Sewell was too canny to keep his assistant if he weighed up lacking. But for a young man of Gill's attainments, the temptations offered by the many rare volumes must of necessity be at times very great.

And the masked assailant could easily have been Gill. He could have made his calls, as he detailed them, but perhaps not at the times he stated. He could have killed Philip Balfour for a number of reasons: either connected with rare books or with the beautiful wife of the great collector. And Gill, like Ramsay, was ingenious enough to compass that mysterious murder with neatness and dispatch.

So much for Gill. And if there was anything wrong about him, Sewell knew nothing of it. That man never would keep an assistant of whom any wrongdoing could be suspected.

So Gill went down second on Stone's list.

Then along came Guy.

During Stone's visit to the rooms which had been the senior Balfour's he had sized up the son to a considerable degree.

And, while he found it hard to imagine Guy guilty of parricide, yet he realized that the friends and the environment of this pleasure-loving youth were not of a sort to steady his character or improve his morals.

It was within the bounds of comprehension that Guy, who admitted being in a place he was ashamed of, might have had more than enough to drink, and might have achieved a spirit of derring-do, or even arrived at a state of mental instability, though physically truculent. What had then happened left room for wide speculation. Perhaps egged on by greedy companions, who would blackmail him afterward. Perhaps only intending to steal the precious Gwinnett book, and driven to murder by circumstances.

Yes, difficult as it was to reconstruct the awful crime, it must be reckoned with.

So the third name was Guy Balfour.

And, Stone told himself, he had no further names to put down.

There were the Balfour servants, to be sure, but after the police report of their interviews, there seemed no one of them in any way implicated. Potter might know more than he had told of family matters, but he was assuredly in the apartment all the evening, and could not have slipped away long enough to accomplish the fatal deed.

There were fellow collectors who might be envious or jealous of some of Balfour's lucky finds in the way of rare books, but as a rule, collectors are not of the murdering class. It may be argued that there is no murdering class, but scholars are not often suspected of murder.

Stone pondered. The two men who lived in the house had

no claim to a place on his list, he concluded. Swinton was not much interested in old books and Wiley, though interested, had no grudge against the greater collector; indeed, rather seemed to think he knew more about the subject, if Balfour did have the larger and more valuable lot.

And then, as Stone had feared they would, his thoughts turned to Alli, the strange beautiful wife of the murdered man, and the secret inamorata of his trusted secretary.

Stone's pencil refused to write Alli Balfour's name, until he realized he was not playing fair and he slowly inscribed it.

He thought hard and long.

He couldn't conjure up a vision of Alli, the embodiment of dignity and grace, killing or having any part in the killing of her husband.

He would have cast the monstrous idea from his brain, save that he was a conscientious reasoner, and he knew that he strove to get away from the notion because it was so repugnant to his own feelings.

He made himself consider it seriously.

It was idiotic to say Alli couldn't have been the murderer because she was so beautiful or so graceful or so dignified! He had to admit that in all stages of the world's history wives had murdered their husbands in fact as well as in fiction.

And Alli, he had already discovered, was as clever as they come.

Moreover, her love for Keith Ramsay, concealed, as she thought, was palpably evident to him.

Fleming Stone's long career in the investigation of crime had brought him into contact with all sorts and conditions of women and he knew for certain that there is no human being, of either sex, entirely exempt from the possibility of committing a crime.

Great loves have been the cause of many a crime in fiction, as we know, and in truth, as we do not always know.

And Alli Balfour was a strong character, a woman of deep passions and swayed by deep affections.

She had lived three years with a husband twenty years her senior. She had then been thrown with a man who complemented her own nature so perfectly, who was so entirely congenial, so at one with all her tastes and preferences, that it was small wonder she could not bear to think of his leaving her.

As to the details of this view of things, Stone cared little. If Alli Balfour had made up her mind to do away with her husband, the ways and means would be duly and properly attended to by the lady herself. Whether she chose to strike the blow or hire an underling to do it or persuade her lover to attend to it, it would be accomplished with wisdom and foresight.

Stone couldn't see it, couldn't get it at all, but he knew he must not evade it.

To a stranger it would not sound so unbelievable.

The circumstances were far from unique. The conditions far from prohibitive.

Stone remembered every word of what Ramsay had told him when he so frankly confessed his love for Alli and honourably announced his decision to go away.

Then, supposing Alli could not let him go and suppose she alone, or in collusion with him, made his going unnecessary?

Well, it had to be followed up. And followed up by the wretchedest means. Means that included prying, listening, secret questioning, equivocation, spying and traps.

Then, he concluded, if so, he would set about it at once. If Alli Balfour killed her husband or was in any way implicated in his killing, Stone wanted to know it, finish up the distasteful business and get out!

He determined to go to see Sewell. He could ask him about Mrs Balfour, and also pump him a little, very carefully, about Gill.

He found the genial bookseller in his front office, but they at once adjourned to the back room as being more secluded.

Gill was out on some errands, for which Stone was grateful, as he wanted to see Sewell alone.

'Who killed Balfour?' Stone said, as they sat down in two comfortable as well as valuable old chairs.

'Well, who did?' echoed Sewell. 'Didn't I drag you into this case on purpose for you to find that out?'

'What price Mrs Balfour herself? Or her hireling.'

Sewell stared at his guest.

'Are you serious?' he asked, speaking slowly.

'I am. I have just had a thinking spell and while I'm not putting this idea forth as a theory, nor even as a proposition, I consider it a suggestion that must be met.'

'I'll agree to that,' said Sewell, whose logical mind saw this necessity at once. 'What are your arguments?'

'Only the usual formula: young wife, elderly husband; attractive young man in the household; sympathy of interests, deepening and broadening into love. So one or other or both at last yield to the urge of their affection and remove the barrier that keeps them apart.'

'There is no positive repudiation to your data and it does follow the routine course of such a situation. But I can't—'

'Stop there. I know you can't. I don't ask you to. I'm here only to ask you what you know definitely and positively of the relation of the two Balfours.'

'I didn't really know much more than all the world knows. I watched the three shaping the usual triangle, but I hoped their fine minds and their clean hearts would bring them through free of smirch or stain.'

'You're my idea of a first-class optimist. Think you they were brought through?'

'I don't know, Stone—I don't know. But I begin to have doubts.'

'I'll tell you what ails you, Sewell. You don't want to suspect Mrs Balfour or Ramsay, because you feel very friendly toward them. But—and here's the rub—you know if you don't suspect either or both of them, you'll have to turn your thoughts to one toward whom you feel even more kindly, your own assistant, Gill.'

'Never!' and John Sewell looked belligerent. 'You don't know Gill as I do. Why, I'd believe in Ramsay's guilt far sooner than I would in Gill's! That chap is a one-er! He's been with me five years and I know his worth.'

'Hasn't he, now and then, sold some little item, and—and forgot to record it?'

'If he did, it was his own book. I often give him a book to do what he likes with. Sometimes he sells them and sometimes he keeps them. He has a fair collection of his own. Never you mind about investigating Preston Gill. He's true blue. Now, look here, Stone, I've had a letter.'

'A ransom letter? About the Button book?'

'No. About the two people we've been talking of, Mrs Balfour and Ramsay.'

'When did you get the letter? It's only mid-afternoon now. Quick work on somebody's part! Come by mail?'

'No, that's the queer part. It was tucked under the front door, like a valentine.'

Stone held out his hand in silence.

Also without speech, Sewell handed him a letter.

Stone studied it a moment before taking the sheet out.

He saw an ordinary Government-stamped envelope addressed properly, to the book dealer, in an illiterate but painstaking hand.

'Clever,' Stone said, nodding his head at the superscription. 'That is not the disguised handwriting of one who can write better, it is the work of an ignorant and unpractised writer, presumably a woman. What's inside?'

'Read it and see.'

Stone drew the letter carefully from its envelope and looked curiously at the page.

'See what it is!' he cried.

'A fly-leaf,' and Sewell smiled; 'and first-rate paper, too. Can you deduce the author, publisher, title and date from that?'

'That's your business,' Stone retorted. 'I'm not a publishing expert. But I'd say it's a fly-leaf from a novel put out by one of our best publishing houses. Or maybe a book of poetry or belles-lettres.'

'You're pretty well right. I might add it's one of Finch and Hallon's books, but I'm not sure.'

Stone was scanning the contents, greatly interested.

The letter was not written, but was made up of words cut from a printed page and pasted into place.

'An old dodge,' he observed, 'but one of the best if the clipped papers are carefully destroyed. But what's all this?'

'Read it out,' advised Sewell.

'It begins merely "Sewell" with no other word of address. That looks as if he—or she—doesn't know you but wants to pretend acquaintance.'

'Why do you think of a woman?'

'This pasting trick is more like a woman. I can't see a man fiddling with these tiny scraps of paper.'

'Unless he's an editor or a compiler. It would come natural to them.'

'Good point. Well, it starts off breezily enough. "Don't you worry about your precious Gill. He is all right. He is one of my boy friends and he has too much character to commit any crimes. If you want to find the villain who killed the rich man, look nearer home. His death lies at the door of his lady-wife. I don't say she struck the blow, but her parrymore did. The three went to your shop, sneaked in a window, ostensibly on some book business, and then, the two conspiritors chlorryformed the poor man and one of them made the dagger play. All this so they could be rid of him and marry each other. You watch them scoot for a licence as soon as its fairly decent and maybe not that long. Anyway, turn your goggles on them and not on innocent Preston Gill. From a Lover of Justice." How's that for a faked-up letter?'

'I know, Stone, but it may be true in the main. Ramsay has been the outstanding suspect from the start. Oh, I'm not saying he did it—or she either, but it makes a plausible story.'

'Of course it does, and we'll look into it thoroughly. Let's do a little on it now. What paper do you think these words were cut from?'

'Oh, some city newspaper. Looks like the type of *The Times* to me.'

'Yes, it is *The Times*. Chosen, doubtless, because of its ubiquity. Hard to trace words cut from a daily paper. And you see, the determined author of the letter would use no other print. If she couldn't find the word she needed, she did the best she could. See, conspirators is not spelled wrong purposely. It is made up of three parts. Our artist in paste couldn't find the word, so she used *con*, then added *spirit* and then clipped *ors* from some other word, like doctors or motors, and tacked it on. Not difficult but very ingenious. I like that *chlorryformed* even better than the way the dictionary has it. She found *lorry* and *formed* and then picked up a *ch* from some word and tucked it in. Put that letter among your rare documents—not holograph, though. What do you make of the sender?'

'A lunatic, I'd say!'

'Far from it. A well-ordered brain devised that ruse, and I'm hoping it will be his undoing.'

'I thought you had already deduced a woman correspondent? How you jump about!'

'Yes, it may be a woman, but I don't think it so likely as I did.'

'Why not?'

'A little too logical for one thing. But of this I'm fairly sure. It is from the criminal—from the person who stabbed Philip Balfour. Who else would write that note? Who else would care whether Gill was suspected or not? The criminal knows that the evidence against Preston Gill is too slight, while the evidence against Ramsay, as the letter-writer states it, is damning. Now to discover who that letter-writer or, rather, letter-paster is. I know I suggested that a lot of pasting meant a woman's work. But it doesn't, necessarily. Make-up men, in a newspaper office, use paste all the time. These words are not perfectly pasted, but they are not amateur work, either. You can see by the way they are clipped, evidently with long clipping shears, and the way the ends are butted together that it is not the work of a careless flapper.'

'Maybe Preston will know something about it.'

'I doubt it, for I don't think the sender of this note knows Gill at all.'

'Now how do you get that way?'

'It just seems so. I think it is somebody who has it in for Mr Ramsay or Mrs Balfour. Oh, looky now! It might be young Balfour!'

'In the name of common sense, why? Where's any possible hint that Guy is fond of Mrs Balfour?' Sewell seemed bewildered.

'That's it. He may desire to get Ramsay so caught in the meshes of doubt and uncertainty that he may be convicted, while the lady would, of course, go free.'

'Purely speculative, old top. Try again. At any rate, the anonymous one hasn't harmed Gill any, whatever he has done to the lovers. And I suppose you've noticed that Guy Balfour also is in love with his stepmother?' Sewell looked at his friend inquiringly.

'Yes, I've noticed indications to that effect, but the whole thing is getting to be too much of a *crime passionnel*. I mean to turn my attention to the theft of the book, first, and I fully expect that will lead us straight to the murder motive.'

'All right, then. Who benefits by the possession of that book? Only someone who can so manage its sale that he will profit financially. Who can do such managing? Only one who knows quite a bit about selling rare books, but not necessarily one who knows what's inside them. Who are such in this case? Nearly everybody. Mrs Balfour, Mr Ramsay, young Balfour, myself, Gill, and, incidentally, the butler up at the Balfours', and one or two of the other servants. A sharp-witted man can't be around such a bookish house without getting more or less wise to the values.'

'Right, from start to colophon! So, it seems we have plenty of suspect fodder. Can't you help me, Sewell? I mean, take over some of these suspects, weigh 'em up and give me a final decision as to their guilt or innocence?'

'I'll have a try at it if—if you'll leave Gill to me.'

'Sure I'll leave Gill to you, you're the one to do him. Now, I take it you're going to hand that letter over to the police, pronto?'

'Well, yes—I suppose so.'

'Why not? It'll put Gill square with them.'

'That's just it. I'm afraid they'll think he did it.'

'Lord, man, you are cautious. Well, give the letter to me, and I'll use my judgment about it.'

'Yes, I'd rather do that. You take the responsibility.'

'And what shall we do about telling Gill?'

'He ought to know it—'

'I think not. Suppose you tell him the gist of the part about himself but not about the other two? I don't want that to get about, yet Gill ought to know of his friend's kindness. Besides, he may be able to state where it came from.'

'Very well, you take the letter along, you may puzzle it out. I'll tell Gill to keep it under his hat. I rather fancy he'll think it tells pretty strongly against Ramsay. He's felt mighty sorry for Alli for a long time. He has an old-fashioned love for her. Chivalric, you know, and all that. I believe he'd be glad Balfour died if it ensured her happiness.'

'With Ramsay?'

'Oh, Preston doesn't think Ramsay was the criminal at all. He says he suspects some intruder that none of us knows. Some enemy of Philip Balfour, unknown to the rest of us. Of course, that may be. It's hard to know which way to look.'

'The first thing to do, John, is to discover for certain who is the Lover of Justice. Anonymous letters are reputed to be easy to straighten out. But they are far from that. If they are clever, it takes a very clever wit to untangle them. I'll have a go at this; it may fall to pieces in my hands and it may stump me utterly.'

'When have they decided to hold the funeral services?'

'Sunday evening, I believe. At the mortuary chapel. Balfour was not a churchman and he left explicit directions as to his funeral. I shall not attend, as I want that time to do a little good-natured searching of some few places. I daresay there'll be a large gathering.'

'Yes, I daresay. Balfour was rather popular with those who knew him well. And while he had no real or known enemies, he did have acquaintances who will not grieve overmuch at his passing.'

'And we'll find the book. I'm positive that affair will end happily. But if not, whose loss will it be?'

'That's a complicated matter. Wait till I learn my lawyers' opinions. If you're going up to the Balfour house now, I'll go along with you.'

CHAPTER VIII

THE PASTED LETTER AND ANOTHER

WHEN Fleming Stone and John Sewell reached the Balfour home, they found Manton and Burnet there.

Several relatives and friends were house guests, and callers were in one room and another, waiting for some member of the household.

Ramsay was around, acting as a sort of major-domo and making excuses for Alli and Guy, who refused to see anyone.

Fleming Stone collected the two policemen and Ramsay and, with Sewell, went to the safe room to conduct a conference.

'Mr Sewell has received a communication,' he said, 'which he will show you. I think you should be informed of it, Mr Ramsay, but not necessarily Mrs Balfour, as it may be a hoax. So many misguided people write what may almost be called fan-mail to those involved in a criminal case. Show it up, John.'

Sewell laid the letter on the table at which they all sat, and the Inspector eagerly picked it up.

'For Heaven's sake!' he exclaimed, 'what's all this?'

With Burnet looking over his shoulder, he scanned the pasted words and then read it again, aloud.

Ramsay listened, unmoved, to the part about Preston Gill's innocence; then as his own name and Alli's were brought in, he showed an expression of fear. His eyes stared and blinked alternately. His lips quivered and his hands clenched themselves tightly together.

'Who sent you that letter?' he exclaimed, looking at Sewell as if he were to blame.

'I've no idea,' the book man replied. 'It reads as if from one of Gill's friends, and I'm not sure but it is just that. The reference to you and Mrs Balfour is absurd, for she was here in her home and I was here, too, at the time Mr Balfour was killed.'

'And you all know where I was,' Ramsay said. 'I was right there in Mr Sewell's shop, and I did not kill Mr Balfour, though I have no way to prove my statement.'

'This letter may be of some help.' Manton spoke a little dubiously. 'What do you make of the thing, Mr Stone?'

'Not much of anything as yet. Mr Sewell and I noticed that the notepaper is merely a fly-leaf torn out of a book, but that isn't very enlightening. The words are cut from a morning paper, and were pasted on by someone accustomed to the use of a pastebrush. It may well be from some young lady of Mr Gill's acquaintance who hopes to help him by suggesting other ways to look.'

'Pretty quick work!' declared Burnet. 'It isn't yet twenty-four hours since the murder took place.'

'It was in the papers this morning,' Stone reminded him. 'There are always busybodies ready to jump at a chance for a little excitement. Do you gather anything from the note, Mr Ramsay, that gives you the faintest idea of the sender?'

'Not the faintest. But it seems to me rather an enemy of mine than a friend of Mr Gill's.'

'That's what I think,' Sewell declared. 'But we must find out for sure. Can't you detectives track down the note by sheer ingenuity?'

'The detective instinct is useful,' Burnet told him, 'but it won't work miracles. I defy anybody to trace the sender of that letter, with no more information than the letter itself.'

He stared at Stone with a suggestion of truculence.

'Oh, I think we can manage it sooner or later,' the investigator said. 'But it will take time. You see, with all that pasting process it stands to reason there must be some fingerprints. It would be difficult to paste those tiny scraps with gloves on, and if ungloved, there probably are prints, even though invisible to us now.'

'And what earthly good would prints do us if we've no suspicion whose fingers made them?'

'Remember, we've only just seen this note,' and Stone took possession of it. 'If you'll leave it with me for a few hours, I don't promise a revelation, but I think I can make some progress toward it.'

'Take it, for all of me,' retorted Burnet. 'You want it, Inspector?'

'Not till Mr Stone gets through with it,' Manton said. 'Then I want it to file, if nothing more.'

'Let's think it out a little,' Stone suggested. 'Isn't it probable that not many of Mr Gill's friends know Mrs Balfour or Mr Ramsay? Isn't it certain that whoever sent that letter does know that those two are friendly?' A smile of apology to Keith Ramsay took the sting out of Stone's speech. 'And isn't it likely that Mr Gill can tell us which of his acquaintances are familiar with the details of the Balfour ménage? I'm not sure, just yet, that we want to show this letter to Mr Gill, but we can question him blindly about it.'

'Of course we must hunt the careful paster,' and Manton looked rather hopeless at the thought. 'And we must find out if any of Gill's friends had it in for Mrs Balfour or Mr Ramsay. What about the boy? Young Balfour, I mean.'

'There are lots of possibilities.' Stone looked pleased. 'I hope more curious letters will come. This Lover of Justice may be of real help to us as well as to Gill. Then I'll keep the letter for the present; call for it when you want it, Inspector. Don't mention it to Mrs Balfour just yet. I think she should be allowed to rest and be free from police anxieties until after the funeral. Of course, if there's any pressing necessity to consult her, we can do so. Otherwise let's try to leave her in peace. The guests in the house, the funeral, the responsibilities, leave her little spare time. She seems very much alone, but perhaps some relative will stay with her for a while.'

'Not much of anything will be done until after the funeral,' prophesied Inspector Manton. 'Tomorrow's Sunday and then the funeral in the evening—what can we do?'

'I expect to put in some work,' Burnet said, with a superior air. 'There's always something to be done in the way of gathering points here and there. I'm not through with the servants yet, either. The two chauffeurs may be able to tell us something. Did Mr Balfour use his cars much, Mr Ramsay?'

'Not very much,' Ramsay returned. 'When he went to see Mr Sewell, he usually walked. If he went down to the Public Library, or to more distant bookshops, he went in one of his cars. Mrs Balfour used them more than her husband did.'

Then the Inspector summarily dismissed all present except Fleming Stone.

'What about this letter, Mr Stone?' he said, as he returned from fastening the door.

'What do you think? I can say frankly, I've no definite idea about it as yet. Give me a cipher message or a cryptogram and I can usually unravel it at once. But this word-pasting business is the hardest kind of puzzle to solve. Imagination pushes to the fore and sometimes runs away with you. I don't think it is from a girl friend of Gill's, the wording is too sophisticated. But of course the paster had to take such words as were available. Still, with all that, whoever made up the message must have known about the friendship between Mrs Balfour and Mr Ramsay. I spoke of the matter before him without apology because, to my mind, that friendship may be the pivotal argument. Both he and she practically admit their affection, and while we can't applaud it, yet it is there and must be accepted in our calculations. Now whether the theft of the rare book is connected with the murder or not, I haven't yet made up my mind. But I can't think they are two entirely disconnected crimes.'

'Nor I. Nor do I think Gill implicated in either one. I did, but I feel now that Gill had no motive in the world for the murder, and as to the theft, I can't conceive of Sewell putting such implicit confidence in a man who would steal that treasure of a book. And yet, my experience has taught me that things and deeds we can't conceive of often do occur, and afterward we wonder why we thought they couldn't.'

'Right enough, but I've known John Sewell for a long time, and I've always been impressed by his power of sizing up people with astonishing insight and intuition.'

'That's something, of course. I don't know the man at all, but if he's like that, then Gill may be out of it. You don't think it was a young lady friend of Gill's that pasted up the letter?'

'I'm almost sure not. A young girl, anxious for Gill's welfare, wouldn't go about it that way. She would consult her people or some wise friend. I think the paster, as we call him, adopted that role of a young girl in order to divert our suspicions and stir up suspicion of Mrs Balfour. Or Ramsay, but I incline to its being an enemy of the lady. If, however, it was the murderer himself, then there was enmity toward both Mr and Mrs Balfour, and Mr Ramsay was merely caught in the meshes of the net. I have never held the opinion that Ramsay committed the murder, though I must admit the seriousness of the evidence against him. The invention of the masked man is not plausible, and yet, were he guilty, something like that would be imperative. Now, Inspector, I want a session alone with Mrs Balfour. I will tell you the results, if any, but I want a *tête-à-tête* interview. Won't you go and find her, and if she will see me, bring her back here?'

'Of course I will, and I make no doubt she'll come.'

A few moments later Alli Balfour appeared at the door. Stone greeted her gently and offered a seat.

'I know it is a busy and a sorrowful day for you,' he began; 'and I would not have troubled you but that I want a little important information which you may or may not be able to give me. Will you look at this letter?'

He handed her the pasted letter, watching her intently all the while.

She looked at the scrawled address, and said, 'I certainly don't recognize that handwriting anyway.'

She drew the letter from the envelope, and though watching closely, Stone was only almost, not quite, sure that she gave a little gasp of surprise.

In fact, he concluded he must have been mistaken, for her features changed instantly and she scanned the pasted words, while a puzzled expression appeared on her face.

'What a queer letter,' she said. 'What's it about?'

'Read it, please,' and as she obeyed, Stone again tried to catch the meaning of her bewildered look.

'It suggests nothing to you?' he asked, disappointedly.

'Why, no. Ought it to?'

'I only thought—hoped, rather, you might know someone who used that method instead of writing.'

'I? Oh, no, indeed. Why would anyone do it? It must require time and patience.'

'Go on and read it, please. Take time to finish it.'

Alli read the thing through. She grew paler as she went on, but she made no pause until she reached the end.

She handed it back to Stone, with a dignified gesture.

'That is untrue,' she said, calmly. 'I never went to Mr Sewell's shop in the evening and I was here at home all the time last night. Do you consider anonymous letters?'

'Not as a rule, but in this case we have so little to work on, I must let no chance escape me.'

'Tell me, Mr Stone, do you think that Keith Ramsay killed my husband?'

'My own personal convictions tell me no. But there is much reason to suspect him, and very little reason to suspect anyone else. Therefore, whatever my own opinion may be, I have to investigate thoroughly the possibilities of Mr Ramsay's connection with the affair.'

'Yes, I understand that, but I am disappointed to hear you say there is no other suspect. What about the person who stole the book? I can assure you Mr Ramsay never would have done that, for he was as interested as Mr Balfour himself in getting it for our library. Quite aside from the fact that Mr Ramsay is incapable of such a crime, he was desperately anxious that Mr Balfour should get it and did all he could to help. And as to Mr Ramsay being the murderer, it is out of the question.'

'But we must have proof that it is out of the question. I speak to you frankly, Mrs Balfour, because I want so much to get evidence against someone other than Ramsay. That is what we must have. As it stands, we know that Mr Balfour and Mr Ramsay went to the Sewell place together, and except for Ramsay's unsupported story, we have no knowledge that any other human being entered the shop until the police came. This masked man must be found, or we cannot expect the law to accept a story which is just what a guilty man might invent.'

'I do realize that. That is the situation I want you to clear up. Now, you think, and I am sure you are right, the book was taken in a kidnapping sense. I think the thief means to demand ransom money. I think he will not delay long his letter to that effect. Can we not wait a few days to hear from him?'

'You have given your heart to Keith Ramsay?'

'I have. I'm sure you will understand my telling you that I fought against it, but it was too strong for me. We realized how wrong we were and we decided he must go away. As you know, he confessed to Mr Balfour the situation, but you do not know that when Mr Balfour flouted the idea of his leaving, he said he would rather I should go than his efficient librarian. Mr Ramsay didn't tell me this at first, but he concluded to do so, that I might better realize the way my husband felt about the matter. I don't think for a minute that Philip would have sent me away rather than Keith, but he used that as an argument in favour of Keith's staying. Mr Balfour was a selfish man, and since Mr Ramsay was such a valuable aid, he couldn't bear the thought of losing him. I know Mr Ramsay is innocent of any crime, but as you put it, it seems to me he is in great

danger. So you must free him from suspicion. You must! Mr
Sewell thinks highly of your powers, so do many other of my
friends. Now won't you use your most ingenious, most subtle
efforts to find the criminal? Ask me anything you like—about
my husband's son, Guy—or about Mr Sewell's assistant,
Preston Gill—they seem to me possible suspects. And don't
think me cruel to Guy. He is weak and easily led. He has fallen
in with a bad set and though I would stand up for him against
my own suspicions, I cannot do so when Keith Ramsay is
involved.'

'I do understand and I thank you for your frankness and
your confidence in me. Now, suppose we do nothing further
until after the funeral. Let us wait till Monday morning before
we speak of it again. I can't answer for the police people, of
course, but I'm sure, if you request it, they won't interview you
again until after the funeral. Do you propose to ask some relative or friend to live with you?'

'No, I prefer not to. My position as Philip Balfour's widow
gives me a right to live as I choose. The presence of my stepson
supplies the need of a resident relative, and Mr Ramsay must
stay long enough to look after the library until I decide about
selling it. It is too soon yet to consider those matters and I shall
allow myself a little time to recover from the shock and excitement of this tragedy before I take up my life again. Of course,
I must obey the wishes of the police, but I want assurance of
your continued interest and effort in the case.'

'That, of course. Now I may not speak to you again about
these things before Monday. Certainly not, unless something
new turns up.'

'I am, naturally, much disturbed about that anonymous letter
that came to Mr Sewell. I had hoped no one knew of the
friendship between Mr Ramsay and myself.'

'Don't worry too much about that. I think that letter will be
a help to us, not an obstacle. And if the book kidnappers send
us a ransom letter soon, we may polish things off quickly. I

hope they show up soon, for whatever their message or however hard to decipher, we shall have something to work on.'

Fleming Stone's hope was fulfilled.

During Sunday morning, as he sat thinking over the Balfour case, a letter was brought to him which proved to be from Alli Balfour.

A mere note from her said that she was enclosing a letter that had just come to her. She added that she had read it, but wanted to make no decision regarding it until she could see Stone on Monday morning.

Stone looked at it curiously.

It seemed so innocuous in outer appearance, he could scarcely believe it was from the thief.

An oblong envelope of moderate size, addressed simply, in good-looking handwriting, stamped properly and mailed at a downtown station. Fleming Stone always noticed the way a stamp was affixed. If out of alignment with the edges of the envelope he set the writer down as a careless or untidy person.

This one, however, was so meticulously placed that it seemed as if the one who put it on had taken especial care.

The paper was white and of good quality, though not super-fine. There was no stationer's mark under the flap of the envelope and no return address on it.

Slowly, Stone took the letter out. He laid the envelope care-fully aside, though he had small hope of indicative fingerprints. Anyone as careful as this writer would not be likely to leave them, and if he had, subsequent handlings would confuse them beyond use.

The double sheet matched the envelope and the date was correctly written, though without address.

It began: 'Mrs Philip Balfour: Dear Madam:' in approved fashion, and the penmanship showed no look of disguise, no faltering and no undue haste.

If from the criminal, Stone granted his admiration to one

who used his own handwriting so freely, or so cleverly disguised his hand as to show no apparent hesitation or awkwardness.

This is what he read and he marvelled afresh at the *savoir-faire* shown.

'We have in our possession the book on the subject of certain taxation laws, rather dull reading, but made valuable by three signatures and some annotations by a previous owner. We are holding the volume at a ransom price of one hundred thousand dollars. We want to effect the exchange of the book and the money quickly and slickly. No shilly-shally work and no backing and filling. We annexed the volume for the sole purpose of getting ransom money, and we propose to get it with neatness and despatch. We are willing to state our terms and if you accept them at once the deal can be put through. If not, we shall immediately take the book apart and sell the three autographs separately. This can easily be done, and we can perhaps get as much that way as the book is worth intact. Yet you may prefer it as it is. In that case you must put a notice in one of the prominent morning papers. Any one, we shall read them all. Just say: "Your proposition will be considered," and sign it "B.G.", which will mean the name of the great signer. Unless this offer is accepted within three days, it is withdrawn, and the incident is closed. As proof that we have the book, you will find enclosed a copy of one of the annotations—your book dealer will recognize it. We do not want cipher letters, mysterious messages, go-betweens or any of the usual foolishness shown in such deals as we propose. We write frankly, and if you can trace our identity by this letter you are welcome to do so. We regret the forced omission of our signature and adopt that of—Button Gwinnett.'

The letter filled nearly the four pages. Stone read it through and then read it through again.

It seemed to him that from a letter as long as that one he should be able to deduce everything there was to know about the writer, including what he usually ate for breakfast.

He decided the stationery might have been bought at any department store or small stationer's and was useless as evidence.

The writer, he thought, had obviously used an ordinary pen and not a fountain pen, as he could note almost every time the ink in the pen dwindled and necessitated another dip. This convinced him that the man who wrote the letter was accustomed to a fountain pen, and likely a typewriter, but used the farthest remove possible from those implements.

The accuracy of the margins and spacing showed him afresh a methodical, fastidious nature, but after all these things meant little.

An educated man with tidy and careful habits, who had a good vocabulary and knew how to spell it, was not sufficient data on which to build up a criminal.

In view of the details the letter gave him, though, he tried to fit it to someone he knew.

It would do for Ramsay. Doubtless the man never used a pen, but if he did, he would, Stone thought, produce just that sort of precise writing.

The same thing could be said of Gill and of Guy Balfour, both of whom were tidy writers and scrupulously exact.

He had unostentatiously taken occasion to look at their writing, with a view toward any graphological hints.

But he must get more from this letter than any of those nebulous ideas.

Such a lot of text must give him indications of practical and definite traits that would help him find the writer.

Yet nothing appeared of any interest. Nor could he decide positively on the writer's breakfast food. If the grocers kept any cereal that quieted the nerves, that was probably the one chosen. For never had he read such an illuminating letter in such calm, casual words.

He gave up the thought of a woman writer—it was too masculine of touch for that. He didn't believe more than one person was concerned in the composition. He thought the plural form was used to mislead, or else it was used in an editorial sense.

He ran over the names of all the people who knew anything about that book. He had questioned all the principals, and this letter seemed to him to put it out of the question that the servants might have been guilty.

But the criminal was taking shape in his mind.

A collector, indubitably. But a collector base enough to steal a book and cut it up for scraps to sell, rather than stick to legitimate barter of properly accredited treasures.

He wondered if he must turn to the well-known collectors. There were doubtless many who had all the Presidents' autographs and all the signers except the coveted Button Gwinnett.

Those three autographs, cut from the book, could be sold, if judiciously marketed, for a very large aggregate.

He must take some immediate steps in the matter. In a few moments he had reached his decision, made himself ready and started off for Sewell's bookshop.

CHAPTER IX

THE OTHER

STONE knew that his friend Sewell was usually in his shop Sunday mornings, instead of going dutifully to church with his wife.

So when the investigator tried the back door and found it unfastened, he stepped inside to find Sewell almost buried in what looked like an avalanche of news sheets.

'Hello,' his host said, and swished a pile of papers from a chair for his guest. 'Sit down and tell me everything you know.'

'And I can tell you quite some,' Stone returned. 'We are in receipt of a missive from the petty thief who picked up a stray volume from your rubbish heap.'

'And to think,' Sewell groaned, 'when I hid that book in that pile of old pamphlets and magazines, I thought I was choosing the safest hiding place ever! Sort of Purloined Letter stunt, you know.'

'Yes, and it's my opinion that those smart tricks don't always get over.'

'Apparently not. Well, if the thief also wrote your letter, it must be a pretty good screed.'

'It's all of that,' and without further word, Stone handed over the letter.

Sewell read it through in silence.

'It is a good letter,' he said, speaking slowly. 'A very good letter. The writer is about as smart as they come. And it lets Gill out. Gill is a smart chap and a good letter writer, but this screed is a peg above Gill's correct but less cultured style. If a gentleman can be a thief, I'd say this is written by a gentleman. I can't help admiring his style, but I'd like to put him where he belongs. Where's the slip he enclosed? Yes, it's copied verbatim, and correctly, of course. Now, where do we go from here?'

'We ought to get a lot from that epistle,' Stone told him. 'And I think we shall. You say it lets Gill out and I'm glad of that; and I think it lets Ramsay out, too. Although Ramsay is clever enough to do that letter as it is done, I feel he couldn't write to Mrs Balfour like that.'

'No, he couldn't; Ramsay is a bit of a puzzle to me; he seems capable of daring, and I can imagine him doing a wrong, but he is not hard-boiled.'

'Nor is the writer of the letter. He says nothing rough or rude, but he shows that he means to have quick action. I'm glad of that, there's more chance of catching him off guard. As I see him, he's entirely capable of coming to the shop here, masked and perhaps otherwise disguised, and carrying out exactly the programme that Ramsay described. But the thing is to get at his identity. It does little good to say he's clever and gentlemanly and adroit and all that, but if we don't know his name, where are we? And the calm way he dares us find it out from that letter is too confident to suit me. But I propose to meet him on his own ground. I propose to find out his identity, his name and address from that letter. If I can't do it, I'll take a hard fall in my own estimation.'

'What are you going to advise Mrs Balfour to do about it?'

'Nothing, until I learn what she wants to do. She sent me the note as soon as she received it, but I'm not expecting to see her today and I want time to think it over, anyway. Do you think the thief wrote it, or had somebody write it for him?'

'I think he got it done by someone else.'

'All right, if he's only the thief. But if he's the murderer, then it isn't likely he had a confederate or a confidant of any kind.'

'Well, he has the book all right. Let's try to get that before he ruins it. The death of Mr Balfour is a much more terrible crime than the theft of the book, but the police are after the murderer and they won't pay much attention to the book until the murder case is solved.'

'That's so. We must look after the book ourselves if we can. Now, John, when did you put that book in that pile of worthless junk?'

'Thursday afternoon. I just got it and I would have taken it to Philip Balfour Thursday evening, but they were having a musicale or something. So I concluded to wait till Friday night and then, if Balfour didn't ring up and ask me about it, I was going to take it to him. But things turned up and I was busy, and so it turned out—the way it did turn out. When Balfour and his secretary came over here, they didn't know whether I had the book yet or not. You see, the owner didn't want to sell it, but the enormous price Balfour offered was too strong a temptation.'

'Did he, perhaps, get it back?'

'Lord, no. An agent was acting for him. That part of the business is right as a trivet.'

'Then when was the thing taken?'

'Why, I figure it out like this. I hid the book in the pile of papers Thursday evening and also fixed up the packet to look like the book and put that in a dummy book on the shelf. Ramsay found that, thought it was the real one, and pocketed it, meaning to get Mr Balfour home before he showed it to him. Ramsay had a right to take it, it was, of course, Balfour's property, but he had become so excitable of late, that Ramsay feared he'd have a conniption fit of some kind and he'd better be at home. But Ramsay had scarcely found the fake parcel and stuffed it in his pocket when the lights went out.'

'And from there we proceed by ourselves,' Stone said. He often included Sewell in his statements, both because he was glad of his help and he knew it pleased him. John Sewell was himself of a reasoning nature, and Stone was glad when they worked together. 'Now, we have to admit, if we grant the masked intruder, that he was someone who knew where the book was hidden. How come that, Mr John Sewell?'

'Well, he needn't have known exactly where it was. He may have come here, not knowing but I was here myself.'

'And then, perhaps, he would have killed you?'

'Why, yes, he might. You see, we've got to admit his determination to get that book even at the cost of taking a life, and he did take a life. I can think of several who are crazy about that silver skewer but that doesn't seem to point to the killer.'

'No, it doesn't. Can you think of some of your customers who would be crazy to get a Button Gwinnett signature?'

'I can't think of any who wouldn't be crazy to. But they wouldn't pay anything like what Balfour was ready to pay, nor would they be likely to kill him to get it.'

'I don't think anybody killed him to get it. He did get it, or at least we think so. We don't *know* the murderer was the thief. But I think it more likely he killed Balfour because Balfour recognized him. Then, knowing—for he must have known—he went and got the book, turned on the lights and went away, fully satisfied with his evening's performance.'

'Guy Balfour?'

'I begin to think maybe. At first I didn't suspect him at all, but since I've talked with him, and find him such a sybarite, such a lover of creature comforts, I can see how he might be so eager to inherit his father's home and a share of his father's money that he hastened the time. He's not altogether an admirable character and I'd suspect him long before I'd suspect Ramsay, other things being equal.'

'I think Alli suspects him a little.'

'She's trying not to,' Stone said. 'But after the funeral is over and she can quiet down a bit, I shall ask her to watch Guy a little and perhaps learn something. We're so desperately in the dark. We have positively no evidence against anybody in the world, except the surmises against Keith Ramsay. I'm not going to the funeral, but I shall do a little prying in the rooms of Mrs Balfour and Mr Ramsay and the suite of the late Philip Balfour, now occupied by his son.'

'Suite fit for a prince,' remarked Sewell. 'When Balfour bought that apartment, it was in process of construction, and he had it built just as he wanted it. His own rooms are palatial. And Guy is like him that way. The lad fell into his father's place as if he had always lived in splendour. He showed me all through his rooms yesterday. I like the chap, but there's something about him I don't quite understand. He's well-mannered and all that, but I wouldn't trust him as far's the corner.'

'Now, do you feel that way?' and Stone looked at his companion. 'Well, so do I. It seems as if he was positively transparent, and yet I feel he's concealing something.'

'That's come on since he hooked up with those Bohemians he admires so much. If he's connected with this trouble in any way it's owing to their influence or insistence.'

'Oh, I don't see how that can be. Well, if Mrs Balfour decides to hook up with these canny book-kidnappers, we may learn—'

'More than we want to,' Sewell interrupted.

'Yes,' Stone agreed, 'far more than we want to. I should hate to advise her to give them their head, but it can do no harm to receive his next advices and see where they lead.'

'Kidnappers of human beings are cold-blooded creatures,' Sewell observed, 'and while I suppose kidnappers of inanimate things are not so fierce, yet I wouldn't want to see a woman try to get the better of them.'

'Nor I,' Stone said, emphatically; 'I hope Mrs Balfour won't see anyone alone regarding the ransom.'

'I doubt Ramsay would let her do that. I hope for her sake he won't be arrested, but I think it quite possible he may be. And owing to the utter absence of another suspect, he may be railroaded through. It seems to me the man who wrote that letter you have should be looked up. Even if it means danger to Mrs Balfour, she could be guarded, and her experiences might solve the problem.'

'I wish I could think so, but it seems problematical. Would you advise Mrs Balfour to go to meet these people alone? Anything might happen to her. But we can't cross that bridge till we come to it. They may be willing to make terms with her without meeting her.'

'Remember all that about no go-betweens, no mysterious errands—or whatever it was?'

'But it all pointed to simple plans and not complicated proceedings.'

'Then, a lot depends on how she feels about it.'

'True enough,' Stone agreed, 'and even more depends on what Keith Ramsay thinks about it.'

'If it's Guy Balfour's doings it ought to be easily discovered—or not?'

'I don't know. That note could have been written by Guy. If he committed the murder, he wouldn't stop at theft. But he'd have to be a monster to drive that great skewer into his own father's breast!'

'And he's not a monster. But he is a creature of impulse. I've seen quite a lot of him, for he's always trying to sell me some book his father gave him. He thinks I'll pay him more than other dealers.'

'Do you?'

'Well, yes. I suppose I do. I sort of like the lad, only I wish he were a bit more trustworthy. Why are you going?'

'I have to go now. I've errands to do and a few statements to check up. I shall have to show this letter to the police tomorrow and I want to do all I can about it before I give it up. I shan't try very hard to trace the paper, but I mean to look around a bit.'

Going home, Stone spent a long time considering the mysterious letter. He enjoyed this sort of thing as a puzzle worker enjoys a particularly fine puzzle. And too, he was on his mettle to discover the identity of the writer from the letter itself, as the sender seemed to think that not likely.

He had sized up the stationery while at Sewell's and had also given attention to the penmanship. He studied that again and noted the easy swing, the carelessly tossed off words, and felt still convinced that it was the natural handwriting of someone, and not a careful disguise of his own hand nor a close copy of another's. Stone had often detected forgery after experts had declared a signature genuine and he had no hesitation in pronouncing this the work of a man untrammelled by any restriction as to shaping his letters or arranging his words. Indeed, he noted small peculiarities which he felt sure would be of help in corroboration, should he find a suspect.

For instance, he saw that invariably the dot was far ahead of the 'i' it belonged to, and the cross mark above and far ahead of its 't'. In graphology these things mean haste and also ambition and vivid imagination, and as he progressed, Fleming Stone found many points that would quickly prove for or against any other letter questioned.

The words too were taken into account. Always well chosen, and of dignified effect without being stilted, they were almost friendly in their calm straightforwardness.

And the declaration that unless something was done about it inside of three days the occasion was past.

The letter had been mailed on Saturday with a special delivery stamp that brought it to Alli Sunday morning. Stone didn't know whether three days meant until Wednesday or only until Tuesday, but he assumed the former, as the writer evinced a certain consideration.

It was mid-afternoon before he gave over his study of the problem and concluded to go to the Balfour home after all.

He walked all the way up, thinking of the letter as he went. Thinking, too, that in this case there seemed more scope for cogitation than in any crime he had solved in a long time.

His suspects remained the same, and in the same order. Ramsay, Gill, Guy Balfour—and Alli. The last he held in reserve until the rest should be freed, and he hoped he never would be called upon to accuse her directly. But she must be considered if developments called for it.

At the apartment, he found many people and much seemed to be going on. Groups here and there whispered what were apparently important bits of information and young friends of Guy's stood apart from older friends of the late Philip Balfour.

Keith Ramsay was obviously at the head of affairs. Servants went to him for instructions, guests asked him for information, curiosity seekers made him impertinent requests—all of which Ramsay managed with admirable generalship.

Guy was there but he was engaged with some friends and showed no interest in the occasion.

Ramsay made a chance to speak to Stone quietly.

'Watch Guy,' he said. 'I don't like his actions. He's all wrought up and may go to pieces at any minute.'

'I will,' and Stone looked across the room and back to Ramsay. 'How is Mrs Balfour?'

'Holding up bravely. She's in the morning room with some of her friends.'

'Has she considered what she will do about the letter from the book thief?'

'Oh, no, not yet. She says she won't even think about it until tomorrow.'

'No, of course not. What's happening tonight after the funeral?'

'There'll be supper here for anyone who cares to come. Shall you be over?'

'Not then; I'm coming here during the funeral to prowl a bit in one or two places. Leave your rooms unlocked, will you?'

'Of course. But remember, Stone, I'm not the murderer.'

'No. Who is?'

'Wish I knew! There's Guy now. Looks ill, doesn't he?'

'Yes. Who's that with him?'

'Swinton, the chap who lives downstairs. And behind him is Wiley, he lives in this house, too.'

'Yes, I know them both. Couldn't see them plainly for the moment. Mr Wiley is a collector, I believe.'

'Yes, there are several collectors here. They're all dying for a look at the library. But I've locked it up. Too easy to annex a book in a crowd.'

Stone quickly remembered that the letter in his pocket used the word 'annex' for stealing a book, but it was too slight a coincidence to implicate Ramsay.

'There goes Guy,' he said, 'going upstairs with Swinton. Are they chums?'

'I think so,' Keith returned. 'You see, Swinton lived in the same home town with Guy before they all moved to New York.'

'Where was that?'

'Trentwood, way down East. Massachusetts or Connecticut, I forget which.'

'The Balfours lived there?'

'Yes, father and son. That's where Philip Balfour met Alli and married her and then they came to New York. That was three years ago. I've only been here a year. I daresay people think me presumptuous to be taking charge here as I am, but there's no one else to do it. Somebody has to. I thought there would be some relative, old maid aunt or someone like that, to look after things. But there's no one. Alli isn't to be troubled about anything today, even the police let up on her, though they're quizzing around the city.'

'About what?'

'Oh, I don't know. Among Mr Balfour's friends, mostly. They took a lot of addresses. Probably Guy has a lot of young fellows up in his rooms, entertaining them in his own way. So somebody must look after the crowd and I've taken over.'

'Good for you. Now I'm going to look round a bit. I shall peep into your rooms but don't let it alarm you, I doubt I'll dig deep.'

'Go to it, but don't mess up the drawers of my chiffonier. I'm by way of being a tidy chap.'

'And I shall look into Mrs Balfour's rooms a little. Don't alarm her, I'm sure she'll never know I've been there if no one tells her. And it's better for her to have me rummage than old Manton or Burnet.'

'Much better. Go to it, man.'

So Stone went on his way and stopped first at Keith Ramsay's pleasant rooms, pausing longest in his sitting room, which was also office and library, for the young man had amassed a few shelves of books of his own and was justly proud of them.

Stone was after letters and he carefully looked at various packets and boxes of them, stacked away in desk drawers and cupboards. But nothing incriminating did he find, nor had he expected to.

He thought, what a farce 'searching' is! If Ramsay had anything he didn't want me to see, he would have hidden it so thoroughly that I would take hours to find it, or if very dangerous to his well-being he would have destroyed it. A few notes from Alli Balfour he left untouched, knowing if they held anything of importance they would not be there.

The only other paper that held any interest for him was a scribbled page torn from the desk pad which, interlined and crossed out by turns, showed such phrases as: 'I realize the dishonour of every hour I spend beneath your roof'—'I therefore propose to resign my position'—'My confession is forced from me'—'I trust you understand'—and other similar phrases that could only mean a rough draft of a letter he meant to write to Philip Balfour or a speech he meant to make to him.

The attitude taken by Ramsay in that matter was admirable and quite natural to a man of his temperament. But the attitude of Philip Balfour amazed Stone. He wished he had known the collector. A man who would say he would let his wife leave him rather than his assistant must be queer in his head—unless, of course, Keith Ramsay made that up!

It was dawning on Stone that many speeches and acts

accredited to Keith Ramsay might be taken with a grain of salt or—perhaps might better not be taken at all.

He left Ramsay's rooms and started toward the suite occupied by Alli Balfour.

His hand on the door, he was about to turn the knob when a voice at his elbow said:

'Just a moment, Mr Stone; you won't find Mrs Balfour in there.'

'I know it,' and Stone coolly proceeded to open the door.

'Oh, you're prospecting—I see.' Guy looked quizzical.

'Yes,' Stone said, 'and I am very busy about it. Don't detain me unless absolutely necessary.'

'It seems necessary to me,' and Guy teetered on his toes like an impatient child. 'That snooping business can wait. Do step in my place for a moment and have a little pow-wow.'

'I thought you had a flock of cronies in there.'

'I had, but one of them declared it wasn't right for me to entertain a pack of hoodlums on the day of my father's funeral.'

'Did you think it was?'

'Well, no. But they came of themselves. I didn't invite them.'

'And who was the somewhat forward guest who put them out?'

'Oh, it was Rollinson, a stickler for proprieties.'

'Well, I agree with Rollinson. And now we're here, don't you want to have a little talk with me?'

'About what?'

'About your future—your near future.'

'Anything the matter with my near future?'

Guy looked troubled, and as he turned back to his own front door, which opened into a little foyer, and ushered Fleming Stone inside, he said:

'I'm glad the fellers went and I'm glad you came.'

'So'm I,' and Stone seated himself while Guy lounged on a divan.

'You see,' Guy began, 'I want to know if I'm suspected of the death of my father.'

'By whom?'

'Well, first, by you?'

'No, I don't suspect you, or, at least, I haven't so far. But it does show a lack of reverence and respect for your father to have a bunch of cronies up here, smoking and drinking and telling stories, just before the funeral services. It shows a shocking heartlessness that would go far to strengthen the suspicions of anyone who held them.'

'Yes, I daresay. Now, Mr Stone, you're beginning to think I did in poor old Dad. Is that right?'

'Not quite. I'm only beginning to think I must pay a little more attention to your qualifications as a suspect.'

'Well, I'm sorry to say you're too late for that. You should have begun last Friday.' And then Potter came to summon Stone to the telephone.

CHAPTER X

THE DEATH OF THE SCION

FLEMING STONE had no opportunity to take up again his conversation with Guy. He left the Balfour house to keep a dinner engagement and afterward, when he knew the funeral services were being observed, he returned.

He searched Guy's rooms but found nothing of any significance. The contents of the desk were almost entirely letters and papers of Philip Balfour's and only a few notes of condolence and some bills indicated a change of occupants. Stone glanced over them, looked through Guy's personal belongings and gave up hope of finding anything incriminating.

And, as he asked himself, what could he expect to find? If Guy had killed his father he was not the sort to leave any evidence about.

Philip Balfour had employed a capable valet, but the man had left the morning after the murder and declared he would not stay in the place another minute. Guy had never had a man of his own and proposed to do so, but had not yet engaged one.

But the ever ready Potter looked after the young man, and all his personal belongings were arranged properly in the places of those his father had used. As Stone looked at the brushes and other implements on the dresser, he noticed they were blond tortoise-shell, whereas Philip Balfour had had silver ones.

'The world moves,' Stone told himself, and after another look around he concluded a better place to look would be the rooms Guy was living in before his father died.

He determined to do this as soon as might be and went downstairs to the lower floor of the duplex. He found Potter and asked him a few questions about his new master.

'Mr Guy is a fine young man,' the butler said, but Stone felt sure he would have said the same thing had he known Guy for a villain.

'Yes,' agreed Stone. 'I'm sure of that. Is he much like his father?'

'In a few ways, yes, but in the main, no. A good-natured chap, Mr Guy, but with no ambition. A lovable sort, but lazy as they come. He's never worked a day in his life. If he wanted more money than his allowance he could always wheedle it out of his father.'

'You have no suspicion of his guilt, have you, Potter?'

The grave friendliness of Stone's voice had the effect of producing a serious answer instead of a mere indignant denial.

'Well, no, sir,' Potter said. 'I did, at first, but I've watched him these two days and he's innocent, I think. But I can't say he feels deep grief because his father's gone—'

'Does anybody?' Stone spoke significantly.

Potter sighed. 'I'm afraid not, sir. It's known to all of us in the house that Mrs Balfour and Mr Ramsay are by way of being in love, and it's my opinion that Mr Balfour knew it and didn't let on.'

'Why?'

'Well, Mr Ramsay was a most useful man to the master. He helped him with his books like nobody else could. And he could manage his wife. A strong man was Mr Balfour and a wise one. Those two couldn't go very far without Mr Balfour gettin' on to it.'

'Therefore, you think Mr Ramsay might—'

'Or Mrs Balfour—' Potter said, and stopped there, as one of the under servants appeared.

Fleming Stone went home.

He was not ashamed of having tried to get some information from a servant. He had long ago discovered that the knowledge of a menial is well worth listening to. And he knew that Potter was a reliable source of enlightenment who honestly felt it his duty to help the investigators all he could.

Stone thought for a long time over Potter's suggestion of Alli Balfour's connection with the crime.

If Potter really suspected her, he must have some reason for it, and the reason in all probability was the affection between her and Keith Ramsay.

Though he had thought of this, he had not really suspected Alli, nor did he do so now, but it must be looked into more deeply, which he could only do after the funeral rites were over.

He went to bed Sunday night feeling that he had a hard row to hoe. He seemed to have so many suspects, and every suspect seemed to have means and opportunity in addition to an obvious motive.

Monday morning, as was not unusual, he was wakened by the sound of the telephone bell on his bedside table.

Inspector Manton was calling and the gist of his message was that he felt the police had shilly-shallied long enough and that he proposed to arrest Keith Ramsay that very day.

Stone smiled as he heard the word shilly-shally, for the writer of the letter to Alli had used the term. Still, he could scarcely suspect Manton of having stolen the Button Gwinnett book so he let it pass. He asked the Inspector at least to delay the arrest until his own arrival and promised to be at the Balfour house inside of an hour.

As good as his word, Stone arrived in slightly less than an hour and found Manton and Burnet in conference with Keith Ramsay and Mrs Balfour.

The latter was pale and greatly disturbed, Ramsay was indignant.

'You have no right to arrest me,' he was saying as Stone entered. 'It is surely a fifty-fifty chance that the theft of the book and the death of Mr Balfour are the work of the same hand. Now, you have had communications from outside, which indicate pretty clearly that the book is or may be available. Yet you ignore this possibility and accuse me, with no evidence whatever, of murdering Mr Balfour. If the masked man, of whom I told you, stole the book, I hold that you should get in touch with him on the chance of proving him the murderer as well. I hold it is my right that you should run down this very important clue of the letter from the thief, before you so positively assert my guilt.'

'That seems right to me, too, Inspector,' and Fleming Stone looked at Manton with real scorn. 'Where is Guy Balfour?' he went on. 'That young man is more or less under suspicion and should be present at this time.'

'Where is he?' Manton asked of Mrs Balfour.

'I suppose he is not up yet,' she returned. 'He always sleeps late.'

'Then get him up,' directed Burnet. 'Shall I go and do it?'

'No,' and Alli spoke with dignity, 'I will attend to it.'

She touched a nearby bell push and Potter appeared.

'Is Mr Guy downstairs, Potter?' she asked.

'No, madam, he has not yet come down.'

'Then go and fetch him, please. If he is still asleep, waken him and ask him to join us as soon as possible.'

Potter departed on his errand and few words were spoken until his return.

Then he said, 'I cannot get into Mr Guy's apartment at all, madam. He has locked the hall door from the inside, and there is no other way to enter. I knocked repeatedly, but received no answer.'

Mrs Balfour's face paled, but Ramsay spoke quickly. 'I don't believe there's anything to be alarmed at, Alli,' he said. 'Guy is a keen one for sleep and he must be awakened. Shall I go and rouse him?'

'What can you do more than Potter?' asked Manton. 'No, Mr Ramsay, stay where you are. We must break in, if necessary.'

'That isn't necessary,' and Alli spoke with dignity. 'There is another way in. There is a door between Guy's dressing room and my own. When my husband was alive, that door was always open. Now that Guy has the rooms, that door is locked—and I have the only key.'

'That is fortunate, Mrs Balfour,' and the Inspector looked relieved. 'Will you tell Captain Burnet where he can find that key? Or call your maid?'

'Captain Burnet can get it,' Alli said. 'Let him get Potter to go with him, and they will find the key in the small top drawer of the Chinese cabinet in my dressing room. They can knock again on the locked door that opens into Guy's dressing room and if he doesn't answer, they may unlock the door and look in.'

'Oh, I don't apprehend anything wrong,' Manton declared, 'but young men are hard to get up in the morning.'

It seemed to those waiting that it was a long time before Potter appeared at the door and said that Captain had asked for either the Inspector or Fleming Stone to come to him in Guy's apartment.

'You go, Stone,' said Manton, quite obviously unwilling to leave his potential prisoners. 'Find out what's the trouble and fix it right or let us know.'

Stone went with the butler, saying, 'Another tragedy, Potter?'

'I don't know, Mr Stone, but there's something devilish going on.'

The hall door of the suite was now open and the two men entered.

'Come on in here,' Burnet's voice sounded from the bathroom. 'Hurry.'

Stone went first into the large bathroom, and saw that Burnet was in the small compartment which held the shower bath and beyond which was the steam room. The policeman turned to greet them and silently pointed to the closed door that gave entrance to the steam room. From under this door came tiny puffs of white steam, hissing and smoking. The rug that lay in front of the door was wet and soggy, and the tiled floor showed wet places here and there.

'The door will not open,' Burnet said in a low voice. 'I fear Guy Balfour is locked in there by some accident, and is—'

'If he is in there, he is most certainly dead,' said Stone, solemnly; 'that steam is scalding hot. We must open the door as quickly as possible, but keep away from it while it is being opened. Potter, telephone down for the manager to come up here at once, and also order the chief engineer and a house plumber to hurry along. Make them understand it is a fearful emergency and they must rush! Tell them to shut off the steam.'

'Shall I use the house telephone call in Mr Balfour's office?'

'Yes, yes, but move quicker! Burnet, something terrible must have taken place in there. Guy must have gone in there for a steam bath and accidentally locked himself in, turned on the steam and for some reason couldn't turn it off again—and—it's too awful to think of! I wonder if he was subject to spasms or anything of the sort. Do you suppose there's really no way to get into that room but to break in?'

'Better call a carpenter, I'd say. And I think the lady should be sent for—and—'

'No, wait a few moments for that. But I'll get a carpenter.'

Stone stepped into the other rooms and found Potter just cradling the telephone. He bade the man call again for a carpenter of skill and advised that he bring a helper.

It seemed but a few moments before the place was filled with people. The engineer took one look and rushed back to telephone that the steam pressure be turned off all over the house.

The manager, a big man named Latimer, took in the situation at a glance.

'How long has he been in there?' he cried. 'Potter, call Doctor Kelsey from six-o-three. Lord knows how we may find the poor fellow!'

'Not alive,' Stone said, sadly. 'There's no other way to get in, Mr Latimer? We must break in?'

'Yes, yes! Go to it, men. Boss the job, Mike. Break in, or cut out the lock, as you think best, but hustle!'

An electric drill soon cut out the knob and lock, and at a push the door opened about half way.

The men sprang away from the flood of steam that issued, and waiting impatiently, tried to peer in through the clouds. But having been turned off in the basement, the supply soon ceased, and the vapour began to disappear.

Burnet was the first man in, and Stone quickly followed.

Waving back the others and holding a Turkish towel to his face, Stone saw what had kept the door from opening fully. The nude body of Guy Balfour lay on the floor, dead from the effects of the escaping steam.

'Get the doctor in here,' Burnet said, 'we can't wait for Jamison now.'

Stone held the door, allowing Doctor Kelsey to enter the steam room. It was still too warm to be pleasant, but the danger was past, and better visibility obtained.

The physician knelt by the body, and shook his head. 'Nothing to be done,' he said. 'Poor chap, he was trying to reach the door sill, in hope of getting air to breathe. He was suffocated, you see, and died before he was greatly affected by the burning steam. Give a hand, Burnet, we'll lay him on the couch for further examination.'

'Want any of these workmen any more?' Latimer asked.

'Let the carpenters go,' Burnet directed, 'but hold the plumber. We may want him.'

The carpenters, cautioned to say nothing about the matter, were dismissed, and then Burnet said Manton must be called.

'Of course,' returned the manager, who was nearly beside himself with dismay and anxiety. 'Such a thing to happen in this house! The head and front of all fine apartment houses in the city!'

'Captain Burnet,' Latimer went on, pleadingly, 'when the Inspector comes, can't you and he get the body away at once? You know what these high-class tenants are. And this thing is an awful blow. I hope you can take him to the morgue right away. I want to do anything I can for Mrs Balfour, of course, but this—coming right after her husband's—er—sudden death is too much! He, thank goodness, died away from home, but this horror right here on the premises is not good for the house—no, not at all.'

'I'm sorry, Mr Latimer,' Burnet told him, 'but there is a police routine that must be carried out. The Medical Examiner must come here and give his permission before the body can be removed. Also, the Inspector will have something to say; I can only promise that after police regulations are carried out and Mrs Balfour's wishes consulted, I will do all I can to have your request granted. But, unless your workmen chatter, the story need not get out until much has been accomplished. Now, someone must tell Inspector Manton, also Mrs Balfour and Mr Ramsay, what has happened. Will you do this and send them all up here? Doctor Kelsey must remain until the Examiner comes. Sorry, Doctor, but it won't be long.'

Latimer hurried away, glad to get matters started, and running down the curving staircase he flung open the door of the room where the Inspector was still waiting the return of his associate.

'There's another murder,' the manager announced explosively. Then as he saw Alli pale and tremble, he turned his back on her and whispered to Manton, 'Guy Balfour is dead—you tell her and look after things, I must get to my office.'

He fairly ran from the room and all but slammed the door behind him.

Ramsay took the situation in hand. 'Latimer is a very excitable person,' he said. 'Suppose I go and see what is the matter?'

'We'll both go,' Manton said. 'Please remain here, Mrs Balfour. I will send for you.'

'Latimer told me young Balfour is dead,' the Inspector said to Ramsay as the two went upstairs.

'Did I do it?' asked Ramsay, sarcastically.

'You're quite likely to be suspected, I imagine,' returned Manton.

'Don't let your imagination run away with you,' Ramsay advised, and no further word was spoken.

Burnet met them in the bedroom, gave a brief recital of what had happened and led the way to the bathrooms.

Stone watched Ramsay's face as he took in the scene and heard the particulars, but, as the investigator had anticipated, there was no definite expression of emotion on that immobile countenance.

Ramsay was exceedingly angry at the Inspector's attitude toward him—and if he were innocent he had a right to be angry. But was he innocent?

He showed a decent amount of regret and sorrow at the passing of young Balfour, but made no observation nor asked any question regarding the strange circumstances of his death.

Feeling no vital interest in the conversation going on, Stone wandered off by himself. He paused in the dressing room, which was between the bedroom and the main bathroom.

He saw only the traces of the most natural actions on the part of Guy Balfour. The suit that he had worn was hung in a clothes closet. His underwear was tossed on a chair and his shoes and socks were untidily thrown on the floor. The bed was turned down, but had not been used. In the bathroom Stone had noticed a flung bathrobe and a pair of kicked-off slippers, for Guy had stepped into the steam room unclothed.

In the bathroom, too, Stone saw the lock that had been taken from the door. This he took with him and went on to the small room that had been Philip Balfour's office, which his son had planned to turn into a bar.

Stone's attention was attracted to the lock he was holding.

As far as he could see the lock was unimpaired. It was the type of lock often used in apartment houses, the kind that has in the edge of the door a small catch or bolt which pushed in will lock the door, and another, just below it, when pushed in will leave the door unlocked.

But, and this is what engrossed Stone's mechanical brain, it was positively certain that the way that lock was arranged, when the latch was off the door could be opened from either side, but when it was on the door could be opened from the outside only.

Absurd, Stone thought to himself. No sense to it at all. But I must be mistaken about it, for Philip Balfour lived here three years, presumably using that lock, and he must have turned it on or off at will. I'll see what the police mechanicians make of that.

Also, he thought, he would see where this new tragedy was leading them.

Ramsay was the pet suspect of the police. Could he have managed this horrible crime if he had so chosen?

Stone had to admit that he could have done so. He didn't for a moment believe Ramsay did do it, but it was within the possibilities.

Indeed, who else could have managed it? Ramsay, living in the apartment, having lived there a year or more, had ample opportunity to fix up the lock of a door to suit himself.

But the steam business—what about that?

Stone had been tacitly taking for granted that that was an accident. He argued that Guy, unaccustomed to such elaborate plumbing fixtures, might easily have turned on the steam at a greater pressure than he meant to and had been unable to turn it off again. A further examination of the pipes would settle that question, but now it must wait.

Stone thought further. The doctor had said Guy was suffocated. Quite apparently he had fallen to the floor, and had crawled toward the door either in hope of getting air or to call for assistance.

So he was conscious up to then, anyhow. The steam suffocated him and he died, then and there, unable to call out or to reach the door. But where—and this is what baffled Stone—where was any hint or sign of foul play?

Why did the manager immediately lament the direful stigma

of murder on his house? Why did Burnet assume murder? Why did he, himself, Fleming Stone, feel sure it was a murder?

But that must be settled later. He was basing his present thoughts on the crime, if it was a crime—on the murder, if it was a murder.

And he would go on, for a few moments, investigating the circumstances.

If a murder, then a perpetrator. Who? The police would surely say Ramsay. But was it necessarily Ramsay? There was still Gill to suspect. Could Gill get in the house and get into Guy's rooms and fix up that steam gauge? Oh, ridiculous! Of course he couldn't!

Then—and Stone knew he now had to face it—then how about Alli?

The word was out, in his mind, and he felt as if he had blazoned it to a thrill-hungry crowd.

He had to keep on. Alli? Why, yes, many people would say she had motive, all would say she had opportunity, and if the means, including as they seemed to, mechanical knowledge— well, Ramsay was known to be a handy man at mending books, why not at a bit of simple plumbing?

It was out, and Stone faced it squarely. He didn't believe it at all, but he had to know if such a theory would hold water.

Still and all, did Alli have such a strong motive to be rid of Guy? Her husband was a different consideration, he stood in the way of her happiness with Ramsay. But Guy didn't do that, unless—oh, that trite old reason—unless Guy knew some secret detrimental to Ramsay or, even, to Alli.

Now he was started, Stone pursued his thoughts further, knowing he could have no peace till he did so.

It was all such an easy solution; such a plausible, such a likely solution. The two young people in love; the much older man, so careless of the situation that he scoffed at Ramsay's confession. The ready-made opportunity—all three under the one roof—oh, he'd considered all that before. Say it was true, say Alli had killed her husband with or without Ramsay's assistance. Then say Guy had discovered it; that meant that only Guy's death could save the guilty pair.

Stone rose, shook himself and walked to the window.

I won't have it, he told himself, emphatically. I discard all such deductions or suppositions or beliefs. Whoever committed that murder or those murders, it was not Mrs Balfour and I do not think it was Keith Ramsay, either.

My God! He suddenly remembered: today, Alli was to see about that ransom letter! I wonder what the poor girl is doing in there with the police! I'm going to see.

Stone went back through the rooms and found the two policemen, Alli and Ramsay in the dressing room.

'Have you reached any conclusion?' he spoke to Manton, but he sat down beside Alli.

'Not a definite one,' the Inspector said, 'but Jamison will be here any minute now and he may be of some help.'

'Young Balfour's death is a murder,' Burnet declared, shortly. 'I have no doubts as to that.'

'Why are you so sure?' Stone inquired, urbanely.

'Because it couldn't be anything else. Philip Balfour used all these dinky gadgets—these gauges and stopcocks and pressure meters for three years and they never bothered him. Along comes his son, who is nobody's fool, and he falls dead in forty-eight hours or so. What's the answer? Somebody preferred his absence to his presence. That's all.'

'No, Captain,' Stone said, 'that isn't all.'

CHAPTER XI

ALLI RESPONDS TO THE LETTER

'As I see it,' Stone went on, 'the first thing to do is to find out for certain whether this is accident or murder.'

It was afternoon now and they were again downstairs, presumably undergoing an inquisition by the police, but really deferring to Fleming Stone's leadership.

The Medical Examiner had been and gone. He had merely corroborated the statement of Doctor Kelsey that Guy Balfour had been suffocated by the escaping steam and had died a swift and probably painless death. He had given permission to remove the body and it had been sent to the mortuary.

A buffet luncheon had been arranged in the dining room, of which both the policemen had partaken separately.

Alli Balfour refused food with a mere shake of her head and sat like one benumbed, gazing out of a window and saying no word.

Keith Ramsay sat beside her, also silent, but alert and watchful.

They were in the library, Alli having chosen to go there, and they were grouped round a table on which were a few notes or lists belonging to the two policemen.

Stone had a few notes on a card in his pocket, but he did not display them.

'I have spoken with the plumber and the electrician,' he said, 'but they seem to have no definite or personal knowledge of the fixtures in Mr Balfour's steam room. They are new men, I think, and had nothing to do with the installation of the special plumbing Mr Balfour had put in. But I am even more curious about the lock on the steam room door.'

'There's no lock on the steam room door,' said Alli, still looking and speaking like one in a daze. 'He said no one could come in except his valet, and he never wanted to lock him out.'

'There isn't a lock on the door exactly,' Stone explained, 'but there is a catch which may be pushed in, that prevents the door being opened from the inside.'

'Oh, yes, I remember now,' and Alli suddenly became alert. 'When the steam room was installed—you know Mr Balfour had all those bathrooms built to his own order—the knob or the scutcheon or whatever you call it was of a very elaborate type, and somehow the workmen put it on wrong, and the result was you could open the steam room door from the outside but not from the inside, unless the catch was off. Then it would open from either side. Mr Balfour always intended to have it fixed, but he procrastinated and after a time, he wouldn't bother about it, for, as he said, the catch was never turned on, it was always off, and so the door would open either way. Now, in some way that catch must have got turned on, probably Guy did it himself, not knowing about it. I never thought of it, of course, and Victor, Mr Balfour's valet, was here only one night while Guy was in those rooms—that very first night, you know, and he left the next day. He never liked Guy. I don't know why, I'm sure.'

'If the valet didn't like young Mr Balfour, might not he have turned the catch to make trouble for him? Not thinking, of course, of tragedy.' The Inspector asked this question, but Alli made no reply. She just sat and stared, seemingly at nothing.

Keith Ramsay answered.

'I'm sure Victor never did that. I've known him more than a year, and he is an honest, reliable chap, devoted to his master and careful about his work. He had no real quarrel with Guy, but he was a superstitious sort, and he was terribly upset by Mr Balfour's death, more because of the mystery and gruesomeness of it than because of personal sorrow. He came to me and told me he must leave at once, he was afraid to go into Mr

Balfour's rooms any more. I urged him to wait a few days, but he said no, and he gave me an address which would always find him and went off early that next morning.'

Manton gave the speaker a glance of disapproval.

'And you didn't care to report that episode to me? Seems a bit strange. Were you a special friend of his?'

'No,' Ramsay spoke coolly, 'I have no interest in the man. Nor had I any thought of his implication in the matter of Mr Philip Balfour's death, nor do I now think of him as connected in any way with the death of Mr Guy Balfour.'

'He must be thought of, and seriously,' Manton said. 'He was the only one who would have had opportunity to adjust the latch of the steam room door so that it would make anyone shut in there a prisoner.'

'No,' Ramsay said; 'several of the other servants could have done that. The chambermaids, the cleaning women and the man who takes care of all the tiled floors and the bathroom fixtures. Any of these could have fixed that catch had they wanted to. It was probably done by Guy himself, unconsciously or unthinkingly. He may have known about it but forgotten it. I'm sure his death was an accident.'

'I'm not sure of that,' Fleming Stone said. 'I am here to investigate the death of Mr Balfour, Senior, and I think that death and the death of his son were brought about by the same hand. It seems to me that Guy Balfour after a shower bath went into the steam room, closed the door, not thinking of lock or catch, and turned on the steam. Unfamiliar with the gauges and dials of which there is a bewildering array, he turned on what he thought was right, but which was not right, because, to my way of thinking, the murderer had so manipulated the pressure gauge that it gave higher pressure than was indicated by the dial. Then, as I see it, Guy became more and more frightened and confused and, beginning to lose his breathing power, he fell to the floor and endeavoured to reach the door either to open it or to get air from under it. This may not have been his exact procedure but it must necessarily be just about what he did. Now, it may be all accidental or it may be the premeditated work of a heartless fiend. If the latter, we must discover his identity; if the former, we have to prove it.'

'I suppose you realize, Mr Stone,' the Inspector spoke slowly, 'that all you have just said points unmistakably to Mrs Balfour and Mr Ramsay who are here with us?'

'If it points to them, it points mistakenly,' and Stone began to show a spirit of contradiction. 'If you suspect them, Inspector, please say so openly and not make use of my words.'

'Very well, then, I do suspect them, either separately or in collusion. I came over here today expecting to arrest Mr Ramsay, but the excitement of Mr Guy Balfour's death interrupted all else. We have now to discover the truth about that as well as the truth about the death of his father. I have grave suspicions of Mr Ramsay's guilt and I have fears that Mrs Balfour is also implicated. But owing to this new tragedy, I shall postpone any action until some further investigation. In the meantime these two are forbidden to leave this house without my consent and are under strict surveillance.'

'You may as well own up, Inspector, that you are postponing your threatened arrest because you have not sufficient evidence to justify such a proceeding.' Stone said this lightly, but he saw from Manton's face that it was true.

And then Alli, speaking with dignity and a certain independence, said, 'I am in no way involved in either of these tragedies, Inspector, and you know better than I do the penalties of a false arrest. Yet I have no objection to your surveillance, if you will leave me free to attend to one highly important matter. And that is, the recovery of a very valuable book, which is missing and which you doubtless know all about from Mr Sewell. The abductors, that is what they call themselves, have directed me to take certain steps toward getting the book back if I choose to do so.'

'You have had a communication from the thief who took that book? Why have I not been informed of it?'

'There really hasn't been time to tell you, Inspector,' and Alli gave him a sad little smile. 'Yesterday I was a nervous wreck and declined to see anybody. The funeral last evening left me almost in a state of collapse. On my return home I went to bed at once. I intended telling you about the letter this morning, then this second death occupied all our attention to the exclusion of everything else. Here is the letter if you want to read it. If I answer it at all it must be done tonight.'

Inspector Manton read the letter through, then handed it over to Captain Burnet for perusal.

'What do you intend to do in the matter?' Manton asked her.

'I have not quite decided but I think I shall put the advertisement in the paper as he suggests. I feel that it is my own affair and that I am quite competent to handle the situation.'

'May I warn you that you are probably running into danger? An abductor of a human being is one of the most formidable of criminals, and in some ways an abductor of a book may be equally dangerous. I beg of you, Mrs Balfour, do not run unnecessary risks. Report to me any important step you contemplate taking and let me see to it that you are duly protected.'

Alli's icy attitude thawed a little.

'You are kind,' she said, 'but I've no idea what plan the thief will suggest to me, if any. Moreover, Mr Stone is working for my good and will doubtless be amply able to look after my interests.'

'I've no desire to intrude but I will remind you that many situations can be met only by police assistance and should not be handled by citizens however capable and willing.'

'There can be nothing definite done in the matter of the book today or tonight,' Stone said. 'If Mrs Balfour puts a notice in the paper it must be in tomorrow morning's issue. It will then take some time for an answer to reach her and you may rest assured I shall let her take no chances where her personal safety is concerned.'

'So you see, Inspector,' Alli went on, coaxingly now, 'I must have permission to keep any appointment in regard to that book, without being under this strict surveillance of yours, or the abductors may get frightened off and I may not be able to arrange for the return of the book. See?'

The girl looked very wheedlesome, and in truth the Inspector was glad to be relieved of the responsibility of finding the book. He felt he had quite enough to do with two murders on his hands and the two people he suspected of the crimes showing no inclination to confess!

He and Burnet had agreed that the guilty parties in the first murder must be Ramsay and Mrs Balfour. In the second murder—if it were a murder—they were so palpably the criminals he felt no need to look further.

But proof or at least strong evidence must be obtained to establish his beliefs and how could he hunt for proof, if all bound up in the entanglements of a very complicated theft?

'Very well, Mrs Balfour,' he said, at last. 'Consider yourself free to hunt for your missing book, but have a care for your own safety and do nothing at the behest of people you do not know, however plausible their arguments and however promising their plans. You understand me, Stone? You know how desperate a bold thief can be. And this book theft has all the villainous possibilities of a kidnapping case. Look out for the welfare of Mrs Balfour in preference to retrieving the book.'

'Yes, Inspector,' and Stone spoke sincerely, 'I do understand and you are entirely right. I shall use most extreme care and discretion. And in case of need I shall be glad to call on you for assistance.'

Some time later the Inspector asked Stone to go with him for a conference in the safe room.

Stone went, and they found Burnet already there.

'We have reached a conclusion, Mr Stone,' Manton said. 'We

have carefully investigated the circumstances of Guy Balfour's death and we must conclude that it was brought about by foul play.'

'That was my opinion from the first,' Stone said. 'Have you also discovered the criminal?'

'There can be no doubt that it was the work of Mr Ramsay or Mrs Balfour, or the two in collusion.'

'There is doubt of that in my mind,' Stone returned. 'Will you tell me why you are so sure?'

'Yes. Mrs Balfour had a key that would open a door into Guy Balfour's dressing room. There was no other mode of entrance as the hall door was locked last night.'

'Yes, I know that. But that does not prove that the dressing room key was used—until it was used to open the door by us this morning. What time do the doctors set for Guy's death?'

'They agreed that it must have taken place soon after midnight.'

'But don't you see that the arrangements in the steam room could have been made much earlier than that?'

'What do you mean?' asked Burnet. 'Guy was in his rooms with some of his cronies before he went to his father's funeral at the mortuary chapel.'

'Yes, and he was there for some time before those friends came. Anyone could have been with him and could have fixed the lock of the steam room door and also have turned the steam pressure gauge a few pounds higher. The criminal, a caller let us say, could have done this without Guy's knowledge, or could have done it while Guy was at the funeral.'

'It is possible but far from probable.'

'Not possible, either,' declared Burnet. 'A caller couldn't have marched into the steam room in front of Guy's very eyes and fixed up the place.'

'Yes, he could, if other callers were there all talking and jesting among themselves, as I'm told they were.'

'Cut it out!' Burnet showed his annoyance. 'Don't make up

fairy tales when the truth lies open before you. Who wants that
young man out of the way? His stepmother and her lover. Why?'

'Well, why?'

'I'll tell you why! Because it was Keith Ramsay who killed
Philip Balfour down at the bookshop. Guy Balfour found that
out and was about to expose him, so they had to put him out
of the way. Of course, Mrs Balfour was not at the shop when
her husband was killed, but she knew all about it and knew
Guy had found it out.'

And then Stone suddenly remembered that Guy had begun
to tell him something just before the funeral the night before,
but just then Potter had called him, Stone, to the telephone,
and he never had heard what Guy was about to tell him.

It could be that Guy had learned who killed his father and
had told Alli or Ramsay, and together they had conspired to
kill him.

The fact that Alli did have a key that gave access to Guy's
suite was a damning fact against her—and therefore against
Ramsay.

Stone's heart was heavy as he realized the score they could
count up against the two lovers. Yet it was absurd, too. Had
they chosen, either of them could have found a chance to enter
Guy's rooms through the day, Sunday, and do whatever they
chose unheeded.

Stone said this to the policemen, but Manton said: 'Well, yes,
of course that could be, but the easier way was for Mrs Balfour
to slip in, from one dressing room to the other, by means of her
key. If she had been seen, she could have said she was taking
fresh towels or some special soap or anything like that.'

'I don't believe Mrs Balfour would kill her husband's son!'
and Stone showed a trace of anger.

'Well, all right, then Ramsay did it,' Burnet said. 'She gave
him the key, and he could choose his own time.'

'But, Burnet, you're just imagining all that. Stick to facts.
There were those young fellows in Guy's lounge. How many?'

'I d' know, five or six, I guess.'

'Well, anyone of those could have met the conditions. Could have fixed the door catch and the pressure gauge and then gone off home. Of course, the steam room wasn't used until Guy used it late at night after his return from the funeral. I asked Potter, and he found out from the clean-up people that the steam room was all in order when the bathrooms were done up. So later on, when they all came home, Guy, as I learned, excused himself rather soon and went up to bed. Weary and worn out, he took refreshing baths and after a shower went into the steam room and just as his father had done for three years, he flung the door shut behind him and turned on the steam, giving neither gesture a thought beyond its routine. Then, the door latch having been set, so that it would not open from inside, and the steam pouring out so fast he could neither check it nor turn it off, he fell to the floor and was suffocated. No imagination there. Just the facts as they must have happened. But I am sure you agree to all that. Where we disagree is the name of the one who did all this.'

'That's right, Stone,' Manton said, speaking positively. 'We do agree to all that. But Burnet is set on the guilt of those two. You seem to have someone else in your head—who is it?'

'No, I haven't anyone else in my head. But I do think it was not one of the pair you suspect, nor do I think it was Gill or any of the servants here. I'm speaking now of the first murder. And I think Guy's death was by murder, too, and I think the same person committed both murders. I mean to look for him among Guy's crowd or at least among Guy's acquaintances. What about that man called Rollinson?'

'I saw him,' Burnet stated. 'He's of no interest. He's sort of ringleader of this gang Guy had fallen in with, but he's a well-mannered chap and he tries to keep the others in order. Some of them came over here to see Guy late yesterday afternoon, but I don't think they went around fixing death traps.'

'What about those two men who live in the house?' Stone asked. 'Aren't they friends of Guy's?'

The Inspector gave the information. 'One is; Swinton used to know the Balfours in Johnnycake Corners, or wherever they lived in Connecticut. He went to see Guy quite often before his father died. But he'd have no reason to kill either of them. Wiley, now, he is a parasite sort. He'd fawn on Guy or the old man either, in hope of getting a present of a rare book. Or if not a present, then as a bargain. He was, like many collectors, anxious for high spots, as they call 'em, but not anxious to pay high prices. I've talked to both those men and they gave me no slightest reason to suspect them.'

'Same here,' Stone said. 'I called on them both, but got from them exactly nothing. Now, Inspector, you won't make any arrest until after this next funeral, will you?'

'Oh, no, not before Guy is buried. Well, Stone, go about your kidnapped book, but be careful of the lady. I'd rather see her under arrest than in the clutches of a kidnapper. They are ruthless, you know.'

'Yes, when they abduct a child, or an adult; but a book is merely a theft.'

'I hope it will prove so. Do you know when the funeral services will be held?'

'No, Inspector, I don't. Most likely tomorrow night or Wednesday. Poor Mrs Balfour, she will be ill if things go on like this!'

'She's ill now. Well, Stone, I'd like to see you pull off one of your surprise stunts, but I see no sign of such a thing.'

'The game's never out till it's played out. You can't tell what may happen. But don't make any arrests for a few days. You can keep your suspects under the strictest surveillance and yet learn a lot if they think they're free. I'm going to see Mrs Balfour about the missing book now and perhaps I'll learn something. I say, Burnet, did you say you saw that Rollinson chap at his home, or just over here, yesterday?'

'I stopped in to see him a minute about noon today. I had to go out on another errand and I looked him up. He was amiable enough, but he seemed to have nothing to say. Not surly or taciturn, you know, but just sort of blank. Couldn't believe Guy was dead. Knew nothing about the steam room, wasn't there when Guy was showing off his new home. He was shocked at my news, said it must be an awful blow to Mrs Balfour and then shut up and waited for me to go. I was in a hurry, so I went.'

'You think him innocent because he was so unconcerned?'

'I think him innocent because I see no reason to think him otherwise. Why don't you go to see him?'

'I am going as soon as I get a chance. And you mark my word, there are others to consider before you pounce on Keith Ramsay. Don't forget Preston Gill. If he was guilty in the first case, or if he is mixed up in the missing book business, you'd better get him clean before you arrest innocent people.'

Stone left the room and went in search of Alli.

He found her with Ramsay in the library.

He looked around at the great, beautiful room, and wondered into whose possession it would pass if—if Alli Balfour were arrested.

This thought gave him a shock, and when he entered the room, Ramsay exclaimed:

'For Heaven's sake, man, what has happened now?'

'Nothing new,' Stone returned, forcing a smile. 'What is going to happen is the question. Mrs Balfour, are you still determined to answer the letter about the book?'

'No,' said Alli in a low somewhat frightened tone, 'I am beginning to feel afraid. Suppose the bad men want me to come to see them alone, or at night, and then abduct me as well as the book!'

'Don't talk nonsense, dear,' said Ramsay, who took but slight pains to hide his affection before Stone. 'You see, Stone, I look at it this way. That book *belongs* to Mr Balfour's library—I mean, the library needs it. It is a rounding out book. It completes the lot of the signers.'

'And is a set of signers' autographs of such national importance?'

'That's just what it is—of national importance. And this splendid library,' he looked around, 'has its signers complete, save for Button Gwinnett. It has most of its items complete. You know, often a book demands another book to make it perfect. I want Alli to put that notice in the paper, even if she never follows it up.'

'Oh, I'm willing to do that,' and Alli looked at Keith, 'but if their next directions are too hard, I won't meet them—alone.'

'You needn't,' Stone told her; 'we won't allow you to do that.'

'Then all right,' Alli agreed. 'But I won't do anything till after Guy is buried.'

'Of course not,' Keith said; 'shall we word it just as he said?'

'Yes, why not?' and Stone began to think the librarian rather insistent.

'Then I have it here already written. But I think I'll telephone it. Shall I have to give my name?'

'Yes.' Stone looked at him. 'Why don't you go to the newspaper office and deliver it yourself? It's no secret, you know.'

'That would be better. Here, look it over.'

Stone read the typed slip, 'Your proposition will be considered.' It was signed 'B.G.'

Ramsay took it again and left the room.

CHAPTER XII

WHERE DID ALLI GO?

MORE than a week had passed since Philip Balfour had come to his untimely end. And nearly a week since his son had followed him.

It was Saturday morning. For some reason known only to themselves the police had not yet arrested Keith Ramsay. It was obvious that the reason implied was merely a lack of sufficient definite evidence and they hoped to achieve that soon. Whether such hopes were well founded only the future could tell.

Fleming Stone, not depending on the efforts of the Inspector and his aides, worked tirelessly after his own fashion.

He had gone to Trentwood seeking information among those who used to know Philip Balfour and his son. He found many who knew them, but none who knew them well or who knew anything against them.

They described Balfour as a book collector and a bookworm who kept himself very much to himself, associating with only a few friends who were also bibliophiles.

Guy seemed of no interest to anybody. He was spoken of as one who would never set the North River on fire and, indeed, few people are expected to do that.

Carl Swinton had lived there for a brief period, but he, too, had left no mark, shining or otherwise.

Starting with the postmaster and the shopkeepers, Stone received hints as to the friends of these men, but when he hunted them up, they were either dead or moved away, or, if available, they remembered no definite or helpful details about their one-time fellow citizens.

Stone might well have said, 'Well, this is the hardest case I ever tackled!' But that was not his attitude toward his work. Instead, he said to himself, 'Guess I'll have to put my most desperate energies on this problem!'

His temptation was to assume some person or persons unknown and endeavour to make their acquaintance. But first, he must exhaust every possibility of the suspects now claiming his attention.

He favoured Gill because of his exceptional opportunities, then Ramsay, because of his strong motive, then the unknown intruder who left no trace, because of his mystery, and—at last, very reluctantly, Alli.

Reluctantly, but definitely and logically. Always his nature refused to blind himself to a possible suspect because of his own interest or affection. If from what he knew it could logically follow that Balfour's wife had been instrumental in his taking-off, then he must suspect her and follow up those suspicions.

He tried while in Trentwood to learn more about the girl, but it seemed she had been of Lucy's class—'a violet by a mossy stone, half hidden from the eye'.

Yet Stone knew, none better, that three years' absence is enough to wipe out personal memories, and he sighed as he concluded he could learn more of Alli from her present-day self than by what any of her old acquaintances could tell him.

A good-natured young shopkeeper, whose stock seemed to run to stationery and artists' materials, appeared to know more about the girl than most. In fact, he admitted, he was desperately in love with her himself when she lived in the little town.

'Probably most of the young chaps were,' Stone surmised.

'They sure were!' and the uninteresting historian nodded his blondish head. 'Every last one of them. And she threw over the whole lot for that man old enough to be her father!'

'Why?'

'His millions. Most of us fellows had little to offer her and she wanted lots.'

'Weren't there two men here at that time, named Wiley and Swinton?'

'Never heard of Wiley. Swinton lived here for a short time.'

'Was he in love with the beautiful Miss Cutler, too?'

'I d' know about that. But he was going to paint her or thought he was. He was always trying to get sitters.'

'Could he paint?'

'Not he! But he'd come in here and buy a lot of gamboge and yellow ochre and make out he was a genius. I never saw any portrait he did.'

'And Wiley you don't know? Pete Wiley?'

'Nope. Say, tell me, who bumped off the old man? Wonder if Alli'll marry again?'

'A little soon to think of that, eh?'

'Not for a woman. No, sir. Oh, well, I've some work to do. Can I help you any more, sir?'

Stone didn't say that he hadn't helped him any, as yet, but he couldn't feel that any of the stationer's news was valuable. But he observed the amenities and went back to the railroad station, feeling that he had gained nothing from his trip save a knowledge that there was nothing to be gained in the mildly pretty village of Trentwood.

That was a couple of days ago. He had sent a trusted ambassador to Chicago to track down any rampageous stories he could about Pete Wiley. But though willing and eager, the messenger found no rest for the sole of his foot, and returned with the information that no one in Chicago knew Wiley and no one wanted to.

Stone honourably admitted to himself that he was nearing the end of his rope, but added, also to himself, that in such case he must merely let out more rope.

Near the end of his rope, then, and knowing that at the end he must find Alli, he commanded himself to think seriously of Keith Ramsay.

It seemed an anti-climax after his hopes of stirring up a

hornets' nest in Trentwood, but he took up again the threadbare arguments.

Ramsay had motive and opportunity and a weapon ready to hand.

Yes, he told himself, sarcastically, so he had heard.

He knew every detail of Keith's motive and how strong it was; of Keith's opportunity and how convenient it was; of Keith's weapon and how sharp it was. Those were all concrete things.

Now, as to the psychology of the occasion, could Keith Ramsay, loving Alli Balfour as he did and being the upright, clean-handed man that he was, could he kill the lady's present husband and then expect her to marry him after that? And if he didn't expect her to marry him, why undertake the dreadful and dangerous enterprise at all?

All the fine talk about leaving Mr Balfour's service because of his honourable impulses cut very little ice with Fleming Stone. The criminal of deepest dye would tell some such story in an endeavour to prove his innocence.

He concluded upon his plan of action and started for the Balfour apartment to put it to work.

There he found Ramsay, looking deeply perplexed and even more distressed.

'I'm glad to see you,' Keith greeted him, though looking too perturbed for gladness. 'I wish you'd come into the safe room for a few minutes.'

'Of course,' and the two men entered and closed the door.

'I had a talk with Alli last night,' Ramsay began, not waiting for preliminaries. 'She's all for going to see the mysterious keeper of the missing book.'

'I'd be glad to see her go,' Stone said, slowly, 'but she mustn't go alone.'

'I know,' Keith responded, 'but who can go with her that they would allow? Not you or me, surely.'

'No, probably not. But if they would send someone of their

own crowd, I don't for a minute think they would harm Mrs Balfour, and a guardian from them would assure her safety. They want her only in order to get the money. That's always the trouble with a secret barter and sale. How to effect the exchange of the goods for the price? This time it ought to be easy enough as both parties are getting what they want.'

'But she can't go until they send her some address or some directions about how to go. She's crazy to start off, and has no tinge of fear.'

'I don't think we need have any real fear, but the whole sum is a lot of money for her to carry unless she is very strictly guarded.'

'I don't think she'll get those further instructions. You see, Stone, they thought it would be easy when they began to lay their plans, but now it isn't such clear sailing.'

'How do you know?'

'Only from common sense. They're going very slowly, you may note, and they are finding it hard to keep themselves hidden.'

'Leaving them, for the moment, what is the police attitude— toward you?'

'They throw out a hint now and then that they are about to arrest me. But they don't do it. I'm sure they will, though, just as soon as they can get a trifle more evidence or proof. One more black mark against my spotless character would give them their head and they'd nab me. I'd not care much, in fact I wish they'd do it and get it over. I imagine I'd fare better at a trial than at their everlasting baiting.'

'You might. But think of Mrs Balfour's distress if you should be arrested.'

'I know. But the blessed angel feels as I do about it. She thinks if I were arrested and jailed and tried and acquitted the whole sky would be cleared and the sun shine again. That is—if—'

'Yes, if.' Fleming Stone looked very serious. 'If you're willing,

Ramsay, and if Mrs Balfour is willing, I'd like to have a little confab with you two. Do you ever see her alone?'

'Very seldom. I wish I might, but we think it best to keep apart—'

'Yes, I know. Where is she now?'

'In her rooms, I think. I'll call Potter.'

Ramsay pushed a button and in a moment Potter came.

'Do you know where Mrs Balfour is?' Ramsay asked him.

'No, sir. Shall I find Myra, her maid, and inquire?'

'Yes, and then ask her, or tell Myra to ask her to come to us in this room at once. Is the Inspector about?'

'I haven't seen him this morning, sir.'

'Very well, find Mrs Balfour for us, then.' Potter departed and Ramsay went on: 'If you can advise us in any way, Stone, we'd be mighty glad.'

'I don't mean to advise you two, Ramsay, but I may make a suggestion or two, which you can consider and do as you please about.'

Potter returned, and with an odd look on his face, he said:

'We cannot find Mrs Balfour anywhere.'

Ramsay looked alarmed immediately, but Stone said calmly, 'Who saw her last, Potter?'

'I don't rightly know, sir. She had her breakfast in her room. Shall I send Myra to you?'

'Yes, send her right in here. Tell her to hurry.'

Myra appeared, and from the girl's white face and trembling lips, Stone apprehended some further mystery.

'Tell me of Mrs Balfour's plans for today,' he said, speaking gently to calm her evident fears.

'She had no definite plans, sir, that I know of. She had no appointment with her modiste or milliner and she expected no guest until afternoon, when she looked for her friend, Mrs Metcalfe.'

'Where was she when you last saw her?'

'Sitting in her boudoir. She had had her breakfast served

there, as usual, and was about to write some letters. There are many letters of condolence awaiting acknowledgment and it is a burden on her.'

'To be sure,' and Stone spoke sympathetically. 'Have you any reason to think Mrs Balfour went out anywhere?'

'Not likely, sir. She would have called me to help her dress.'

'What was she wearing?'

'A white morning frock. She could not wear that out of doors.'

'No. Is any street gown or coat missing from her wardrobe?'

'I haven't looked but it would hardly be possible. I always get out her clothes for her—'

'Where were you after leaving Mrs Balfour?'

'I went to the sewing room, to finish a piece of work.'

'From that room could you have heard Mrs Balfour if she had moved around, dressing herself to go out?'

Myra looked uncertain.

'I don't know, sir,' she said. 'I didn't think about it. If Mrs Balfour wanted me she would have rung for me. I never thought of listening.'

'I wish you would go upstairs, Myra, and look in the wardrobes. If any of Mrs Balfour's street clothes are missing, let me know.'

'I suppose, Stone,' Ramsay said, as the girl went away, 'you are thinking that Alli has gone to see the people who have the book. I don't think she would do that without telling me. We had a talk last night and began to plan a little. The situation must be met, you know. And a mode of life must be arranged for. We two love one another and we expect to marry after a decent interval. Meantime, convention will not allow of our living here together without some sort of duenna or companion for Alli. I want to stay here for there is much work to do in the library and it is infinitely more convenient for me to be here than to come every day. And since we have no one to consider but ourselves, why shouldn't we live as happily as we can until we can be married? Don't think I've forgotten the possibility of my arrest, but I am innocent of either of those murders and if I am accused I shall fight to a finish. I am hoping, yes, and expecting to have my innocence recognized, but if I'm in for arrest and trial, let us hope it won't mean conviction. We talked this all over last night and Alli thinks she will ask a friend of hers, Mrs Metcalfe, to come here and live with her, thus satisfying the tongues of gossip. All this is why I think Alli would never have gone off to those people without letting me know.'

Myra came back then and said she thought Mrs Balfour must have gone out, as one of her new black street gowns was missing, also a lightweight black coat and one of her black hats.

'Did you notice as to bag, gloves and such accessories?' Stone inquired.

'Yes, sir; a long black suède bag is not in its place, and a pair of black suède gloves are not in her glove drawer. A pair of walking shoes, also—in fact, all the things she would wear are missing. I must conclude she dressed herself and went out somewhere.'

'How about the things she took off?' asked Ramsay, anxious on every point.

'They are all there in her dressing room—her house gown, her slippers, stockings—all—and that she didn't call me makes me very surprised.'

'Let us go up there,' Stone said, suddenly, rising and motioning for Myra to lead the way.

Ramsay followed, and the three entered Alli's boudoir.

Stone at once noticed a half-finished page on the writing pad, and read it.

'This is to a cousin, apparently in answer to a note of sympathy,' he said; 'I think we must conclude that Mrs Balfour was writing letters when she was interrupted by some thought, or perhaps some message, and decided to go on some hasty errand. Myra, would Mrs Balfour dress more quickly with or without your aid?'

'Without, Mr Stone. When a maid helps dress a lady, there

is more or less formality and detail. When Mrs Balfour dresses herself, she is like a small whirlwind. A garment is whisked off and another on with the lightning's speed. I've seen her and it seems as if in a moment she is garbed as perfectly as I could have done it for her.'

Stone went on into the dressing room. As Myra had said, discarded garments were flung on chairs or otherwhere and white slippers and stockings lay on the floor.

'Mrs Balfour is never untidy,' Myra observed, picking things up. 'She must have been in the greatest haste.'

'Look about,' Stone directed the maid, 'and see if Mrs Balfour took money or valuables with her. Can you tell?'

'I think not,' Myra replied. 'I mean I think I can't tell. Mrs Balfour's bag has a purse inside it, nearly all her bags have. I don't know what was in the purse. Her jewels are in that small safe. I don't know the combination. Also, the upper drawer of the Chinese cabinet is always kept locked. I don't know where the key is. But Mrs Balfour most certainly dressed herself and went away on some errand.'

'Look at her dressing table,' Stone went on. 'Did she take anything as if for an overnight stay?'

'No,' said Myra, after a glance. 'She probably carried a small compact in her bag, but she took none of her brushes or creams.'

'Just gone out on a shopping errand or something of that sort,' Keith assumed, but Stone shook his head.

'Why the hurried dressing and the omission of calling Myra?' he asked. 'No, Ramsay, I don't want to alarm you but I think we must follow up this thing at once. Myra, if Mrs Balfour wanted to go out unseen, how would she manage it? I mean is there any other than the main entrance?'

'Only the tradesmen's and servants' entrance at the back.'

'Would Mrs Balfour use that?'

'She never has.' Myra's eyes opened wide. 'I don't think she would go out that way.'

'It would create more commotion than for her to go out the front door,' Ramsay said.

'That will do, Myra, you may go,' and Stone started downstairs again with Ramsay following.

The detective called Potter, and questioned him closely.

'Tell me, Potter,' he began, 'to your knowledge, did Mrs Balfour get any message or letter not through the mail?'

'Yes, sir; I carried a letter to her myself.'

'Where did you get it?'

'It came under the door, Mr Stone.'

'And you took it direct to Mrs Balfour?'

'Yes, sir, as soon as I found it.'

'Where was the lady then?'

'In her boudoir, sir, writing letters.'

'You didn't hand it to Myra?'

'No, sir. Mrs Balfour gave me strict orders to give her all her letters, personally, myself.'

'She has a very large mail?'

'Oh, yes. She looks it over and picks out the library letters. There are lots of book catalogues and advertisements.'

'But she goes over it all?'

'Every morning, sir.'

'Tell me of this letter you gave her this morning. Tell every detail of your giving it to her.'

'I saw it under the door, picked it up and took it up to her rooms, at once.'

'What was Mrs Balfour doing?'

'She sat at her desk, in her boudoir. She was writing letters. She had already written quite a pile. I took them away to mail.'

'What did the letter you brought look like?'

'It was just a plain white oblong envelope. Not stamped, you know.'

'Pushed under the door, then, by a messenger?'

'It looked like that.'

'What did Mrs Balfour say? How did she look? Be very

frank, Potter. What you tell us may be of very great help to Mrs Balfour. Did she seem alarmed?'

'No, not alarmed, so much as surprised, and—I think, a bit excited. She went pale like, and her eyes sort of stared, then she grabbed for a letter opener, and slit it open. She took out a sheet of white paper and read it quickly; it looked like a short letter. Then she said, "You may go, Potter," and she read it over again. As I was going through the door, she said, "Don't mention this to anybody, Potter, remember that!" But I am telling you because you say it may help her.'

'Perfectly right. Tell everything you can. Did you see Mrs Balfour go out later?'

'No, sir. But I thought I heard the front door close. I couldn't imagine any reason for that, but I went to look and I opened the door, but there was no one about.'

'At what time was this?'

'I couldn't say. But perhaps fifteen minutes after I had left her boudoir.'

'That would make it—?'

'About half-past ten or quarter to eleven. But I'm not sure about the time.'

'What was Mrs Balfour wearing?'

'It must have been a black gown, coat and hat. She wears always black now when she goes out.'

'She was walking?'

'That I don't know. She didn't call any of her own cars, but she may have taken a taxi.'

Abruptly, Stone left the room, and left the apartment. He went to the nearest elevator and asked if it was the one Mrs Balfour used.

The attendant told him it was; and in response to further questioning said that Mrs Balfour had gone down in his car between half-past ten and eleven. She was much as usual, smiled at him pleasantly, but seemed preoccupied, or, as he put it, sorta wool-gathering.

The doorman also told of Alli's exit, saying she went out and walked straight down Park Avenue at a brisk pace. He noticed nothing unusual about her manner, saying she was pleasantly polite, as always.

Stone went back upstairs with his news, which was no news, save the facts that Alli went away of her own accord and that, except for a slight absent-mindedness, she was just as usual.

But the two men most deeply interested felt sure that she had been summoned to meet the thieves, if not the murderers, and were forced to believe that she had walked straight into the lion's mouth.

CHAPTER XIII

RAMSAY GETS BUSY

HAVING told Ramsay all he had gathered from the house attendants, Stone put on his overcoat and hat and hurried down again to the street floor and out to the sidewalk.

The doorman could add nothing to his statement that Mrs Balfour had walked down the Avenue, and as she often went for a walk, he thought nothing of it.

With no definite hope of learning anything more, Stone walked on down the block and on to the next block, there seeing the policeman on the beat, who was walking south.

'Just a moment, Officer,' the detective said. 'Do you know Mrs Balfour, who lives on the block above?'

'The lady whose husband was murdered? Yes, sir, I know her when I see her.'

'Have you seen her this morning?'

'I have; not more'n a few minutes since. She was walkin' alone, all in black clothes, and lookin' that sorrowful.'

'Walking down Park Avenue?'

'That's right, sir. I watched her—'

'You did! Where did she go? Straight on down?'

'No, sir. On the corner below this she turned east and I hustled a bit to look.'

'And what did you see?'

'You're her friend, sir?'

'I am. I'm the detective in charge of the case. The murder case. Tell me anything you saw. I'm working with Inspector Manton.'

Quite satisfied, the man walked by Stone's side and talked. 'She reached this corner, d'ye see, and she stood still a minute lookin' down the cross street, and a showfer who was standin' there stepped up to her and spoke to her. 'Course I couldn't hear what he said, but seemed like he asked her something and she nodded her head and he led her to a car he had parked there and helped her in, and then he hops to it and drives away as fast as the law allows.'

'Which way?'

'Straight along east. I lost 'em in the traffic.'

'Then the lady apparently expected the car to be there? And got in willingly?'

'Oh, yes, sir, she musta known he was waitin' for her. Nothin' wrong, is there?'

'I hope not. What was the car like?'

'A fine one. A top-notcher. I couldn't get the number, I was too far away. The showfer was in a good-looking livery, but not as swanky as that car called for.'

'Well, of course it's hopeless, but if you ever see that car or man again, get their number.'

'I will that.'

'What was the livery and what did the chauffeur look like?'

'A sort of mulberry colour, I guess they call it. And the guy was a smart-lookin' young feller with good manners and all.'

Stone sighed as he walked back to the apartment house. If the policeman had only been a bit nearer and could have seen the car's number, or heard a word or two that was said, how good that would have been.

Yet it was much to learn those few facts. Alli had gone willingly, that was certain, though far from satisfactory. If taken by the enemy, the way must have been made easy and apparently safe.

Of course, Stone realized, the car might have belonged to one of her friends, and the chauffeur well known to her. But in such case, the car would have come to the door of her own house.

Greatly disheartened, Stone went up to the Balfour apartment.

He found Manton and Burnet there, and took them with Ramsay to the safe room for a confab.

After relating his findings, the detective looked at the others to see how they took it.

The two policemen were angry with the lady, and said she deserved anything she might get for being so foolish as to go in search of trouble.

But Ramsay, unheeding the police, turned to the detective with an agonized air.

'Stone!' he cried, 'you must find her! We must find her. Inspector, you must raise the silly embargo you've made—I must go and find her! I can't stay here in idleness while she may be at the mercy of a gang of thugs!'

'I realize the seriousness of the situation, Mr Ramsay,' Manton said, touched by the distress of the man whom he had suspected of murder. Somehow, his suspicions were allayed at sight of Ramsay's grief. 'But don't rush off at random. What would you do? Where would you go? Let us all consider matters and see what had best be done. What do you suggest, Mr Stone?'

'It is hard to think of anything to do immediately. We have no slightest notion of where to look and to rush out to the street would be of no use. I assure you I gathered everything I possibly could from the policeman on the beat, and it is a marvellous coincidence that I happened to see him, or that he happened to see Mrs Balfour. Doubtless, the next step will be a communication from the enemy, and that we shall have to wait for.'

'I can't do it!' stormed Ramsay. 'I want action and I'm going to have it!'

'Calm down, Mr Ramsay,' Manton said, coldly. 'We have enough trouble without having to get a strait-jacket for you. What would your proposed action be?'

'Don't speak to me like that,' and suddenly Keith Ramsay ceased blustering, and became calm, as he pulled himself together and restrained his emotion. 'To my mind, there are quite definite efforts to make. Mrs Balfour walked at least two blocks and then turned a corner. That means she must have passed at least six or eight doormen standing outside or just inside of their doorways. I'm sure someone of these could have seen something that would be helpful for us to know. She may have met someone she knew, and may have been seen pausing for a moment to chat. Such chances must not be neglected. Let me have a try at them. I pledge you my word, Inspector, to return in a short time and report. And isn't it time you let up on this idea you have of arresting me? Don't you know me well enough by now to be sure I never would kill a man whose wife I loved? Do you think I could offer a woman the hand of a murderer? The soul of a murderer? There are some things beneath possibility!'

The Inspector looked at him coolly.

'You're doing your cause no good, Mr Ramsay, by that line of talk. As you know, I have grave suspicions that you are the murderer you disdain, and in my opinion, this whole gesture is a planned affair. If you go out, you will join Mrs Balfour and the pair of you will disappear for good and all.'

Fleming Stone looked shocked.

'Oh, come, Inspector,' he said, sternly, 'that isn't quite fair. I admit you have imagined a clever little dodge, but if you have the faintest knowledge of character, you must know better than to attribute such a game to Keith Ramsay. And again, why should he and Mrs Balfour concoct such an absurd and unnecessary plot? If they wanted to run away, they could make a dozen plans of escape with far less trouble and bother than this one. Why the note under the door, the hasty dressing of Mrs Balfour, the mummery of the chauffeur and the grand car, just to get away from a house she might have left in a simple and ordinary way?'

A slight nod of his head was all the response Ramsay gave to this good-natured argument, and centred his attention on the Inspector.

'You have had me watched,' he went on, 'followed, quizzed,

baited—yet you have found out nothing to corroborate your charges. You have been through my files of letters, my library accounts, my confidential work on Mr Balfour's affairs and you have found only proofs of loyalty to my employer and helpfulness in his avocation. In your heart you have exonerated me, but you are unwilling to admit it because you have no other human being to suspect. You can find no evidence of my guilt, but you accuse me for lack of a just suspect. I am tired of it all and I demand either a removal of your espionage or a straightforward arrest, incarceration and trial. If the trial be fairly conducted I have no fear of the outcome. Nor have you and that is why you do not precipitate it.'

'Your ranting moves me not at all, Mr Ramsay,' and Stone looked with amazement at the Inspector's hard face as that worthy spoke. 'It is, as you yourself must recognize, just what you would say if you *were* guilty. The only thing that could prove your innocence would be to find the real murderer—'

'Just a moment, Inspector,' Stone interrupted; 'you give yourself away right there. When you say, "Find the real murderer," you tacitly admit that you are not at all certain that Keith Ramsay is the man. Now, it seems to me that Mr Ramsay's plan of speaking to the doormen who might have seen Mrs Balfour on the street this morning, is a good plan. The doormen in this vicinity are alert, capable men, and may easily have taken notice of Mrs Balfour and know something of interest to us. Let Ramsay try out his own suggestion, and I'll guarantee that he won't run away.'

Manton began to argue the matter further, but Stone cut in.

'If you're going to agree, Inspector, do it now. The trail will be cold very soon—if anything is to be discovered, it must be looked into at once.'

'Go to it, Ramsay,' Manton said, a trifle grudgingly, but with a distinct effect of hopefulness. 'Communicate with me inside of an hour, even if you stay out longer.'

Keith Ramsay left them and then Burnet lifted up his voice.

'Not so good, Chief,' he growled. 'You'll never see that baby again. She's waitin' for him around the corner and they'll be in the Newark aerodrome before you can say "knife"!'

'Well, he's gone now,' said Manton. 'What shall we fly at next, Mr Stone?'

'I'm in rather a peculiar position, Inspector,' Stone told him. 'I seem to be stranded. I have no employer, no case, no *raison d'être* of any sort. The lawyer, Scofield, is probably in charge of the estate, so I think I shall ask him to let me carry on, for I can't drag myself away from the case at this stage.'

'I hope you will remain, Mr Stone,' and Manton spoke sincerely. 'I'm sure something must break pretty soon, and it may be that we can find a surer suspect than the impetuous Ramsay.'

Stone smiled to himself over that 'we', but he replied cordially enough:

'And just now,' he said, 'as I see it, we can do nothing but wait for some message from the enemy's headquarters, from Mrs Balfour or from the knight-errant, Ramsay. I shall, for the present, remain in this house. I want to be right here if word comes from anybody. And someone must look after things as a whole. Potter is a blessing and he will look after the servants. If anyone in authority comes along, I will step aside. But for the moment, I'll man the deck.'

Neither of the policemen raised any objection to this plan, and soon they went away, with Stone's promise to advise them if anything transpired.

Whereupon Stone called Potter and informed him that he proposed to be a guest at the Balfour apartment for a time, and that he would like to be installed in the suite used successively by Mr Philip Balfour and his son Guy.

Potter listened to instructions and then sent for Mrs Lane, who was housekeeper in general, though Alli Balfour always had a judicial eye on the management.

Stone at once took a liking to Lane and felt he could leave

all arrangements for his own comfort and convenience in her hands.

He went into the great library, and on into the small office, which room he adopted for his own. He knew the importance of being right on the scene in case of any emergency and he realized it afresh when the Inspector sent for him.

He found Manton and Burnet busily engaged in quizzing Wiley and Swinton, whom they had summoned for an interview.

'Good morning,' said Stone to the witnesses, who, he thought, looked rather bored. 'Anything new?'

'No,' said Wiley, a bit pettishly. 'A repetition of the timetable element. I'm sure I've told all I know over and over.'

'Timetable?' and Stone looked at Manton, inquiringly.

'Yes, I want to get at the hours more closely. I mean the night of Philip Balfour's death.'

'That sort of information is often useful,' Stone agreed. 'Can I help?'

'More than a week ago,' Swinton complained, 'and we're hauled over the coals again. Oh, well, I'm willing. It was in this very room that I sat talking with Mrs Balfour while her husband was being killed. At least, that's the way I figure it out. And there's the little clock that told the time.'

He glanced toward the timepiece on the table—a lovely little Swiss travelling clock, cased in fine, tooled leather. 'I don't come here often, but I always notice that clock. It's always right.'

'Who takes care of it?' Stone asked, suddenly.

'Potter does,' Manton said. 'He told me he winds it and sets it by the big electric clock in the hall. Mr Balfour was very particular that it should always be correct.'

'Yes,' Swinton agreed, 'I've heard Mr Balfour speak of it myself.'

'Call Potter, will you?' the Inspector said to Burnet, who pushed a button, and the butler appeared.

'This clock, now, Potter,' Manton said, 'it's always correct?'

'Always, sir. It's one of my duties and I never neglect it.'

'Think back to the night Mr Balfour died—Mr Philip Balfour. Was the clock right that night, to your personal knowledge?'

'It was, sir. I remember well.'

'All right, Potter, you may go.'

'Reliable man, Potter,' commented Swinton, as the butler left them. 'Now, Inspector, I've said this before, but I want to repeat it. If I can be of any help in this affair, do let me. Isn't there something to do like going to see people or hunting some information where you don't want to send any of your men? I'm sure my tact and judgment would carry me through such an interview successfully, and it might help you a lot.'

'I can't, at the moment, think of any assignment for you,' Manton returned, 'but I'll bear your offer in mind and I may be glad to take advantage of it. Just now, I'm checking up on the alibis. I'll frankly confess that's why I asked you two men to come up here just now.'

'Perhaps you could help us out on those, Mr Swinton?' and Stone looked at him inquiringly. 'Your own alibi being vouched for by the steadfast little clock, can't you investigate some of the other alibis that stand in the way of nailing our suspects? Mr Wiley, I understand, gave the Inspector a satisfactory account of his doings that evening.'

'Of course,' and Wiley waved an aristocratic hand as if to push away all contact with sordid matters. He had made no offer of assistance, and Stone was glad of it. Amateur helpers were always a nuisance.

But he knew that Swinton was a long-time friend of the Balfours and hoped he might prove of some slight use.

'Why, yes,' Carl Swinton showed a decided interest. 'Who are your quarries? I might run one of them to earth.'

Whereupon, with serious directions as to secrecy and discretion, Stone mentioned the names of Preston Gill and Jack Rollinson. He told Swinton if he cared to investigate the alibis of these two men, he would be given whatever data the police had on the subject.

Swinton's enthusiasm seemed to cool a trifle as the plan took shape, but he stood by his offer and listened to instruction.

Then he said, 'Is Mrs Balfour at home? I'd like to see her, as a friend. I've refrained from calling, but if she will see me, I'll be very glad.'

Stone looked at Manton inquiringly, and the Inspector looked uncertain.

Captain Burnet settled the question by blurting out the truth.

'Mrs Balfour is not at home,' he said, bluntly. 'We don't know where she is.'

'What!' cried Swinton. 'Has she disappeared?'

Wiley, staring, seemed beyond all power of speech and Stone took hold of the situation.

'Mrs Balfour dressed for a walk and went out this morning, and has not yet returned. But I see no reason to use the word "disappeared".'

As a matter of fact, Stone saw very grave reason to use that alarming word, but he frequently passed up truth in favour of diplomacy.

'I see,' and Swinton exhibited no further excitement. 'She often goes for a morning walk, I frequently see her in the elevator or lobby. I will go, then, and after thinking it out a bit, I'll see what I can do as an investigator. I promise every precaution and care.'

Swinton left them, and Wiley began to lament.

'If there is the slightest uncertainty about Mrs Balfour's safety,' he said, 'how can you all sit here idle? You should be making the most strenuous efforts to rescue the lady—'

'Bell-ringers are out of date, Mr Wiley,' and Stone frowned a little. 'Nor would we profit by a "calling all cars" order. We have no reason to think Mrs Balfour is in need of rescue, as you term it. Nor do we want you to spread the news of her absence. Please understand the whole affair is strictly in the hands of the police and any ill-advised move of yours will be a matter for their consideration.'

This gave Wiley pause and he changed the subject.

'Doubtless she will return soon,' he said, 'meantime, I will await her in the library. I can occupy myself there.'

'I think not, Mr Wiley,' and Stone again frustrated his intention. 'The library is exclusively in charge of Mr Ramsay and Mr Sewell. Without an order from one of them, no one can be allowed in the library.'

'Are you in charge here, Mr Stone? I thought matters were in the hands of the police.'

'Mr Stone is working with the police,' the Inspector told him, 'and for the present, he is one of us. In this house, his word is law, until Mrs Balfour returns, at any rate.'

'Your manner makes me think you desire me to leave,' Wiley said, with great hauteur. 'I take no offence at that, and I will remind you that in case you want any assistance with the books in Mr Balfour's collection, I am both able and willing to lend a hand. Of course, my knowledge is far greater than Mr Ramsay's, who is merely a librarian; I am a collector.'

When a famous king remarked that he was the state, he could have shown no more vanity and importance than Pete Wiley showed then.

And on this bumptious note he left them.

'Notwithstanding your denial to Wiley,' the Inspector said, as they were alone again, 'I know you do think Mrs Balfour was, in some way, induced to go out this morning by some request or command of the people who killed her husband or stole the book, or both. I think you take a great deal upon yourself, Mr Stone, when you take that for granted. And I think you quite overstep the bounds of wisdom and propriety when you spread abroad the news of the lady's disappearance.'

Stone kept his temper, and even smiled a little at the irate Inspector.

'Now, now, Mr Manton, remember, first of all, that I am not working with you officially, and certainly not under your orders, or even suggestions. I am distinctly on my own and I am conducting my own investigation as I see fit. But in passing, let me say that a mysterious note coming under the door, an unusually hasty dressing and a swift, silent departure are so unlike Mrs Balfour's habits and so like her probable behaviour if she had been obeying a summons, that I consider it full justification for a belief that she did not go entirely of her own volition. I sincerely hope you are right and that she will soon return, but it is my unwilling opinion that we shall not see her soon again unless we accomplish it by our own efforts. This feeling on my part will by no means retard my activities. On the contrary it proves to me the necessity for immediate and drastic action. If the lady returns, well and good, but we dare not wait to see. We must get busy at once. As soon as Keith Ramsay comes back I shall go out, and I can't say, as yet, just where I shall go or how long I shall be gone. And I beg of you do not curb Ramsay's efforts, for beside his strong affection for Mrs Balfour, he has a wise head and an ingenious brain. Give him full freedom and you will be far more likely to find the lady.'

'I don't agree with all you say, Stone, but I do think we are up against it and that Ramsay is in a position to help.'

Keith Ramsay, coming in just then, heard Manton's last words and answered them.

'I fear I am not in a position to help,' he confessed as he sat down. 'I did pick up a few words of information but nothing of any importance.'

'Tell us about it,' said Stone, kindly. 'It may mean more than you think.'

'I did just what I said I'd do,' Ramsay said, a hopeless look in his eyes. 'I spoke to perhaps half a dozen doormen, standing outside. I didn't go inside any house. Two had not seen Mrs Balfour at all. Two saw her, but took no especial notice of her, saying only that she was dressed in very deep black. One chap, on the next block, spoke to her.'

'What did he say?'

'He asked her to come in and sit down for a few moments. He told me she looked so ill and distressed, he feared she was going to faint.'

'Did she go in?'

'No. She thanked him and said she was all right. Then she walked on, he said. Well, the next doorman was round the corner, the first house on the cross street. It is a Park Avenue apartment house with the entrance on the side. I talked to him, and it seems it was just beyond his door that the big car was parked. I asked him about it—his name is Dorlon—and he said he saw the whole incident.'

'What kind of car was it?'

'He didn't know the make, just said an enormous black limousine, stream-lined, chromium-trimmed and very shiny. He didn't get the number, he had no reason to, and he was watching the doings. He said the lady came along slowly and uncertainly. As she neared the car, the chauffeur slid out of his seat and spoke to her. Dorlon couldn't hear the words except a sort of growly "Get in!" and the lady stepped inside. A voice in the car said shortly, "Sit down!" and the lady sat down. The chauffeur slammed the door, jumped to his place and drove off like a gliding snake—that's what Dorlon said, "like a gliding snake". That's all.'

'Now we know she was kidnapped,' Manton said.

But Stone snapped back, 'No, we don't know that at all!'

CHAPTER XIV

BENSON BUSY TOO

FLEMING STONE had always thought that the phrase 'like hunting for a needle in a haystack' was an amusing bit of over-statement.

But as he sat in his office off the library of Philip Balfour, thinking of the work ahead of him, he concluded that the haystack search was child's play compared with his task.

If one knew the needle was in the haystack, all he had to do was to hunt till he found it. But to know only that Alli Balfour was missing and to have no slightest hint as to her whereabouts seemed to him 'what nature itself can't endure', to quote the words of Marjorie Fleming, one of his favourite authors.

He had just concluded a short interview with Keith Ramsay. That hopeless and despairing young man had seemed to undergo a subtle change. He was as despondent as ever regarding the fate of his loved one, but he was somehow more quietly determined, more ready for persistent and definitely planned work that should be efficacious rather than spectacular.

The nature and details of this work he was quite content to leave to Fleming Stone's direction and offered to follow his advice in every particular.

'All very well,' Stone had told him, 'if I had advice to offer. But needles in haystacks are easy quarry compared with our problem. Don't you know of any friends of Mrs Balfour who might have driven her away like that on an errand having no connection with our case?'

'No,' Ramsay said, 'no friend would have waited for her and picked her up in that extraordinary manner. From what Dorlon said, I gathered a mental picture of the waiting car with a man on the back seat waiting impatiently and telling her to get in in a none-too-kindly tone. She did so and was whisked away. Surely that sounds like the action of an evil-doer of some sort?'

'Yes,' Stone agreed; 'certainly not the action of a well-meaning friend. First, then, to discover the identity of this man.'

'And the destination of the car.'

'Yes, that, too. And, Ramsay, we must plan about this house. I am going to stay here for the present. You and I will be enough to take charge of affairs. Mrs Lane is a marvel of a housekeeper, and Potter is perfection. They will attend to the ménage. Myra must stay, for Mrs Balfour may return at any moment. Mrs Lane will look after the girl, of course. I think we shall hear from Mrs Balfour, or of her, soon. I make no secret of the fact that I believe she was persuaded or forced to what she did this morning, and that as a result she was driven away to some place of conceal-ment. Now, supposing she was promised the book if she would go to get it, what about the money? Do you know if she had it in the house to take with her, or do you suppose she went to the bank after getting in that car?'

'I can't suppose she did anything so open as to go to the bank in that conspicuous car, and yet it would seem right enough. Perhaps B.G.—I know no other name for him—went with her and they collected the money and he took her some place to make the exchange.'

'That won't wash. He could have the book in his pocket, make the exchange in the car and send her home. He said he wanted no elaborate doings.'

'I know. It's too much for me. What do you think?'

'I think that, for some reason, B.G. took Mrs Balfour some-where and is holding her for ransom. We are not dealing with a man as straightforward as he pretends to be. Greed is a disease and it grows with what it feeds on. Having received the price of the book from her, he may have concluded to get more large money by demanding it for her safe return. That is my fear and I tell you frankly, because I want you to be prepared for any event. But, remember, I may be all wrong. It is possible that Mrs Balfour went away with a friend, even though we can't make it seem so. Suppose you call up one or two of her nearest friends and ask discreetly if they know where she is? Don't imply she is mysteriously absent, but just that we can't place her for the moment. Wait, though, till I call the bank.'

But a short conversation with the paying teller proved that Alli had drawn no money from the bank that day.

Ramsay went off to telephone one or two of Alli's friends and Fleming Stone began to do what in lighter moments he called his ratiocination, but in desperate situations he dubbed just plain thinking.

He fully believed that Alli had been abducted and would be held for ransom. He thought this action might have been brought about by the 'abduction' of the book, or, on the other hand, the book might have been a prelude to the greater abduction.

In any case, he must act as if he were sure of the things he surmised. He must fight fire with fire, and the fact that he didn't know where the fire was, or where he could find any fire to fight it with, must in no way impede or delay his action.

He grasped the telephone and put through a call to Benson, his trusty helper.

This individual was, or had been, a street arab, but under Stone's patronage he had become a more civilized member of the human race and was always at the disposal of the detective.

'Hello, Benson,' brought an enthusiastic, 'Hello, Mr Stone; what about it?'

'Come right along, boy, I want you.'

'I'm there. Address, please?'

Benson had caught the serious note in Stone's voice and realized it was no time for chaffing.

He noted down the address Stone gave him, cradled the instrument and was out of his home and into the subway with a speed Mercury might have envied.

Reaching the Balfour apartment, he was shown at once into the safe room where Stone waited for him.

'Sit down, Benson,' he said, after shaking hands with the lad, 'there's bad business going.'

'Spill it, sir, please,' and the earnest interest in the lad's wide eyes removed any touch of flippancy.

'I want you to find a certain new, big, black glory-car, with very streaming lines and chromium decorations.'

'Yessir. I know two.'

'The one I want has—or had this morning—a chauffeur wearing a mulberry suit that didn't fit him, or the car, either.'

'No. Was it too big for him or too little?'

'I'm not sure, but I can doubtless find that out. Or you can.'

'Any more to tell me?'

'Yes, take it all in one. Go to the Benares, a large apartment house, corner Park Avenue and—'

'I know where it is—coupla blocks down—'

'Yes; well, go there and make up to the doorman. That is, the doorman who was on duty this morning about ten and eleven. If he isn't there, track him down. Then ask him everything he knows about a big car that parked near his door, around the corner, you know, on the cross street.'

'Yes, sir.' Benson looked still expectant.

'Then after you squeeze out every drop of information he can give you, find the car or some trace of it. He'll tell you how a lady dressed in black got into the car, the chauffeur put her in and there was a man inside waiting for her and they swung off—fast! Where did they go? Who was the man? Who was the chauffeur? Whose was the car? But principally, where did they go and where are they now?'

'I see.' Benson looked grave. 'I hope I can do it, Mr Stone, but I'll have to have a lot o' luck.'

'Pray Heaven you'll have it,' and Stone spoke solemnly.

'Is that a picture of the lady?' Benson pointed to a framed miniature on the desk.

'Yes, but she looks differently now. She wears all black and her face is white and sad. Bank on the car and the chauffeur, I don't think you'll see the lady. But you run down that doorman, his name is Dorlon, and pump him dry about the car and the driver. Then do your best, Benson, your very best, to get track of something.'

'Yes, sir. When'll I report?'

'This evening, or sooner, of course, if you get anything. It's a hard trick, I know, but if anybody can pull it off, you can.'

'Yessir. Got the gentleman's picture here, sir?'

'No, I wish I had! He's the one I want to meet. I don't know what he looks like. Maybe you can tell me when we meet again. Don't sigh like that, Benson. I don't ask you to perform miracles—if I do come pretty near it. Run along now, and mind you turn Dorlon inside out.'

Benson went off and then Stone went out on an errand.

He was determined to use every effort to get any possible light on the man who signed himself B.G. A nervy thing to do after having stolen the Button Gwinnett book.

He went to the office of a graphologist whom he knew and showed him the neatly written letter.

Berger, the handwriting expert, looked at it.

'Pity you don't learn this science yourself,' he said, being an old friend of the detective. 'You're over here so often asking me, you'd save time and money doing it yourself.'

'Yeah, I know, but you're so handy by, and so reliable, and so honest. Anyway, what about it? Is it a natural handwriting or a faked one?'

'Not exactly either. It's the free writing of a man who writes rapidly and distinctly, but he doesn't always write this hand. You've heard of multiple writers, haven't you?'

'Yes, but tell me more about them.'

'Why, they can write several different hands, as different from one another as can be. Yet they can write each style freely and with ease, showing no hesitation or carefulness as they write this one or that one. They may or may not be good at forgery, most likely they are, but that is not what we're talking about. If you know that the man who wrote this letter does not always write this hand, it is probable that he can write several others equally well and with equal ease. This is a very fine specimen. I should not have supposed it was done by a multiple writer.'

'I'm not sure that it was. But I want to know.'

Berger reached for a magnifying glass, studied the writing and then said:

'Yes, when I look for them, I see faint traces of the pauses and jerks that must be in an unused hand. But they are so few and so hard to see they are practically indiscernible save to one familiar with such tricks. I daresay the usual and well-known fist of this chap is a stiff upright with almost no curves at all.'

'Well, that's that. Can you read a bit of his character in that acquired hand?'

'He's a clever devil. Cold-blooded, ironical, heartless, and without pity or affection in his heart.'

'A criminal?'

'Possibly. But bad enough to be one. I see no redeeming quality here except a suave exterior.'

'That doesn't redeem much, to my mind,' commented Stone.

'No,' Berger agreed, 'not much. But it may help you find him. He is polite, well-bred, meticulous in small details and fond of the ladies.'

'In a nice way?'

'Not very—no. Verging on the sadistic, I'd say.'

'Brainy?'

'Clever in a cunning way. Pretends to wisdom that he doesn't possess. Not a good friend—not at all a good friend.'

'All corroborative but not indicative. It's a help, though, in that it eliminates one or two suspects.'

'Don't bank on it too hard. Remember, graphological intimations often slip up if there are contradictory influences at work in a nature.'

'All right, Berger, I'll run along. I'm up against the worst case I've ever had—'

'But you like a hard case?'

'I do, but not where human life is endangered. Could our scribe be a murderer?'

'Indeed he might. There is a kink in that direction. And showing, as it does, in an assumed handwriting it must undoubtedly be there.'

'All right,' and Stone sighed. 'Put it on my personal bill, not for the police. Good-bye.'

Glad of the few hints gained, but disheartened at having no individual suspect to fit them, Stone went to see Sewell.

He found him in the back room looking over some rare pamphlets.

'How's matters and things?' asked the book man.

'Jumbled,' Stone told him, 'dreffly jumbled.'

Then Sewell listened to the account of Alli's disappearance and the description of the big car.

'That ought to be a clue,' he said. 'But there are lots of big cars running around. Did you ever glean anything from the derby hat?'

'What derby hat? Never heard of it.'

'That's queer; I told Gill to tell you about it.'

'Well, he didn't. You tell me.'

'Oh, it was nothing, I expect. But a chap cleaning out some rubbish here, the day after Paul Balfour's death, found a derby in my ash barrel. He brought it to me, thinking it must have been thrown away by mistake, as it was a new one. I kept it, and told Gill to mention it to you—I'm so forgetful.'

'Where is it?'

'I don't know. Hey, Preston?'

Gill came in from the front room, and Sewell said:

'Whatever became of that derby hat the cleaning man found? 'Member? I asked you to tell Mr Stone about it.'

'Oh, yes. Why, I stuck it up on a high shelf and forgot all about it. Want it?'

'Yes,' Stone said, frowning at Gill, who smiled back at him. One never could chide Preston Gill.

He turned to a crowded cupboard and hunted out a derby hat with a dented crown and a bent brim.

'Here you are,' he said, handed it to Stone and went whistling away.

The detective studied it.

'Maybe and maybe not,' he said. 'I can picture the masked man as wearing a soft hat, and then, as he came here, changing to this for the purpose of disguise and putting his soft hat in his pocket.'

'H'm,' said Sewell, dryly, 'carrying his derby in his hand until he changed it?'

Stone laughed. 'No, of course, he wore the derby and then when he went out he put on the other and threw this in the ash-can. Anyhow, I'll keep this hat; it may be helpful. Give me a bit of paper and call a messenger, will you?'

Sewell did and, wrapping the hat, Stone sent it down to Benson with a note telling him to find out where, when and by whom it was bought.

Though Sewell was deeply anxious about Mrs Balfour's safety and well-being he was sure that among the police, Fleming Stone and Keith Ramsay, she would be speedily found and he could take no active part in that search. As to the book, however, he felt that in the greater crimes the volume might be forgotten or neglected, and he told Stone he meant to do anything he could himself.

'I know,' Stone replied, 'but what can you do?'

'I don't know yet, but I mean to begin a search. Also, there will, of course, be a desperate search for Mrs Balfour and if you find her you can doubtless lay hands on the book. It would be terrible to have that volume mutilated, and I mean to have the unscrupulous dealers learn what will be coming to them if they get chummy with the thief.'

'Perhaps they've chopped it up already.'

'Heaven forbid! But I don't think that, for they are wise to rare books, their letters prove that.'

'Well, where do you think Mrs Balfour is?'

'In the clutches of the thief of the book and the murderer of the two men.'

'And they may murder the lady?' Stone suggested.

'Not likely. They need her in various ways. As a hostage—'

'But she went for the book. At least, it's logical to suppose she did, and that she took with her the ransom money.'

'I can't think she'd be such a fool as to do that. If she did, I'm sorry for her—that would mean trouble.'

'I expect trouble, Sewell, and I think it's imminent. I'm tempted to go out to meet it, but I'll wait a little longer for it to come to me. Now, I'm going home—that is, up to the Balfour place. Ramsay is taking care of the library and I'm taking care of everything else. I admire the way I've taken care of Mrs Balfour! But I'll find her, and I'll find the thief and the murderer. No, this isn't boasting, John, you know me better than that. But I'm desperate and when I let go of my caution, as I propose to do, something has got to happen!'

'Look out it don't happen to you,' said Sewell, gravely.

'Probably it will. I say, John, do you know anybody who writes different hands with equal ease? Multiple writers, they're called.'

'I only know Swinton; he can do that.'

'He can? Then he's our murderer!'

'Not so,' and Sewell shook his head. 'That chap has a real alibi, one that can't break down. He was at the Balfour house that night while Balfour was being murdered over here. I was there myself, you know. And Carl Swinton was there when I went in and I left him there when I came out, so there's not a chance. I thought of him, too. You know Alli Cutler threw him over for Philip Balfour? But you can't get around his being there, calling on her, while her husband was being murdered. He wouldn't do it, anyway. He doesn't care for her now in any romantic way—I doubt if he ever did. It was just a half-hearted affair. He told me all about it at the time and he was glad when Balfour took her off his hands. He's not a marrying man, but he was always proud of his acquaintance with the Balfours and he couldn't have had that except through his earlier acquaintance with her. He's a big bluffer about books and all that, but he'd never have the nerve to push that silver skiver into a man's heart! And he was a real pal of Guy's. They were nearer of an age. Why would he do in Guy's father and then Guy himself—for I think the two murders were the work of the same hand, don't you?'

'Yes, I do. You've pretty well shot away my theory of Swinton, though that was only because of the writing.'

'Lots of people can write multiple. Those are the ones we have to beware of—they forge autographs. Well, you look after Mrs Balfour and the murderer, I want to find the book. Even if we never catch the thief, I hope we'll get the book back. What d'ye think?'

'I'm sorry to say I think one depends on the other and I fear we may never again see Mrs Balfour or the book either.'

'Oh, come now, Stone, it isn't like you to be so pessimistic. A few moments ago you were full of energy and resolve.'

'There are some things that energy and resolve can't accomplish. All the same, John, you've helped me a lot and I'll do my best to get that book back. And I think—can do. So possess your soul in patience and await developments.'

Stone went back to the Balfour apartment and put in a few miserable hours in his *bête noire* of all occupations, waiting.

He was not idle, he was racking his brain for some solution to his problem, some overlooked clue, some unnoticed evidence, but he found little.

He hadn't banked much on Swinton, but, according to Sewell, he had what is so often called, and so seldom is, an iron-clad alibi. He turned to Wiley, for it seemed to him those two men had unusual opportunity.

But so far as he could see neither had motive. Swinton couldn't kill a man and his son, too, because of a long-ago jilting, which, after all, seemed to suit his book. Wiley had shown positively no motive, but if he had one it must have been to get possession of the Button Gwinnett book.

And at last the telephone bell rang and it was Benson.

'Hello, Mr Stone?'

'Yes, Stone speaking. Hello, Benson.'

'I've something to report. Too much to telephone. And I'm starving with hunger. What about it?'

'Where are you?'

'Just down the street a piece. In a drug store on Madison Avenue.'

'All right. Did you get a hat I sent you?'

'Hat? No, sir, I ain't been home since I saw you.'

'Well, you go to the Mansion House, get our private room, order what you want and go to it. I'll be with you as soon as I can get there.'

'Yeppy, I'll do just that. Hurry along. I've got a lot to report.'

Bless the boy, said Stone to himself, what a brick he is!

Getting into his coat and taking his hat, he paused only to tell Potter of his plans.

'I'm going out now, Potter. After I'm away, tell Mr Ramsay that I said I'd probably be back soon, but I might stay longer and I might possibly not return till morning. Tell him I've heard nothing alarming but I'm off on some inquiry.'

'Yes, sir; and the Inspector the same?'

'Yes, if he calls up. Or leave it to Mr Ramsay.'

'Very good, sir.'

Stone left the apartment and took the elevator down with quiet dignity, but once in the street, he jumped in a taxi and told the driver to speed to a certain small restaurant, which he and Benson called the Mansion House, and where the knowing proprietor heeded the request of either of them for a private room.

Arriving at the small eating-place, Stone looked inquiringly at the head waiter who jerked his head toward a closed door, behind which the detective found his famished henchman making good with knife and fork.

Stone sat down, dismissed the hovering waiter and said, 'Did you find her?'

'Yes, sir,' and Benson showed a woebegone countenance. 'Shall I start at the beginning, or tell it hit or miss?'

'Start at the beginning, but don't spin it out too long. Eat your food slowly and don't speak with your mouth full.'

'Yessir,' said Benson.

CHAPTER XV

BENSON managed, very successfully, to attend to his food and tell his story at the same time.

'It was this way, Mr Stone. I had a word with Dorlon, round the corner, you know, and I find out that he watched the car till it was outa sight. It run south on Madison Avenue and I walked along, speaking to some more doormen. They're good talkers, you see, 'cause they just stand and watch what's going on. So a feller on Madison said he saw that big car scoot by, and then another said he saw it, till I just practically follered the route of that car on along down and across, and at last I found it had stopped at a house 'way over east, and a lady and a man had got out of the car and went into the house. Then the big car druv away. A guy next door told me that. So I plants myself to wait and I had my full of it. But after a long time a car came along and stopped at the house I was watching. Not the fine big car, but an ordinary car that you wouldn't notice.'

'All right so far, Benson. Get on with your ice cream before it melts. Want coffee?'

'Yessir, a big cup.'

This was ordered and Benson resumed.

'So then the man and the lady came out of the house and got in the car.'

'Describe them.'

'Just like you said, sir. She was all in black and droopy-looking and he was mejum-sized and no style to him, but he knew what he was about. She didn't wanta get into the car much, but he took hold of her arm and said something I didn't hear and she got in quick. They started off, going west, and I hops a taxi,

which I had waiting, kinda on approval like. I told my man to
foller the car, unbeknownst, and he caught on noble, and we
follered the elopers or whatever they are.'

'Get along, Benson. Tell me all, but speed up a bit.'

'Yessir. Well, the car went across and up town and over the
George Washington Bridge, us follerin', and then we was in
Fort Lee. Then we went north and after a while we was sorta
lost in the woods. Not so good. But I took the paper offen some
cigarettes I had in my pocket, and I dropped bits along the
way, kinda far apart though, 'cause that was all the paper I had.
But it'll be a tracker. Then, the car ahead druv into a kinda lane
that led to a house. A good-looking house it was but seemed
like nobody was living in it. I got outa the taxi, told the man
to wait outa sight in among the trees and I follered the car on
foot. Everything was vacant-looking. The weeds and bushes
was all snarleyow and the gate was broke on its hinges and all
like that. There was such a lot of underbrush and canebrakes
I could keep hid easy, so I pushed as near as I could.'

'Did you see them or hear anything?'

'Not much. It was getting dark, being so woodsy, you know,
and the man was a whole lot muffled up, and the lady had on
a little black veil. She didn't have that on when she started. The
man got out first and he said, "Come along, Allie," not very
pleasant. The lady got out, and then two people came out of
the house to meet them. One was a sorta oldish woman, and
the other was the biggest man I ever saw. He was a reg'lar giant.'

'Did he look cruel?'

'I'll say he did! He looked like an ogger, or what you call it.'

'Go on.'

'Well, the man took hold of the lady's arm and led her up
the steps and into the house, and the other two went in after
them and shut the door.'

'And the car?'

'The showfer druv that around back where I guess there
was a garridge. I watched the house for a bit, but the shades

was all pulled down and there was dim lights in two or three rooms, and I thought I might wait all night without seeing anything. The showfer was fussin' around, too, in and out of the back door, and I decided I'd make for home and mother.'

'You did splendid work, Benson. Now, could you take me to that house this evening?'

'Not in the dark, no, sir. Them bits of paper are few and far between. But I could pick up on 'em in the daylight. How 'bout early tomorrow morning?'

'Yes, that would be better. I can lay some plans and you can get some rest, and we'll start at daybreak. You're in on this, Benson, and it's a big chance for you to make good. If you do, you may yet be my regular assistant. Now, about your taximan. Is he a friend of yours? Is he reliable?'

'He's a friend of mine, but he ain't just exactly what you'd call reliable. But he'd do anything for money. He'd even be reliable if you paid him enough.'

'You're sure of that, Benson?'

'Yessir.'

'What did you pay him for the trip you took today?'

'I paid him fifteen dollars, Mr Stone. The trip was about ten and I guv him five more. You told me to pay what was necessary—and it was.'

'That's all right, lad. What you accomplished is worth much more than that to me. Now, the trip tomorrow morning will be worth quite a lot, and I'll give it to you now, and do you hide it away till needed. This journey tomorrow will be very dangerous for me but not for your friend—what's his name?'

'We call him Tiny, sir, he's such a long piece of goods.'

'Is he strong?'

'One time he was a prize fighter, but he isn't as strong as that now. He knows all the tricks, though. Jew-jitsy and all that.'

'He sounds a useful man. I hope we won't need his strong arm work, but if we do, it's good to know it's there and at our disposal. I've taken a liking to Tiny already.'

'Did you say danger to yourself, Mr Stone? Do you mean that?'

'I'm sorry to say I do. And right here I'll say if you get into any trouble or bother, call the police and if they arrest you, go along with them and insist on seeing Inspector Manton. When you get to him, tell him all you know, truthfully. Tell him about the house in the Palisades woods, tell him about me and he will take entire charge of the situation and give you a medal besides. Don't be afraid; we're working with the police not against them.'

'Huh, I ain't afraid of anything you're mixed up in. Now, you going to tell me things?'

'Yes, I'm going to tell you as much of the story as it is necessary for you to know. And you are not to pry into it any further.'

'I know that. I never have any curiosity about your affairs, Mr Stone. You know that, don't you?'

'Yes, lad, but this is an intricate case, and I want to be sure you keep your own counsel. Don't tell Tiny a word more than you have to. Tell him any curiosity shown will bring him just that much less payment. Make him understand.'

'Oh, he will. He's nobody's fool. Go on.'

'The situation is this, unless I'm on a wrong tack entirely, and I don't think I am. That lady you saw I believe to be Mrs Balfour, the widow of the man who was murdered in Sewell's bookshop.'

'I know.'

'And the man I believe to be the murderer, or one who had the murder done by a paid killer. This man's identity I am not sure of, but I think he has abducted the lady and will hold her for ransom. I am going to that house in the woods tomorrow morning and I shall confront that man if he is there, and if he is not there I shall wait till he comes. Now it is quite possible the big man who seems to be in charge of the house may beat me up or may imprison me or may simply order me off the premises. But I am going to rescue that lady and I shall not

give her up without a struggle. We will call that lady Mrs White
and the man who carried her off we will call Mr Black. The
two in the house already we will call Mr and Mrs Gray. At seven
tomorrow morning I will come out of the apartment house
where Mrs Balfour lives, and you and Tiny will be here in his
car, crawling along. At sharp seven come to the door and stop
and I'll get in. Then we'll go over to the house in the woods,
if you can find the way by your torn papers, and on the way I
will give you further orders. But here is the principal one now.
When we reach that house, or nearly, I'll get out and go to it,
and you two remain in the car. By the way, have Tiny change
the number; he can manage that?'

'Oh, yes. And we stay hid—how long?'

'Until I come out and return to the taxi. But—if I'm not out
in an hour, then you can conclude they've held me and I am
no longer able to control my actions. That means trouble and
yet we don't want to raise an alarm too soon. In such case, send
Tiny and his car deeper into the woods, and you edge round
toward the house, keeping carefully out of sight. If I still make
no appearance then you try to get into the house by some
ingenious trick.'

'Tell 'em I've lost my dog?' suggested Benson.

'Yes; maybe you can work on the old lady's feelings and
she'll let you come in and tell her about it.'

'Guess I could work that. I did once—when it was a real
dog. Then, say I get in the house—what?'

'Try to see me. Or if you're not allowed that, look for a folded
paper lying around. I'll have two or three with me, and I'll put
the one that fits the case best on the mantel or window-sill.
You'll see it. Of course, Benson, all this will mean that I can't
get free. Rest assured if there is a ghost of a glimmer of a means
of escape, I shall use it, but what I fear and expect is a simple
locking in by a means that precludes my breaking out.'

'I see, Mr Stone. Go on.'

'It may be you can't see any note and very likely you won't

be allowed to see me. You'll just have to be guided by your judgment in that case. But if there is nothing to be done at all, then you and Tiny drive away, but keep within seeing distance of the front gate and watch for Mr Black to come. I have reason to think he came back to the city tonight and will go to the house in the wood again tomorrow. I don't know what will happen when he and I meet, but the fur will certainly fly. Now, boy, I'm putting a lot of responsibility on your young shoulders, but there is no one else I know of who can help me as you can.'

Benson's eyes glowed, but he said only:

'Tell me all you can, Mr Stone. It would be terrible if I got a chance and didn't know what to do with it.'

'True enough. Well, supposing you come round again to hunt your dog or something else, you might try to get into the good graces of Mrs Gray. Ask her for a cookie or something like that. Use your winning ways to make her like you, and that way you might get a word with Mrs White. Never use that lady's real name. And here's another thing: there's a very valuable book missing. Listen in to hear any word about that. Find it if you can. And if you think I'm held prisoner in the house, be around at exactly midnight any night or every night, and I'll manage to get out and speak to you. Not to escape myself; that would leave Mrs White unprotected and I am sure I can't get her away too.'

'Maybe you can.'

'We'll see. Run along home now, get a good sleep and be on deck at sharp seven tomorrow morning, just as I told you.'

Benson was not an infant prodigy, nor did Fleming Stone think he was. But the detective recognized in the lad the eager desire to get at the heart of a mystery, the quick-witted questioning toward that end and the ability to coordinate the results that go to make up what is called the detective instinct. He thought that with some advice and some training he would become an able assistant, and he was experimenting.

He went home thinking, not about Benson, but about his

new project and whether he could put it over. He had to admit to himself that the question was open to grave doubt. He stopped first at his own apartment and there picked up a suitcase and a few things he wanted. Then on to the Balfour apartment and to his own rooms there.

After writing some letters he called Potter and told him to ask Mr Ramsay to come to see him.

When Keith appeared, Stone said quietly, 'Any news?'

'No;' and Ramsay frowned and sighed. 'How can there be any news when everything is at the ultimate degree of dreadfulness?'

'Oh, now, don't be too discouraged. I have a ray of hope.'

'A real ray of honest-to-goodness hope?'

'Well, no, not quite that. But a vague dream of a shadow of a vision of hope.'

'That sounds cheering. May I know about it?'

'There's little to know. I'm starting off early tomorrow morning on what is certainly a wild goose chase, and may prove a disastrous one. I may be successful in finding Mrs Balfour and rescuing her from the people who took her away. Or I may be forcibly detained myself and unable to escape or to help her. In such case, you will be notified and can take action. The police will also be notified. But I have learned enough to feel fairly sure of the murderer's identity, yet I cannot prove it without the personal interview I hope to have tomorrow.'

'I think you ought to take me with you. You know my attitude toward Alli Balfour, you know how I adore her, and I feel it is my right to be in on any undertaking that concerns her safety.'

'You may feel so, but I don't. Realize, Keith, I am risking not only danger but death. Do you want to get yourself killed unnecessarily? Do you think Mrs Balfour would rather see you dead or me?'

'If it's as dangerous as all that, I shan't let you go.'

'Don't be silly! I may get off scot-free. But to keep away might give the criminal a way to escape scot-free and that we can't allow. I am not absolutely sure of my man, but if he is the one I think him, he must be put out of commission entirely as soon as possible. I don't want to kill him, but if it is a question of his life or mine, I shall certainly try to remain in the telephone book.'

'I suppose you're after Preston Gill, and if he's the criminal I hope you catch him. I can't help a feeling that he's the man, because no one else knew all about the Button book. Does your dangerous plan include the recovery of the book?'

'If it goes through it means the recovery of the book, the conviction of the murderer and the restoration of Mrs Balfour.'

'Pray Heaven you come through safely yourself. If you can achieve all that, you are indeed a conquering hero. But—it sounds too good to be true.'

'It may not come true, Ramsay. You must hope, but you can't expect. You're a bridge player. Well, you know you may be an expert, you may hold splendid hands, but if the breaks go against you—you can't win. I'm afraid the breaks will go against me. That isn't pessimism, it's only looking things squarely in the face. Now, I'm not telling the police just yet. If I'm home in a day or two, it will be because my plan succeeded. If I'm not, rest assured that you will all know the reason why and can then take action.'

'And Mrs Balfour?'

'Will be far safer because of my carrying out this plan than if I didn't do it.'

'All right, Mr Stone. You know my first anxiety is for Alli, but do believe that I am alarmed about you and only respect for your own judgment keeps me from urging you to drop your plan.'

'No, I shall not drop it. And listen to this: if things go wrong with me, you will get word at once. There is a chap helping me, a young vagabond, who is devoted to me and my interests. His name is Benson. Whatever he tells you, you may believe. Trust him entirely. If there is bad news he will bring it to you or to Manton. I'll ask you to clear out now, I've a bit to do. Send Potter to me, will you?'

Ramsay went and Potter came, and the latter had difficulty in keeping his poise when Stone gave certain orders.

'You know, Potter,' he said, 'we must use every effort to learn where Mrs Balfour is. She may be safely with friends, or—she may not. Tomorrow morning I'm going in search of her. I may be gone overnight and I'm taking this small suitcase. I'm leaving at seven. Come up here a bit before that and bring with you two good big hunks of meat—'

'Meat, sir?'

'Yes, solid raw meat, fresh and good. Don't advertise this, but just bring them. And bring me, too, some good piece of Mrs Balfour's jewellery—a diamond bracelet or an emerald brooch. Something worthwhile, but just one piece. Not in a box, twist it in a bit of tissue paper. No, Potter, you needn't look at me like that, I'm not crazy nor do I mean to steal the diamonds. But, if you obey me exactly, you may play a large part in the saving of Mrs Balfour's life.'

Potter resumed his usual air of a respectful numskull and Stone added, 'Oh, there's one more thing—get me a small atomizer, you know, the kind used for perfumery. But I want it dry and clean. Can you find one?'

'Yes, sir, I'll ask Myra.'

'No, I'd rather keep everybody out of this except you. Find one, or if you can't, then go out to some drug store and buy a new one.'

'Very good, Mr Stone.'

'And—er—Potter, if—if I shouldn't come back at all—you know, you go down to my place and see my man there and he'll give you something in the way of a—er—souvenir for all the staff here. You attend to that, won't you?'

'Certainly, sir, but don't talk like that.'

'All right, I won't. But just remember.'

Potter disappeared and Fleming Stone set to work at his

packing. A strange assortment of articles went into the overnight bag, yet it held nothing personal except pyjamas and a few brushes.

There were pencils and paper, postage stamps, a book or two, several old newspapers, some small bottles and boxes, and a little bag of loose silver coins.

When Potter brought the diamond and sapphire bracelet, the new atomizer and a half-used bottle of French perfume from Alli's dressing table, he put those things in too, and again dismissed the man.

Then he took the atomizer out again, filled it very carefully with something he took from a chemist's package, and dropped it in a pocket of the overcoat he proposed to wear the next day.

A few more such odd jobs and, leaving word to be wakened at six, he called a halt on his rushing thoughts and calmly fell asleep.

And when Potter himself came to waken the detective in the morning he found him up and dressed and ready for his breakfast.

'Bring me some food, Potter,' he said, 'but first, have you the meat I asked for?'

'Right here, Mr Stone,' and Potter set down a small tray bearing two large chunks of fine-looking beef.

'Grand, Potter, truly grand. Now, hold it while I add the seasoning.'

Potter obediently held the tray, and Stone sprinkled the meat lavishly with a greyish powder.

'I don't want you to think my brain is entirely shattered,' he said, 'so I'll tell you what I intend doing with this tasty food. Or can you guess?'

'Is the powder poisonous, sir?'

'Very much so.'

'Then, sir, I take it you expect to present the lunch to a large and enthusiastic bloodhound.'

'Good for you, Potter, you have imagination. You are exactly right. Let us hope he will like it better than he does me.'

'You are going into danger, sir? Is there no other way out?'

Stone suddenly realized that Potter was not a wooden automaton, after all.

'No,' he said, soberly. 'No, Potter, I can think of no other way out. Keep all this under your hat.'

'Yes, sir, of course. Will you have your breakfast now?'

'Yes, and a brave one. I don't know when I shall eat again.'

Potter went off, to return shortly with a noble breakfast and the second man, who remained to serve. Potter was not one to take advantage of a little informality.

It was part of Stone's routine to lay aside all troubling thoughts in order to enjoy a perfect meal such as he saw before him now.

By quarter to seven he was all ready, and Potter returned with the poisoned meat done in two trim packages as Stone had directed.

'You can put 'em right in your two topcoat pockets, sir; they've waxed paper on, and then thick, strong butcher's paper, so they won't soil your linings.'

'I hope they'll soil the dog's linings, if I have to use them. I don't like to kill a dog, Potter, but if it's a toss-up between the two of us, his pedigree won't save him.'

And then, with his parcels in his pockets and his little suitcase in his hand, Stone went calmly out to the elevator feeling reminded of Charles the First stepping out to the scaffold.

Another moment or two and he was out in the street and getting into a taxicab which drew up to the kerb.

He sat down beside Benson, who said, 'Go ahead,' to the driver, and Stone looked at the man in the front seat.

He saw that Benson's description had been true, for the man was exceedingly long as to back, and if his legs were long in proportion, he must be a giant.

'Good morning, Tiny,' he said, pleasantly, but received in return only a gruff grunt.

'He wants you to pay him something on account like,' Benson translated the grunt.

'Certainly,' said Stone, 'he's quite right. Here's twenty dollars, Tiny, as a retainer, you know.'

The change in the man's expression was a shock, even to the experienced detective. Tiny turned round with such a beaming smile that his repellent face seemed almost attractive.

'Yer a court-card,' he said. 'Not many sits as high as you do. A retainer, is it? Yer can retain me till kingdom come, at that rate. Thanky, sir, thanky a whole lot!'

'He's all right now,' said Benson, nodding his wise head in satisfaction.

CHAPTER XVI

THE AWFUL BIG MAN

ONCE in New Jersey they turned north and went along the route Benson had followed the day before. The boy's eager eyes sought the torn papers he had thrown out to mark the way, but few of them were visible.

However, the taximan knew the way and repeated his trip of yesterday.

'That's the house,' he said, pointing to a roof that showed through the trees.

'All right,' Stone said, 'go to it. I say, Benson, did you find that derby hat when you got home last night?'

'Yes, Mr Stone and I'll track it down as soon as I get a chance.'

'When you go back to New, York, you can have a try at it.'

'When am I going back?'

'I can't tell you that, now. I shall leave you and Tiny in the woods while I go to the house. You're sure you heard dogs—'

'I heard the dogs,' Tiny put in. 'The kid didn't. But I'm a bit of a dog fancier and I reckernized a bloodhound's low growl. You better be careful, sir.'

'I'm prepared for them. Now, I don't apprehend trouble, Tiny, but it may come. If it does, you look after young Benson, I'm leaving him in your care.'

'Yessir, I'll see to him. You gimme my orders—'

'Only to wait here for a time. If you hear a shot, don't be alarmed. It will be a signal from me to scoot for the nearest telephone you can find and call the police to come here right away. Then you and Benson go back to the city and keep out of all this business until you hear from me again. I am not afraid for myself, but I've no right to drag you two chaps into what may be a bad quarter of an hour. If you hear nothing at all of me by noon, go along home and forget it for today. You'll get your pay all right, both of you, but it may be delayed a day or two.'

'I'm not worryin' about that, Mr Stone,' and the uncouth man turned round to look at him. 'But I'm fearing for yourself.'

'Do you pack a gun, Tiny?'

'Well, not as a rule, sir, but today—yes. You see, I'm not altogether what you'd call a law-abidin' citizen.'

'You ought to be but since you're not, I must make the best of it. As I say, probably there'll be no trouble at all, but if you think it necessary, shoot one of your bloodhounds, or two, if you like.'

'If necessary, I will,' and Tiny looked so responsible that Stone felt real confidence in him.

'Stop here,' the detective said, after another few feet. They were near the house, but in a spot where the trees were close together and hid the car entirely. He got out taking the little suitcase with him. This he proceeded to hide among the underbrush and then, bidding the two remain in the car, he started up the path leading to the front door.

He saw no dogs but his sharp ears caught a sound of distant growling and he concluded they were confined in some barn or shed, of which several could be seen.

Save for some traces of neglect, the house was habitable-looking, and Stone rang the doorbell. It was an old-fashioned type with a knob to pull out, and this act was followed by a sharp jangle.

No one answered the bell and he rang again. Then the door was opened and a matronly looking woman appeared, wearing a grey dress and a large white apron.

'Well,' she said, but not sharply, 'who may you be and what do you want?'

'First of all, I want to come in,' and Stone looked determined to carry out his wish.

She stood looking at him a trifle doubtfully and Stone scrutinized her face. A first impression was that of a gentle, benign old lady, but a second glance showed she was not as old as he had thought and she was far, far less gentle than his hasty supposition.

'Is the man of the house at home?' he asked, speaking courteously.

'No, he isn't, but he'll be here pretty soon. Don't you know him by name?'

'I don't choose to use it, if I do.'

'Don't you know your own name? I believe I asked you for it.'

'So you did. I am Fleming Stone.'

'Well, well, why didn't you say so? Come right in, Mr Stone, come right in.'

A little taken aback at her sudden change of manner, Stone went in.

The house was of an ordinary type. There was a hall straight through from front to back, with what was apparently an outside door at the other end.

All room doors opening on the hall were closed and a staircase clung to the wall at one side. This was on the right side as Stone entered, and his' hostess with a not ungraceful gesture indicated he was to go up.

'Step right along up, Mr Stone,' she said, 'up to the sitting room. I am Mrs Bindle—I live here with my son—'

'It is your guest I want to see,' and Stone looked her squarely in the eye. 'The lady who has been here since last evening.'

'Go along up, then, if that's what you want. Step lively, please.'

Her sudden changes from grave politeness to slangy informality made Stone think that the former was a pose and the latter her natural self.

He didn't want to go upstairs. It somehow seemed that he lost a certain advantage by doing so. He had yet to meet the awful big man who lived in the house, the head criminal himself, and perchance one or two large and healthy blood-hounds.

To be sure, the dogs were not likely to be upstairs, but he liked it better on the ground floor.

However, he had long ago learned 'needs must when the devil drives,' so he started up the wide staircase. Near the top there was a landing and three more steps at right angles to the long stair.

Here Mrs Bindle passed him and led the way to one of the front rooms, the one on the right as one looked at the house from outside.

A pleasant-looking sitting room with old-fashioned but not antique furniture.

It took Fleming Stone's quick eyes exactly two seconds to see that all the windows, two in front and two at the side, were barred and that in a most workmanlike manner. His leaping mind told him that he was already a prisoner, that he had walked into the trap, and that no doubt Alli Balfour was in similar case.

Annoyance was his uppermost feeling. He was not, as yet, afraid, but if he had to be incarcerated in this silly old house, he felt he should lose his temper.

And his foreboding came true very quickly.

'I hope you will be comfortable here, Mr Stone,' his cicerone said; 'this suite is at your disposal. That door opens into your bedroom, with bath. I regret to tell you it will not be possible for you to leave these rooms until Mr Powers arrives. He will give you the interview you came for and then you and he can agree on future arrangements.'

'I see,' said Stone, politely. 'May I smoke in here?'

'Yes, if you like. Mr Powers may be here today and he may not. If you want any night things or toilet articles my son will get them for you when he goes to the store. You might make a list.'

'I may make a small one. I do not propose to be your guest very long. Which rooms did you give your other visitor?'

By a bit of commonplace psychology, Stone hoped he might lead the woman along in casual talk, and spring this question so simply that she would answer it without thinking.

She did. 'Across the hall,' she said, unheeding her speech. And then, quickly, to distract her attention, Stone said:

'And, by the way, Mrs Bindle, could I have a small table, perhaps a bridge table, to write on. I am writing my memoirs and if I am idle for a few hours I could get some odd pages blocked out.'

'Yes, I'll ask Sam to bring you one.'

'Do you play bridge? Perhaps if Mr Powers is not here this evening we could have a rubber.'

'I don't know—I'll see about it.'

Mrs Bindle was clearly flustered at the way Stone was taking things. Not a word of complaint or even surprise at the situation, no attempt at bribery or at wheedling. The man seemed satisfied to stay and only asked to write his memoirs!

'I must tell you, Mr Stone, that it is useless for you to try to get away. My son is a large and strong man and he is very watchful. The locks and bars are most secure, and should you reach the ground there are two ferocious dogs who will immediately interview you. So don't try to escape.'

'Why should I?' and Stone looked at her in innocent surprise. 'I admit I don't understand this locking in business, but it takes more than that to rouse me to insurrection. Don't let me keep you if you are busy.'

A pleasant smile accompanied this last speech, and Stone bowed a dismissal that it was not easy to ignore.

She went out and Stone heard her lock the room door from the hall side. He listened to her footsteps along the hall and then, dropping into an easy chair, he gave way to a spasm of silent mirth.

The laughter, however, was short-lived. Indeed, it was more a matter of nervous exasperation than of merriment and, physically relieved a little, Stone turned his thoughts to his present emergencies.

Benson and Tiny must first be considered.

It was about eleven o'clock and Stone hastily scribbled a note which he hoped might reach them safely. He wrote:

'Held by the enemy. Go back home but return at midnight and do up the dogs, then bring my suitcase and find some way to get it up to me or I can use sheets. Bring a flashlight. This side of the house, second storey, is all mine. I've no plans yet. The chief may come at any moment. I can't use you till dark, so make it midnight. The lady in no danger or discomfort, I think. My barring in is hopeless but bring oustiti and bunch of skeleton keys. Maybe something to eat away steel bars? If I'm not snuffed out, I'll pull through, but case pretty hopeless.'

Then he folded it and sat by the window to watch for the possible appearance of Benson.

At last he saw a large and unpleasant person get into a car and drive away, and concluded it must be the redoubtable Sam. Soon after that, he saw a head peeping from the foliage and recognized Benson. He cautiously showed the white letter and, as the youth crept nearer, he dropped it between the bars and out of the window. Watching carefully, Benson ran for it and got it and quickly disappeared.

This convinced Stone that since Sam was away and the boss criminal not present, Benson was not watched. No dogs were heard, and, as there was nothing else to do, Fleming Stone lighted a cigarette and sat down to smoke.

He summarized his dangers and his hopes. It seemed to him the former far outnumbered the latter, but he must consider them more closely.

The woman in charge was not awe-inspiring; the awful big man, Sam, though as yet unknown, might prove tractable.

With his unquenchable hopefulness, Stone concluded he was not yet beaten, but he could not persuade himself that the immediate future would be easy sledding.

He had thoroughly investigated his domain and, as he anticipated, there was not, so far as he could see, the slightest chance of escape from this simple locking in. It was maddening to be held by plain, old-fashioned locks and keys. Had he been incarcerated in a tower or a dungeon with a keeper who carried great keys on a clanking chain, it would have better suited his dignity and perhaps have been easier to get out of.

Directly back of his sitting room was the bedroom and an adjoining bath, both decently though not smartly appointed. But such details interested him little beside the fact that each room's windows presented the same immovable steel bars, plain, simple bars that looked easy to cut if one had proper tools and plenty of time.

Stone wasted no time thinking about cutting these bars. He knew that to negotiate successfully with Benson for tools and things was outside the possibilities.

He devoted his thoughts to some more ingenious means of escape. For escape he must. He, Fleming Stone, to be baffled by a common lock! Perish the thought!

But the thought showed no signs of perishing.

At one o'clock a knock came on the door, and automatically Stone said, 'Come in.'

The door was unlocked and 'the very large man', who was indubitably Sam, came in, bringing a big tray.

He set it on a chair, and from the hall brought a folded bridge table, which he opened and set up without a word.

On this he put the tray and stood a moment, looking at Stone. The detective gladly accepted this opportunity to study his visitor, and saw to his satisfaction an expression of awe and admiration in the eyes that stared at him. He well knew this particular look, it was hero-worship, and he had often received it from devotees of detective fiction. There is a glamour, he had found, about a Criminal Investigator, and if this giant felt that way about it he might be a decided asset.

Stone didn't rush things, however. He said, pleasantly, but not invitingly, 'You're Sam, I suppose?'

'Yes. Howjer know?'

'Your mother told me you were a big man and you most certainly are!'

This speech was accompanied by a look of unmistakable admiration. Sam fell for it and drew himself up with pride.

'Yes, I am.' But suddenly he seemed to remember his role and said gruffly:

'Don't you try to soft-soap me. I'm here to watch you and I'm gonta do it. If you try to spring a getaway, you'll be sorry, for I ain't bein' any too gentle with you. And you needn't try to make friends. I ain't that sort.'

'You're a mind reader! I was trying to do that very thing, in the hope that if I succeeded, you'd help me to get away. How can a fellow bust through a door with an honest-to-goodness lock and key on it? And there's no reason for my being here. I thought maybe your sense of justice was oversized, like the rest of you. But I see it isn't. Don't stay, if it bores you.'

'Don't get sassy, you might be sorry.'

'As how?'

'I might hit yer a clip.'

'Not you! I'm a character reader, you know, and you'd never hit without provocation of any sort. You've got a code of honour of your own and I'll bet you live up to it.'

'There you go again—soft-soapin'! I tell you that won't get you anywhere.'

'What will get me anywhere?'

'Nothin' short of a miracle, I guess. And they don't have those much, nowadays.'

'Oh, yes, they do. You'd be surprised to know how often they occur. I have second sight, you know, and I prophesy that what will seem to you a miracle will happen to you in less than twenty-four hours. Do you play bridge?'

'Yes. Is that your miracle? Thirteen spades dealt to me in one hand, I s'pose? Well, I've never had that yet.'

'Nor anyone else.'

'Yes, they have. Why, I know a feller—'

The door opened and Mrs Bindle came in.

'Whatever are you doing here, Sam!' she cried, in astonishment. 'Have you forgotten Mr Powers positively forbade you to speak to Mr Stone any more than absolutely necessary?'

'I jest brought him up his lunch, Ma, and I was goin' right down.'

'His lunch! And he hasn't even uncovered the dishes, and it's cold already! What you two been talking about?'

'I'm afraid it was my fault, Mrs Bindle,' Stone volunteered. 'I'm a gregarious sort, and Sam seemed pleasant to talk to, and so we've had a short chat. No harm done, I assure you.'

'Anything is harm that's against Mr Powers' orders.' But the woman's face softened as she looked at her son, and Stone sensed at once that the great hulk of humanity opposite him was his mother's joy and pride, her idol, the apple of her eye.

'I know, Ma—I won't do it again—but you know I never saw a real detective before, and he seems so jolly talkative and all—'

'What's the harm, Mrs Bindle?' Stone asked. 'Why can't I have an hour's chat with Sam? I'm pretty tired of sitting alone. Why can't I go out for a walk in the grounds? I couldn't get away, with Sam and your dogs in charge.'

'Don't waste your breath, Mr Stone,' and Mrs Bindle looked at him scornfully. 'Understand, my son and I are left here to see to it that you don't leave us. Why then should I put temptation in your way?'

'And what do you think, Ma?' Sam exclaimed. 'He says—Mr Stone does—that he can perform miracles and he's going to perform one on me tonight.'

'Now, now,' and Stone laughed outright, 'that's the way stories go! I didn't say anything of the sort, Sam. Now, see if you can tell truthfully what I did say?'

'That's what I heard you say, and my hearing is all right.' Sam looked sulky now, and Stone realized that he thought he was being held up to ridicule.

'No,' Stone said, seriously, 'I did not say I should perform any miracle. I said possibly a miracle might occur tonight, but it is by no means certain.'

'What do you mean?' Mrs Bindle asked, as she quite noticeably shuddered. 'I'm afraid of such things. I'm even afraid of Mr Powers when he has his mask on.'

'Oh, does he wear it now?' Stone seemed interested in a friendly way. 'Such a nice one, isn't it? Black satin and nicely stitched and all.'

'Oh, do you know Mr Powers?'

Stone looked around as if fearing an eavesdropper, and then said in a low voice, 'Not by that name.'

'I told you so, Sam! I've believed all along Powers isn't his real name! I was just sure of it!'

'What is his real name?' Stone asked.

'We don't know,' Mrs Bindle told him. 'We don't know him so very well.'

'Well, what does it matter? Take away the tray, Sam. I can't eat cold food. And don't bring any other, I don't want anything. I'll make a short list, Sam, for you to buy for me in the village. What village is it?'

'Never you mind,' said Sam's mother. 'You make your list, and he'll get what he can of it, and that'll have to do you.'

'Oh, yes, that'll do me. I'm not a fusser. How's your lady guest? Doesn't she want a lot of things? Make-up, hair-nets, perfumes and what-nots? Better get her a pack of cards and teach her to play patience. She's likely to need it.'

'I'll attend to her, Mr Stone. Don't trouble yourself.'

'No trouble at all. Besides, I haven't done anything yet. Did you say we'd play bridge this evening?'

'I said nothing of the sort! You are not here to be entertained.'

'And yet I am entertained—greatly.'

There was no retort to this. Mrs Bindle went off and, taking a list Stone handed him, Sam went away, too.

Locked in again, Stone made up his mind to enjoy his enforced idleness as much as he could. But the small shelf of books at his disposal failed to show any volume he cared to read. There was no radio. He was reduced to the morning paper, which he still had in his overcoat pocket.

He began on the first page and he read every word on every page, but without feeling he had gained any information or entertainment from them.

He gazed out of the window, until he declared to himself he never wanted to see a glorious autumn landscape again.

But at last the long afternoon wore away, and Sam brought a tray of dinner for him.

It was a good dinner, well cooked and arranged on hot water dishes.

Sam did not stay and the detective ate heartily, after his early breakfast and omitted luncheon.

Then Sam returned with some attractive dessert, and lingered to take the tray.

'You're a good sort,' Stone said, sincerely enough, for Sam's quiet respectful attention pleased him. 'What time do the people turn in here?'

'Whenever they get ready,' and Sam looked belligerent. 'We got a maid in the house but she ain't allowed in here. I s'pose you can turn down your own bed?'

'Of course. No chance of his Eminence coming tonight?'

'Who said so? He comes when he likes. You want to see him, particular?'

'I do, indeed. I suppose I'll be told when he comes?'

'You bet you will. You and the lady across the hall. And what he won't tell you two—!'

'I'll be glad to be told something, at any rate. Perhaps he'll tell me who killed Mr Balfour and his son. Do you know?'

'No, I wouldn't be let to live if I did. If you know and won't tell, you'll be put out of the way of those who do know. But don't be quizzin' me. The boss'll be coming soon—if at all. When he comes, you can ask all the questions you can think of and you can sling 'em at him pretty swift; he'll keep up with you.'

'I just want to know the murderer. I can keep up with your boss all right, but I must get some information out of him.'

'I wish you joy outa that job.'

'It may not be pleasant, but I shall accomplish it all the same. Doesn't your boss ever think he's up against a pretty stiff proposition when he tackles Fleming Stone?'

'Well, he does, but you see, he's got me to help him. He depends a heap on me.'

'Yes,' said Stone, giving Sam an odd look. 'Yes, I should think he would.'

CHAPTER XVII

HELD BY THE ENEMY

AGAIN Fleming Stone was left to his thoughts, unless he could find something to do more active than thinking.

Although November was fast approaching, the autumn air was crisp without being chill and, raising the front window, he sat down to smoke and, incidentally, to watch for Benson. He wished he had told him to come earlier than midnight. Still, he had no wish for the lad to meet up with the mysterious Mr Powers.

Yet he eagerly awaited his own meeting with the man and was fully decided to learn his identity or perish in the attempt.

He smiled sourly as he realized that 'perish in the attempt' might be no flight of fancy, but a true detail of what might happen in the near future.

He had promised Sam a miracle—well, his promise might be made good, but it was likely the miracle would happen to him, and would be a mighty unpleasant one.

His situation was a novel one. Never before in his life had he been made a prisoner. And now to be kept inactive by an old-fashioned door key was a little too much!

He heard the sounds of an approaching motor, and looking out the front window saw a big black car come swiftly up the drive and stop at the house.

He drew a sigh of relief that his enemy had probably arrived. Whatever the interview might bring, it was better than this interminable waiting.

A shapeless, cloaked figure got out of the car and went into the house, but just as the man disappeared under the piazza roof, Stone noticed he wore a derby hat. He wanted to think the expected Mr Powers was the same man who killed Balfour, and this looked like it.

He waited, momentarily expecting to be summoned, but time dragged wearily by with no word from below. At last he heard the door across the hall opened and he had reason to think Alli had been taken downstairs for an interview. He scarcely dared hope that he should be called while she was there and resigned himself to a further wait, but almost at once, Sam came and invited him down to a conference.

'And don't cut up any funny business,' the big man advised, as they went down the stairs. 'You see, I'm under orders to take care of you if you get out of hand and while I sorta like you I have to obey orders.'

'Of course, Sam, take care of me all you want to. But I shall be tractable. I don't want to make you any trouble.'

'You won't. Here we are, sir, step right in the parlour.'

Sam opened the door into the large room directly under Stone's front room above and the detective went in. Sam went in, too, and they sat down. Fleming Stone saw Alli and nodded to her with a smile, then turned to the singular figure who seemed to be in charge of things.

This was the man he had seen get out of the motor car, and he looked at him with interest.

Fleming Stone saw what looked like a large man, but as he was draped in a long full garment, like a black domino, it was hard to guess at his real size. He wore a black satin mask, with a frill that hid his chin, and Stone noticed a glitter in the eyes that shone through the eyeholes.

'You are Fleming Stone?' he asked in an odd voice.

'Yes, as you well know. Don't keep those horse chestnuts in your cheeks if they bother you.'

'They do, a little. I use them to disguise my voice.'

'Unnecessary, since I know you, anyway.'

'Oh, no, you don't, though you may think you do. I am a long-time friend of Mrs Balfour, and I hope both she and you will agree to a proposition I am about to make. I do not want a long discussion about the happenings of the past week, I just want you two to consider my proposal and make your own decision. I am not the killer of Mr Balfour, but that is not the point. This is the case. I am not a friend of Keith Ramsay and as I happen to know—*know*, mind you—that he killed his friend and employer, Philip Balfour, and Guy Balfour too, I want to see him convicted of those crimes. I ask nothing more than justice, but that justice must be done. Now, you, Mrs Balfour, and you, Mr Stone, are in a sort of collusion to save that man and I propose to thwart your plans. If you, Mr Stone, will agree to change your tactics and prove Keith Ramsay guilty, and you, Mrs Balfour, will admit your belief in Ramsay's guilt, you two may walk out of here, free and unmolested. If not, there is a mighty uncomfortable future ahead of you.'

Stone looked at Alli, with a nod, as if handing her the situation, and she responded at once:

'Mr Powers, your proposition and the way you put it leads me to think you are the murderer of my husband, yourself. If so, I hope you may yet meet your just deserts, but as to my part in this matter, I positively refuse to do anything except to reiterate my belief in Keith Ramsay's innocence and to help prove it in any way I can.'

'You are daring, Mrs Balfour; perhaps you'd better have a care. And, Mr Stone, what have you to say?'

'I echo Mrs Balfour's speech entirely. And understand this: I know who committed those two murders, I know who stole the valuable book and rest assured he shall not get away with it. It is you who would better have a care. It is you who have a mighty uncomfortable future ahead of you. So proceed with your threats and your bullying. What do you propose to do?'

It was unusual for Fleming Stone to lose his temper, but he was at a disadvantage and he knew it. The powerful Sam would soon settle any physical attack he might make on the so-called

Powers and no attempt at reasoning or appeal to justice would be of any effect.

The strange glitter in the eyes of the masked man gave Stone an impression of madness and he felt that he could best deal with that by definite accusations.

Yet he was a little surprised at what followed.

Powers suddenly lost his belligerent air, suddenly changed his raucous tone, and in a hard, cold voice said:

'Very well, Mr Stone, you have signed your own death warrant. Tomorrow morning you shall be shot at sunrise.'

'Melodramatics, eh?' and Stone smiled annoyingly.

'If you like to call it that, yes. I shall conduct the act myself and appear in the principal role. As to Mrs Balfour, I have no desire for her death. She is too pretty and alluring to be put out of the world. And in her future, I shall also assume the principal role.'

'Then, if that's all, may I be excused?' Stone said in a casual tone. 'I am told a condemned man always sleeps soundly the night before his execution.'

'You may go, yes, Mr Stone. Pleasant dreams.'

The detective rose to leave the room. Mrs Bindle went out the door with him.

'I want to be sure things are all right in your rooms, Mr Stone,' she said, as they went in, 'and I want a word with you,' she added, as she closed the door.

'Please,' she said, coming nearer to him, 'please don't take that superior attitude with Mr Powers. That sort of thing makes him furious.'

'And why should you care about that, Mrs Bindle?' Stone said, gently.

'Oh, when he gets mad he is something terrible. If he says he'll kill you at sunrise, he will. He is a monster, Mr Stone, and—and I don't want you sacrificed—'

'Now, now, Mrs Bindle, don't be alarmed for me. I can look after myself. It is Mrs Balfour I am bothered about.'

'I can't help you any there.' Mrs Bindle looked stubborn now.

'Oh, yes, you can. Listen a minute.' Stone drew a small parcel from his pocket.

He opened it and revealed a sparkling bracelet of diamonds and sapphires that fairly dazed Mrs Bindle.

'Oh—oh, oh—' she gasped. 'I adore jewels! Oh—let me see it!'

For Stone had gathered the tissue paper about it and stood holding it as he looked at her.

'Mrs Bindle,' he said in a low voice, 'that bracelet is yours if you will manage to let me see Mrs Balfour alone for five minutes. No discussion, now—just say you will or you won't.'

Mrs Bindle seemed not to hear him. She murmured to herself—'What a chance! What a godsend—'

Then, louder:

'Yes, Mr Stone, and I trust you that it's all right. I couldn't wear a piece like that, but Sam, he's getting married, and what a gift for his bride! Yes, I can do what you ask, but I must choose the time.'

'No, that won't do. It must come off right away. Go downstairs and bring the lady up. If you arrange for us a safe five-minute interview, the bracelet is yours. It's genuine, of course. It belongs to Mrs Balfour. But she will be glad for you to have it, if you do your part.'

'Never fear, Mr Stone. Leave it to me.'

He left it to her and the result was that for five blessed minutes, perhaps a trifle longer, Alli Balfour was in his sitting room and he was telling her of his plans and her part in them.

She listened intently, understood thoroughly and willingly agreed to the gift of the bracelet to Mrs Bindle who had made the interview possible.

Stone hurried her away, lest Benson should come and, handing the jewel to Mrs Bindle, dismissed the two women, and heard his keeper lock his door from the hall side.

Then, carefully raising the side window, he dropped out a note.

He was taking no chances with whistling, bird calls, or any sound of communication, and as it was midnight, he knew Benson would be there.

After an interval, he discerned two figures, and then began to let down his two sheets, which he had tied together at the corners, and which he fastened securely to the lowest bar of the window.

Then he pulled up his suitcase, which Benson had attached to the sheets and which was small enough to slide between the bars.

This in his possession, he was all right, and he dropped another note to Benson—a long one this time—which he had written during the day. This gave Benson and Tiny full instructions as to their part in the performance which was to take place 'at sunrise'.

It told them, also, to spend the rest of the night, until dawn, in Tiny's car, and be ready for action in the morning.

The two men obeyed to the letter and curled up in the taxicab, with no fear that they would oversleep.

Fleming Stone fairly gloated over the contents of his suitcase, feeling that now he could face any real or apparent danger.

First of all he tried his staunch little means of escape. This was the oustiti, a clever gadget whereby one can turn a key in a locked door. It is a sort of special pliers that works perfectly on an ordinary lock and key. It is of no use in case of a Yale lock.

But the doors in this old house were fitted with plain old-fashioned hardware, and after a touch of an oiled feather, he cautiously unlocked his door easily enough. Crossing the hall without a sound, he slipped a paper under Alli's door. She pulled it in, and in a moment scribbled an answer, which the waiting Stone saw come slowly out from under the door.

Whereupon, still preserving the utmost silence, he unlocked her door and went in.

Not venturing to stay long, he told her some more details of the assassination scheduled for the next morning. Told her about Benson and Tiny, bade her be of good cheer and went back the way he came.

And then he went to bed and slept soundly until five o'clock in the morning.

At that hour Sam unlocked the door and came into his rooms.

'Time to get up, Mr Stone,' he said; 'sorry to wake you, but orders is orders.'

'Yes—of course. That's all right, Sam. Didn't you bring me any breakfast?'

Sam looked astonished.

'I didn't think you'd want any, Mr Stone.'

'I'd like a cup of coffee. No matter about anything else.'

'Yes, sir. I'll make it. Mother isn't up yet.'

'And Mr Powers? Is he on deck?'

'Yes, sir. I say—I mean—I'm awful sorry about this, you know.'

'All right, Sam. You come near being a good chap. After this is all over, I'd like to think you're parting company with Mr Powers.'

'Oh, I am, sir!'

'Get along, then. Just a cup of hot coffee for me.'

Sam went off and Fleming Stone rose and made a careful but quick dressing and by the time his coffee was brought him, he had dropped a note down to Benson, had seen him pick it up and was calmly waiting for Sam in his sitting room.

When the big man came he looked sorrowfully at Stone, but the detective said, cheerfully:

'Well, old man, I'm glad I'm leaving this place, if I do go out feet first.'

'It's a shame, Mr Stone—'

'Never mind, you can't do anything to help. You make good coffee, Sam—thank you.'

No further word was said and the two men went downstairs.

There was no sign of Alli or of Mrs Bindle, but the so-called Powers was there, wearing his long robe and black mask.

'This is all outside the law, Mr Stone,' the cold voice said, 'but I take the responsibility of that. You are in my way, you hamper my projects, therefore I dismiss you from life on this planet. We will have no talk about it, you are at my mercy, but as you will learn, I have no mercy. I shall shoot you at sunrise, because this is a time when no chance passer-by will come along. I don't care about waiting for the exact moment, let the sun rise when it will, we will start proceedings now. Will you step outside, quietly, or shall Sam assist you?'

'Needs must when the devil drives,' and Stone made a mocking bow to his tormentor and took a step toward the door.

'Lead the way, Sam,' said Powers, and as Stone followed, Powers followed him.

Sam led them round to the back and Stone was directed to stand against the house.

He did so, and looked so carelessly unconcerned that Powers exclaimed, 'For heaven's sake, man! Don't you know what's happening to you?'

'Nothing has happened, as yet,' was the reply.

'Well, it will now!' and the black-robed figure lifted an automatic and aimed it at Fleming Stone's heart.

There was a report, a splotch of red appeared where the bullet struck the condemned man, and Stone fell limply to the ground.

Two figures rushed from the concealing bushes and Benson leaned down over the silent form of the man he worshiped, while Tiny ran toward the man who had fired the shot.

Powers drew back and laughed at him, saying, 'Do him up, Sam!'

Sam made for Tiny, and laughed in his face. Tiny was very tall, but lank and without great physical strength.

But Sam had little more than touched him, than by a dexterous bit of jiujitsu, Tiny turned Sam's great weight and strength against himself, and by his skill broke the big man's leg.

The snap of the knee joint could be plainly heard, and for the first time the black-robed figure showed signs of weakening.

'Who are you?' he cried, staring through the eyeholes of his mask.

'I'm just a passer-by,' Tiny returned, blustering, 'and unless you want a broken bone, too, you'd better—run!'

On the last word Tiny started toward him, and with a sort of frightened yelp, Powers ran!

He fairly flew and was met at the door by Mrs Bindle, who said, 'Scoot up to the barred rooms and lock yourself in! That fellow's a holy terror! What did he do to my Sam?'

Without waiting for an answer, she ran past him, through the door and out to see her son on the ground, groaning with pain.

'Oh, Sam, Sam—what is it, dear? Who hurt you?'

'That great long one! Where's Mr Powers? Tell him to kill that chap!'

'Yes, tell him!' and Tiny glared at the distracted mother. 'Mrs Bindle, you're in a mess here. Now, listen! Your Mr Powers is hiding because if he doesn't, he'll get what I gave Sam. And you'll be in some trouble yourself, unless you do what I tell you. Sam has a broken leg, but a doctor can set it, if he gets at it fairly soon. If you wait too long, it will be too late. So here's your chance.'

For the first time Mrs Bindle noted the fallen figure over which Benson was still stooping.

'Oh,' she cried, 'is Mr Stone dead?'

'Yes,' Benson said, rising. 'And what this man here just told you is straight goods. You have just one chance to get a doctor here in time to fix up your boy. If he waits too long, gangrene will set in and he will probably die. Now, we are going to take Mr Stone's body right back to his home in New York. We are two friends of his, we came here to rescue him. If we'd been

two minutes sooner, we could have saved his life. As it is, we
shall start off at once, and take his body with us. Now, then, if
you will let Mrs Balfour out and let us take her along with us,
we will guarantee to send a doctor back here to look after Sam.
If not, you can take your chances with your son.'

'Oh, yes, yes—I'll let Mrs Balfour out. I'll do anything you
tell me if you'll help Sam. Won't you take him to New York—to
a hospital—?'

'No, we can't do that. We shall be busy with Mr Stone's
affairs—you go at once and send Mrs Balfour right down here.
Tell her she is going home and to bring whatever things she
has here. Hurry, now, or I may change my mind.'

Mrs Bindle hastened to obey the very letter of her orders.
She went softly to Alli Balfour's room and hurried her to get
ready and get downstairs quickly.

Alli was dressed and she hurried on her wraps, asking what
had happened.

'Everything,' said Mrs Bindle, bursting into tears—they
nearly killed Sam, they did kill Mr Stone, they scared Mr Powers
all to pieces, and now they're going to take you away. Come
along.'

'Who are they?' Alli asked, as they went downstairs.

'I don't know. Some friends of Mr Stone's.'

The two women reached the scene of action to find that the
body of Fleming Stone had been placed in the big car belonging
to Powers, and another car that looked like a taxicab and that
had mysteriously appeared from the bushes, was waiting for
Mrs Balfour.

Urged by Benson, Alli got in, seemingly quite content to go
without further words.

'We're off!' cried Tiny, who was driving the taxi-cab, and he
started his car while Benson, getting into the other car which
held the body of Fleming Stone, followed.

'Well, he's dead, anyhow,' the crestfallen Mr Powers said to
himself, as he watched proceedings from a back window. 'Now

all I have to do is to get back to the city as soon as possible. Mrs Bindle can telephone for a car, I'll take Sam to a hospital and then we'll be all right again. With Stone out of the way, I can get Alli again, they'll never find the book, and having ended well—all's well.'

A sound of someone trying to open his door was followed by a banging on its panels and the tearful voice of Mrs Bindle crying, 'Let me in! Let me in!'

He opened the door and in his usual calm, cold tones said, 'Don't make such a hullabaloo. Come in.'

'Oh, yes, all very well for you to be quiet and serene. You have nothing to worry about. Although you will have if I turn against you. And I'll do just that, unless you help me to get a doctor for Sam. Those men said they would do it, but I know they won't. Anyway, I want you to see to it. There's danger of gangrene.'

'What! Who told you that?'

'One of those men. Never mind that, you call a doctor!'

'Don't get so excited; it doesn't do any good. Now, you call a car from New York—those wretches made off with mine. And—oh, good Lord!'

'What's the matter?'

'What's the matter enough! But never mind, I can fix it. You call a car from this garage, here's the number—tell them to come over here at once—emergency case—then you get Sam ready to go to the hospital and we'll all three go over together, then I'll go home and you take Sam to any hospital you choose. I'll pay the bills, of course. He'll soon be all right again.'

'All right. I'll make them come quickly. Shall I shut up the house?'

'Yes, it has served its purpose—and nobly. You and Sam will be well paid, with a bonus for Sam's broken leg. Who'd thought that rough-looking fellow had such knowledge? But he'll get his. I'll track him down and see to him.'

'You'd better be careful. They're a smart lot. That young chap is nobody's fool.'

'I'll make him my fool. Now my only enemy is out of the running, I'll win the race myself.'

'What race?'

'Never you mind, Mrs Bindle. You'd better give me that diamond bracelet to take care of for you. You oughtn't to carry it around in your bag.'

'What diamond bracelet are you talking about?'

'Mighty innocent, aren't you? The one Mr Stone gave you.'

'I don't know how you come to know about that, but no, thank you, I'll not trust it to you; I'll take care of it myself.'

CHAPTER XVIII

AFTER ALL

IT was Benson's boast that he could drive anything with an engine in it, and he easily manipulated the big car he had collected from the Powers' garage, with the result that he soon left Tiny and his taxicab far behind.

He drove straight to Fleming Stone's home and interviewed his man, an intelligent person, with whose assistance the victim of Powers' venomous rage was taken into the house.

There, Benson turned the whole matter over to Plum, who was Fleming Stone's secretary. It was decided that Plum should telephone to the mortician, and advise also, with a cousin of Stone's, who lived in the city.

Benson went away, wondering if he had done all he could for his employer and feeling grave misgivings about the future.

Tiny, meanwhile, had taken Mrs Balfour to her home, arriving there nearly an hour later than Benson had ended his journey.

She gave him a present of money, and took his address for future reference, then, at last in her own home, she controlled her excitement, greeted Potter kindly, and going straight to the safe room, she asked that Mr Ramsay be sent to her there.

Keith came at once and, closing the door, took Alli in his arms.

'Tell me all about it,' he said, after he had persuaded himself that she was really there, safe and sound.

So she gave him a recital of everything that had occurred, and while they were talking, Sewell called.

'Show him right in here, Potter,' Alli said, eagerly. 'I want to see him.'

Then she told Sewell her story, and the three went into conference as to what should be done.

But very soon, Sewell said he would go to Fleming Stone's house and discuss things with his cousin, who would doubtless be there by this time. A telephone message confirmed this, and, as a near friend of Stone's, John Sewell went down there.

'You tell Potter of Mr Stone's death, won't you?' Alli asked him, as he was leaving. 'I don't like to.'

'Of course, my dear, leave it to me. You've been through quite enough mental strain and physical discomfort. I'll see what I can do for poor Stone, and then we must see the police and tell them they'll have to hunt down the murderer. And what about the book?'

'Oh, I don't know. I'm sure Mr Powers has it—'

'Did you take with you the money for it?'

'I took part of it. I thought I could persuade him to take less. But of course, we didn't talk about the book. Had I stayed longer,' she shuddered at the thought, 'I should have taken up the subject and—oh, I don't know what the result would have been! It's all like a horrible nightmare. I think I won't talk any more about it now. You take Mr Stone's place, won't you, Mr Sewell? I'll rest a little and by this afternoon I'll be perfectly fit.'

'Yes,' Ramsay said, 'that's what you need, rest. Go ahead on your own, Sewell, and I'll stand by here and Mrs Balfour will soon be herself again.'

Sewell paused on his way out to speak to Potter.

He told him in a few words of the death of Fleming Stone and said he would advise him as to the time of the funeral.

Alli called Myra and went off to her own rooms.

Keith Ramsay went to the library and remained there to await any messages or calls.

After a while Sewell telephoned, speaking from Stone's home.

'Everything is being done that can be done,' he said. 'Stone's cousin is here—his name is Knight. He's looking after everything. The funeral will be tomorrow, from the funeral chapel. At two o'clock. It seems soon, but Mr Knight thinks it's best. I'll see you again tonight.'

In the afternoon Wiley came and asked for Ramsay.

'Thought I'd come in, on a little matter of business,' he said. 'I've been wondering if perhaps Mrs Balfour wouldn't like to sell some of her books. Not the important ones, you know, but some of the lower lights. It must be a great care to her to have so many and I thought she might welcome a chance to sell off some at an advantageous price.'

'Nice of you to think of that,' Keith said, blandly. He detested Wiley, but he saw no reason to tell him so. 'Perhaps, later on, Mrs Balfour may be interested. But not at present. She is pretty well done up with all the sorrow and excitement of the past fortnight, and she couldn't possibly take up the question now.'

'You know a lot about her.'

Though spoken quietly, the remark had an insolent sound which Ramsay promptly resented.

'Why not?' he said. 'I've lived here more than a year. I am, of course, well acquainted with her.'

'Very well,' and Wiley looked unpleasant. 'I say, Ramsay, I know quite a lot about you two and if you could manage to let me have some of the books from the library, at a cheerful price, why, I could forget any gossip I may have heard.'

Keith Ramsay reached out his hand and pushed an electric button.

Potter appeared, and Ramsay said, coldly, 'Show Mr Wiley out, Potter, and should he call again, say to him that you have orders not to admit him.'

'Oh, *pshaw*, now, Keith—don't take a little pleasantry like that! I didn't mean anything.'

Ramsay had picked up a book and was seemingly absorbed in its pages. He paid no attention to Wiley and with a shrug the visitor turned and went out into the hall.

Potter preceded him and opened the front door. As Wiley went through, he smiled at Potter, and said, 'Some people can't take a joke.'

'No, sir,' said Potter.

Not long after, Swinton came and asked for Mrs Balfour.

'Mrs Balfour is not seeing anyone today,' Potter told him.

'Then I'll see Mr Ramsay. Is he in?'

Ramsay was in the library and directed that Swinton be brought to him there.

'I won't take a moment of your time,' the caller said. 'But I just heard the tragic news and I came up to offer my services, if I can help in any way.'

'What tragic news?' Ramsay asked.

'About Mr Stone's death. It's in the evening papers.'

'Is it? I haven't seen the papers. I know about it, of course. It's good of you, Swinton, to call, but Mrs Balfour isn't seeing anyone. And I don't think there's anything to be done here. The funeral will be tomorrow afternoon. Shall you go?'

'Oh, yes. I've long admired that man's genius. Do you think they'll ever find Mr Balfour's murderer now?'

'Why, yes, I think so. Wiley's just been here. He didn't seem to have heard about Stone's death.'

'Didn't, eh? You know, Ramsay, between you and me, I've always had a feeling that Wiley might have been the murderer.'

'Good Lord! Why?'

'Well, for one thing, he hasn't any real alibi.'

'Be thankful you have, for they're suspecting lots of new people. You are sure about that time business of yours, aren't you?'

'Oh, yes. That is, I know I was in this house with Mrs Balfour at ten-twenty, and the doctors say that's the time poor Balfour was killed. But I've no need for an alibi. They are for criminals and I've heard they are always fakes. Ever found the valuable book?'

'No. But I think they have a trace of it.'

'That so? Well, let me put in a word while I can. If it ever turns up let me see it, won't you? Oh, I don't mean I want to buy it. I couldn't afford one page of it. But I'd like a look at it. Well, remember me kindly to Mrs Balfour and after things get more settled, I'll hope to call on her again with better luck. Mind, now, if I can do anything, let me know.'

So then he went away, and Ramsay sat meditating on the two men that came to see Alli.

Though he could never get anyone interested in the idea, Keith Ramsay had always thought there was a strong chance of one or other of them being the murderer, just because they lived in the same house as the Balfours. But, as he realized, Philip Balfour was not killed in that house, and so his theory had no rational foundation.

Alli did not come down to dinner, so Keith dined alone, lost in a maze of wonder at the moil of strange circumstances in which he found himself.

He tried to avoid looking into the future, for he well knew the police still suspected him of the murders and he had no idea what or when their next move would be.

The evening dragged along and at last Myra brought him a little note from Alli. She wrote she was still suffering the effects of her unpleasant experience and thought it wiser to wait until tomorrow before coming downstairs. But she added some words of affection and Keith Ramsay felt cheered and realized that he should have no sadness now that Alli was safely home again.

The next day the doctor was even more insistent that Mrs Balfour should be kept very quiet. She must not go downstairs at all. She could see Mr Ramsay or any intimate friend in her boudoir. She must not think of going to the funeral of Fleming Stone.

'You see,' the doctor said to Mrs Lane, 'Mrs Balfour is on the verge of a nervous breakdown and a nerve-racking scene like that tragic funeral might bring about her utter prostration.'

'Also,' the doctor added, 'she must not see the police people for some days yet. If they want to question her, it must be done through Mr Ramsay or Myra, or yourself, Mrs Lane. Keep her very quiet, and don't let her thoughts dwell on the last few days. Send her off on a longish motor ride today, accompanied by Mr Ramsay or some pleasant woman friend.'

These advices were carried out in part. Alli and Keith went for a short drive before luncheon and then Ramsay started for the funeral.

It was held in the private chapel connected with the mortuary company. Not many people were present for Fleming Stone was not of a gregarious nature.

The scene was solemn but not depressing. The lights were dim and as they shone on the white waxy face in the casket, it seemed to take on an ethereal radiance of its own.

A quiet, simple service, and after it was over the audience dispersed.

Andrew Knight, the cousin of Stone, introduced himself to Ramsay, whom he knew from description, and inquired as to Mrs Balfour.

Keith told him what the doctor had said and then the cover was put on the coffin and it was taken away.

Ramsay and Sewell went home together in one of the Balfour cars, but they said little about the outlook.

'Leave it to simmer a little,' Sewell advised. 'Then we can tell better where we are at.'

That very same night, Mr Powers, or the man who called himself Mr Powers, was lying in his comfortable bed in his New York apartment.

He was not sleeping, he had too much on his mind for that.

He was not altogether pleased with the way things had turned out at the house in the Palisades woods. But at any rate Fleming Stone was dead and he had no more to fear from that very inquisitive personage. And nobody could suspect him of any hand in the killing of the detective, for nobody knew the real identity of Mr Powers.

It was some time after midnight when he heard a faint sound. At least, he thought he did—and he sat up in bed, listening. But no one appeared and he heard no further sound so he concluded he was imagining and lay back on his pillows and closed his eyes.

Still sleepless, he moved uneasily and opened his eyes again to see a tall figure standing at the foot of his bed.

His nerves at high tension, he almost shrieked, for it seemed to him what he saw was an apparition, not a human visitor.

The personage was garbed in a long black robe, which threw off luminous glints as it moved, and the quaking man in the bed shivered with fear, for he was terrorized by any hint of the supernatural.

As he watched, he saw the figure wore a black mask, and a queer glitter shone through the eyeholes.

The thing drew nearer, and spoke in a faraway, hollow voice. 'Murderer!' was the only word that broke the silence.

But from the folds of the black drapery there came forth a long, bony hand—a skeleton hand, and its bones gave a faint rattle.

The fleshless forefinger pointed directly at him—it came nearer until it almost touched his face, and again came the whispered word—'Murderer!'

'Who are you?' cried the tortured listener. 'What do you want?'

'I want you! I am the ghost of the man you killed—I am the spirit of Fleming Stone!'

'Oh, spare me—leave me! Why are you here?'

'I am here to get your confession. Until you give me that, I shall haunt you, day and night—all your life!'

Nearer came the menacing shape, and the man in the bed cried out, 'I'll give you my confession! I'll do anything if you'll only go away!'

'You confess, then, that you murdered Fleming Stone? That you shot him down in cold blood? Why did you do that?'

'He knew too much—he would have told—'

'Told what? Tell it yourself! Confess that you murdered Philip Balfour and Guy Balfour, too.'

'I—I confess! Go—go—!'

The room was nearly dark, but sufficient light came in from the street to make visible the terrifying figure.

And now, the phantom slowly pulled away the mask it wore, disclosing the face of a grinning skull with deep, empty eye-sockets that yet showed a strange glitter from their depths.

'I am the man you killed,' the hollow whisper continued. 'I am the disembodied spirit of Fleming Stone and I am here now for the book you stole. Give me that, and I will leave you.'

The man moved as if to get up, but sank back in a spasm of fright.

'Coward!' was the scornful comment. 'Stay where you are, craven! Tell me where the book is and I will get it myself.'

'Then will—will you g-go away?'

'Yes. Where is the book?'

'In that French cabinet. In the middle division. Open the door; it isn't locked.'

The awful shape glided across the room to the escritoire and softly drew open the door of the central compartment.

'There is nothing here,' and the low tones were menacing.

'Yes, yes—feel up against the top—against the roof—'

Draped in the long black sleeve, a hand felt about inside the desk, and hidden from view, felt the book fastened up inside the top of the hiding-place. It was held by strips of paper, which soon gave way under pressure, and feeling certain that it was the right volume, the nocturnal visitor hid it somewhere in the folds of his robe and waved the rattling bones of his skeleton hand. Then he held some further conversation with his frightened victim and faded from sight.

At ten o'clock the next morning, a number of people had arrived at the Balfour apartment, by special invitation.

Inspector Manton and Captain Burnet were in charge of the

meeting, and Alli Balfour, seated between Keith Ramsay and John Sewell, seemed to have recovered her usual poise and serenity.

Preston Gill was there, and Wiley and Swinton, who lived in the house, and Henry Scofield, the Balfours' lawyer—quite a gathering in all.

Pete Wiley had at first refused to come, as he said he had been ordered out of the house, and forbidden to come again. But the police sent him a peremptory order to appear, and so he was among those present.

Inspector Manton began by saying he had at last learned who had killed Mr Philip Balfour and his son, Guy.

He said that the discovery of the criminal's identity was largely due to the clever detective work of Fleming Stone.

'And,' he said, further, 'I think that since the credit is Mr Stone's, that gentleman should be given the opportunity to tell about it himself.'

At this point a door opened and Fleming Stone walked calmly into the room.

Had anyone of the audience chosen to look about, he would have seen varying expressions of amazement, consternation and satisfaction on the faces of the group, but everyone was looking at the man who entered and had eyes for no one else.

'Perhaps,' Stone said, gravely, 'some of you are surprised to see me here. Others already knew that my death and funeral were merely pretence. But I discovered that the course I pursued was the only way to outwit the clever and ingenious villain who is responsible for two murders and who planned another. Who is also responsible for the theft of a very valuable book, which I have retrieved and am happy to give it back to its owner.'

Stone handed a small parcel to John Sewell, who eagerly opened it and nodded his head in confirmation of the book's identity.

'My work on this case is now finished,' Stone went on. 'I am a detective and I discovered the criminal. But I now turn the matter over to our police force, who will take what steps they think best.'

'I know,' Manton said, 'that you are all interested in this case, and that you want to know, first, who is the criminal, and second, how Mr Stone discovered his guilt. In answer to the first question, I order the arrest of Mr Carl Swinton for murder in the first degree and for robbery. If you have anything to say, Mr Swinton, I caution you that it will be taken down in writing and may be used as evidence. Do you wish to say anything?'

'Not here and not now,' was the reply, given in a scared and broken voice. 'You are all wrong, but I must get a lawyer before I undertake to prove my innocence.'

Several policemen appeared, there was considerable fluster and fight but after a short time Swinton was taken away, and, knowing he was safely in custody, Manton turned his attention to Stone.

'Tell us about it,' he said; 'we're eager for details.'

'It was a desperate case,' Fleming Stone replied. 'I have never known of a more determined and more evil-minded criminal. Nor a more ingenious brain for accomplishing his ends.'

'When did you first suspect him?' Manton asked.

'Not all at once. The conviction grew on me, although I couldn't imagine how he contrived things. But I think I felt positive when I went to Trentwood, where he used to live, and where the Balfours used to live. Do not be alarmed, Mrs Balfour,' for Alli's eyes showed a vague fear; 'we all know that you were engaged to Mr Swinton when you met Mr Balfour, and that you really threw over one man for the other. But I know, too, that you were about to break off your engagement to Swinton, anyway, and that the wooing of Philip Balfour only hastened it. It is my opinion that Carl Swinton is not entirely normal, but the doctors' examinations will settle that, I do not feel that he is insane or abnormal enough to explain his crimes that way. But the truth is that when you jilted him, as he expressed it, he declared he would some day get even. And when, later, you found your heart was not entirely devoted to your husband, but was given to Mr Ramsay—forgive me, but plain speaking is necessary to make all clear—when you found this out, he learned it, too, and he vowed to himself that he would make you suffer. He thought it over and concluded that the best way to bring sorrow to you was to get the man you cared for arrested, convicted and executed for a crime he did not commit. This is the true motive for Swinton's murder of Philip Balfour. He killed Guy, also, because the boy had found out the truth and was going to denounce him. He looked forward to complete success in his diabolical schemes and then I began to discover enough to make him fear exposure and he began a scheme to murder me. This plan was at the bottom of his renting the house over on the Palisades. It is a good house, but it has stood vacant for years. The last family who lived there included a woman afflicted with dementia praecox, and that explains the barred windows. Swinton rented the place, put in a couple of trusty caretakers, installed the dogs, and when the time was ripe he abducted Mrs Balfour and took her over there. Benson found out about that by his cleverness and perseverance, and of course I followed up his findings, and, as I fully expected, was made a prisoner myself.'

'A prisoner! In an old-fashioned frame house!' exclaimed Manton. 'With your experience and your prowess, it does seem as if you could have broken loose somehow! Couldn't you call the police? Fire a pistol? Do something to bring help?'

'Now, now, Inspector, think what you're saying! The first thing Sam did was to search for concealed weapons. Said Sam is an enormous piece of humanity, capable of twisting me into kindling-wood. I am not a timorous man, but I wouldn't care to try to get the better of that brute! As to calling anybody, I had no telephone and no means of communicating with the outside world. No, the simple bars and locks of that old house were just as impossible to negotiate as if it had been a medieval castle. And then, too, remember, I went there to get Mrs Balfour.

Even if I could have managed my own escape, I could not have carried her off under their noses! I had ample opportunity to think and I concluded some sort of trickery must be attempted.

'I learned from the man Sam, who was strong in muscle but not in brain, that Mrs Balfour was in the house, and I paid no attention to any plan of escape that did not include her. Of course, when Mr Powers, as Swinton called himself, kidnapped Mrs Balfour, he knew that if I discovered his hiding place I would follow to rescue the lady. And when I did so, I was lured into the barred rooms and the great, old-fashioned key turned upon me. And aside from saving my own life and that of Mrs Balfour, I had to pin the crime on him and produce evidence and proof of his guilt.'

'I'll say you were up against it,' Sewell remarked, sympathetically.

'Yes, I was. Of course, I managed to get out and to get Mrs Balfour out, but the great difficulty was to convict him of wrongdoing. He had come to the conclusion that he would never be safe from suspicion and discovery so long as I was in the world, so he concluded I must be put out of the world.

'This he would have succeeded in doing, had I not had a trusty young helper, a chap named Benson who is a marvel at obeying orders. I managed to communicate with him, got what I wanted and put over my somewhat desperate plan for getting away.'

'Tell us about the shooting,' urged Sewell. 'I can't get that.'

'I may as well admit,' Stone said, 'that it was not an entirely original plan with me. I lately read some French history, which chanced to include the story of Marshal Ney, that fiery aide of Napoleon's. You may remember he was sentenced to execution, but those members of the Assembly who voted for his death did so with the understanding that the sentence was to be commuted.

'It was Wellington who saved Marshal Ney's life. The firing squad were instructed to fire over his head, but not until he should give the signal by pressing his hand to his heart, by which action he burst a bag of red fluid secreted beneath his shirt. After falling in apparent death, he was hustled off by his friends, and history says he was helped away to our own South Carolina where he ended his days. I resolved on a similar plan, but circumstances being different, I provided myself with a bullet-proof undervest, and having selected a good one, Mr Swinton was balked of his plan. I had a cellophane bag of red fluid, which I managed to break as he fired, but not much was required, as a bullet in the heart does not cause a great gush of blood. Then Benson and another of my helpers rushed forward and took the "body" and I think by that time Swinton was so thoroughly scared, he ran for safety himself. This second helper of mine had already overcome Swinton's helper by a neat bit of jiujitsu and then we had nothing to do but collect Mrs Balfour and come home. I, being supposedly dead, could take only a silent role, but I was so gratified that the lady and myself were free at last that I was satisfied to rest on my laurels.

'I admit it was all a melodramatic stunt and I regret the necessity of it, but I could think of no other way. Swinton is a very strange man and has to be managed in unusual ways. He is childishly susceptible to fright at anything seemingly super-natural, so I knew that a visit to him last night as the ghost of Fleming Stone would put the fear of God in him—and it did. That was the way I got the book. It was he, of course, who came masked to Sewell's shop that night and killed Mr Balfour with the silver skewer, or skiver as some call it. He wore a derby and carried his fine soft hat in his pocket. After leaving, he dropped his derby in an ash-barrel and put on his customary soft hat. This was a bad move, for my smart Aleck traced the derby with no trouble at all.'

'What about this unimpeachable alibi?' asked Manton, who was listening, enthralled.

'I looked into that first thing. When he went into Mrs Balfour's reception room that night—going there straight from his killing of her husband—he waited for her to appear, and while waiting he set that little clock back twenty minutes. This made him *seem* to be there during the time of the stabbing, but he wasn't. Then just before he left he moved the hands of the clock back again to correct time. This I proved to my own satisfaction by having all the fingerprints on the clock looked into, and his were discovered amongst them. He would not have fingered that clock except for that purpose but I bided my time until I had stacked up enough bits of proof, then I plunged. I found out that he had ample opportunity to adjust that steam gauge, so that it resulted in the death of Guy Balfour. In fact, he had fixed up that deadly device for the purpose of killing Philip Balfour, and all he had to do was to set the door latch and adjust the steam regulator to bring about the murder of Guy. I got all this out of him last night, when I frightened him into confession.

'You ask me how I know all the minor details. I am a detective, and it is my business to detect. Some things I diligently dig for, some I overhear or learn by chance, some my helpers drag to light, and perhaps some things come to me intuitively. Also, one thing brings about another. I gathered from the first pasted note that the sender was a man extremely fastidious about having things straight and orderly. I went through Swinton's place, and I found stamp albums with every stamp in alignment as true as a die. The letters he sent out invariably had the stamps on straight. Everything he had to do with was so neat and orderly that I checked up a lot by that, even over in that awful house across the river. You knew, or suspected, didn't you, Mrs Balfour?'

'Yes,' Alli said, slowly. 'When you talked about straight lines and such things, I remembered that was like Carl in the old days. But I never dreamed he was so wicked. He told me more or less over there in that house before Mr Stone came. He said unless I would promise to marry him eventually, he would see to it that Keith was railroaded through—that's what he called it—and sent to the chair. He said he could do that. I don't like to think of the days over there.'

'You needn't, dear,' and Ramsay rose. 'We may be excused for a time, Inspector?'

'Yes, of course, and we must go now, too. I'll be over this afternoon for a short time to look into a few details, but I won't ask for you, Mrs Balfour, until absolutely necessary. Mr Stone will help us out a little further, I'm sure.'

So they all went away, except Stone and John Sewell, who stayed for a few minutes longer.

Fleming Stone was praised and applauded until he begged them to stop it.

'I'll tell you about my playing spook,' he said, 'and then we'll be jogging—eh, John?'

'All right,' Sewell agreed. 'Go ahead with the spook yarn. How did you get into his place? Down on the second floor, isn't it?'

'Yes; but as I could think of no other way to get that book I had to cut up that ridiculous trick.'

'Not ridiculous at all, if it served its purpose.'

'Well, I had a confab with the manager down in his office, and I showed him beyond all doubt that he could obstruct the course of justice and get himself into a moil of trouble, or he could act the part of a decent citizen and help to convict a murderer and thief. I made him see it right, and he lent me the duplicate key that he keeps in his safe, not a master key, you know, but a duplicate, such as he has for almost every apartment. So all I had to do was to bring my paraphernalia with me, slip it on in the hall outside Swinton's door, adjust my two masks, a black one and, beneath that, one made like a skull, and use my borrowed key to walk in.

'Swinton nearly died of fright. I doubt if any other pressure brought to bear would have made him give up the book. But in his pitiable, shuddering terror he told me where to find it. Such a clever hidy-hole! I might have stumbled on it myself, or it might never have been found. Pasted by paper straps up against the top, inside a compartment of a desk, invisible because of a piece of carved wood-work in front of it. Very clever work. Then, what nearly finished the frightened man, I had a skeleton hand with me, and covering my own hand with my robe, I pointed the articulated bones at him and he just about collapsed. Of course, since he thought he had killed me and had been to my funeral, you can't wonder at his belief in my reappearance from the dead.'

'Tell us more about that funeral,' urged Ramsay.

'That was too easy. Some years ago I had a wax bust of myself made. It is a perfect likeness, beautifully made and modelled just like me. So as I persuaded the mortuary people to look on it as a business deal, they agreed to put it over. It's been done before, and if it causes me some criticism, I'll stand it because of the results. I had to disappear or I never could have captured Carl Swinton. And after all he was about to kill me—'

'Why?' asked Alli, who, with Ramsay, had returned. 'Why did he want to kill you?'

'Because I knew too much. I had sized up the whole thing. I knew his motive, and yet I couldn't nail him nor make him confess. Had he succeeded in killing me, Mrs Balfour, he intended to keep you there until you had to marry him or be deeply compromised. As it is I still have his car, which I shall restore to him. But his two valuable dogs I cannot restore. I hate to kill an animal, but they had to be sacrificed to my own safety and that of my helpers. Tiny killed them with poisoned meat. He also had an atomizer of poison, but he didn't need that.

'Also, as to Guy. I burrowed into that matter until I learned almost positively that Swinton had planned and arranged the pressure gauge in order to kill Mr Balfour the way he afterward killed Guy. Swinton was here a good deal and he took his chance to fix things. Then, he decided to commit the crime elsewhere, but after he learned that Guy had found out quite a lot, he used the steam process on him. Swinton found opportunity that Sunday afternoon to slip into the steam room and set the gauge at the higher pressure. He may have gone up and down in a small private elevator that belongs to the Balfour suite of rooms, but he found a way. When I intimated this to him, I was sure from his looks and actions he was the criminal. He saw I knew this, so altogether he decided I must be snuffed out. But, somehow, he didn't quite pull it off.'

'Come along, Stone,' Sewell said, rising. 'We must get along and let these people have a chance to get calmed down. But I hope, Alli, all this excitement won't be too hard on you.'

'Not now,' and Ramsay smiled. 'We've hope for the future now, and plenty of time to make our plans.'

Stone and Sewell went off and walked down the avenue.

'You had to cut up that funeral hoax, I suppose?' Sewell said, musingly.

'Yes, John. Swinton never would have rested till he brought about my death. Nor would he be satisfied with anything but ocular evidence. With me dead, he could make up any story he chose and no one could contradict him. I had mighty few methods to choose from, I can tell you! But that Marshal Ney performance has always seemed to me a slick piece of business, and I have often felt it might come in handy on occasion. You see, I had ample opportunity to communicate with Benson. I could drop notes out of those barred windows and the lad always found them. That side of the house wasn't watched at all. In fact, Swinton was so sure of himself and his plans, it never occurred to him somebody else might be shrewd too. His only weakness, so far as I knew, was his fear of the supernatural. I am positive I could never have extorted his confession or retrieved the Button book except by that spook method.'

'You're a good one, Stone. I should have said the whole plan of yours was implausible, improbable and impossible. But you sure put it over. Was Alli terribly frightened?'

'I think she was, but when I arrived, she told me afterward, she felt sure I'd bring it all to a successful conclusion. I worked the old lady caretaker by means of the diamond bracelet, and cheap at the price. Sam had to be done up by the clever jiujitsu of that scientific fighter, Tiny. Sam's great bulk stood no chance against the twist that caused him to break his own leg. Well, I hope Swinton gets all that's coming to him, and that Mrs Balfour and Ramsay needn't wait too long to step into their earthly paradise.'

'Alli's a good girl,' said Sewell. 'I've known her from childhood.'

'A lovely lady,' Stone agreed, 'but she was to blame for the whole performance.'

'Just because she didn't know her own mind?' suggested Sewell.

'No; because she did. She was engaged to Swinton, but when the rich and influential Balfour came along, she jilted her fiancé. Then, not really loving her husband, when the fascinating librarian appeared she fell in love with him, and then Swinton, catching on, conceived his devilish plan of making her see the man she loved die in the electric chair for a crime of which he was innocent. One of the most fiendish motives I have ever run up against!'

'The most fiendish case all through!'

'Yes, and mark my word, that man will boast of it. To anyone who will listen, he'll crow over how clever he was and how smartly he hoodwinked the police and me. Of course, I'm not imagining all these things. I picked up a lot of knowledge here and there. Why, when I went to Trentwood, I learned much from the principals, who lived there only a few years ago. I learned how hardly Swinton took it when his girl threw him over, and that set me to work on that tack. She has acted nobly since her marriage, and when Ramsay came into the game, they both behaved honourably, telling Balfour about it and all that.'

'Well, I'm mighty glad I called you in, or I don't know where

Keith Ramsay would be now, and, too, I don't know where this blessed book would be!' Sewell patted his breast pocket where the small volume lay in safety.

And at that very moment Ramsay was saying to the woman he loved:

'Bless the kind fate that sent Fleming Stone to our aid. Otherwise we might have no future to look forward to.'

'Don't refer to such things. Come, my Keith, let's go for a walk, without a care as to who sees us or what they think of us. We are free at last from all suspicion or criticism.'

And, smilingly, they went out into the clear bright autumn sunshine.

THE END

THE SHAKESPEARE
TITLE-PAGE MYSTERY

'THAT's the way with you collectors! You were just crazy with joy when you got a first *Leaves of Grass* in wrappers. And now you want a first *Venus*, and I don't suppose you care whether she has her wrapper on or not!'

'I do want a first *Venus and Adonis*, but I have not forgotten my other treasures—my true first—'

'I know, your 'fifty-five *Alice*—'

'No, Sherry,' Herenden corrected him gently. ''Fifty-five *Leaves* and 'sixty-five *Alice*. You know nothing of rare books.'

'Rare! Rare!' Young Sherry Biggs enjoyed heckling those two famous collectors, Garrett Sheldon and Leigh Herenden, their host. 'Why is a thing valuable because it's rare? An honest man is rare, does anyone care for him? A good woman is rare, who collects those? O Boy! As Shakespeare says in *Merry Wives*, Three, four, thirty-six, you collectors are an unmixed evil. This craze for rare books breeds crime. You're always guarding against theft.'

'No, Sherry,' his host smiled at him, 'you're wrong there. I've guarded my treasures once and for all. Want to see my book room?'

Like many another good American, whose wealth piled itself up after the manner of Ossa on Pelion, Leigh Herenden had built a house for himself on Long Island, and the library occupied a large wing. They had to go down two or three steps to it, as seems to be the case with most self-respecting libraries.

'Your stenographer is a pretty girl,' Sherry Biggs noticed in passing.

'Muriel Jewell,' Herenden said carelessly. 'I have little to do with the girl. I've little to do, anyhow. Herbert Rand is my secretary, and Gorman is my confidential book-buyer.'

'It must be nice,' Sheldon said, musingly, 'to have a lynx-eyed librarian like Gorman to nose out rare volumes for you. But somehow, I'd feel I was losing half the fun if I didn't make my own discoveries.'

'Everyone to his taste,' Herenden conceded, and his grey eyes were kindly, with no hint of criticism. 'I know,' he went on, 'there is a noble sentiment that decrees "not the quarry, but the chase; not the laurel, but the race", and yet, I do not enjoy poking around in the rare bookshops as much as I do having my quarry in hand.'

He led the way into a steel-lined safe, the size of a small room, and showed Sherry its hidden devices to balk both the moth that corrupts and the thief who breaks through and steals. As Sheldon was about to leave, Herenden turned to him.

'I have an announcement to make this afternoon.'

'I'll stay, then,' his neighbour and rival collector decided. Garrett Sheldon had a feeling that the news would concern a new acquisition to the already famous Herenden library, and he prepared himself to feel jealous pangs, which he would conceal at all cost . . .

'You know,' Leigh Herenden began that afternoon, 'that among other favourites, I am specializing in Shakespeare. And only now have I been able to find a first edition of *Venus and Adonis*.'

Their excited hubbub of questions and exclamations obliged him to pause.

'Go on!' cried Sheldon. 'Don't stop at the most interesting point! Where did you get it? And—' he almost said, 'how much did you pay for it?' but changed his question to—'how did you hear of it?'

'It was a heaven-sent boon,' Herenden smiled happily. 'I was asked if I wanted it, and I said I did.'

'I'll bet there was something shady about your getting it!' Sherry Biggs exclaimed.

'Maybe.' Herenden showed no offence. 'If so, I sin in company with Cardinal Mazarin. I have read on good authority that "a little pilfering here and there was never known to upset Mazarin—if the book he coveted was worthy of it".'

Sherry turned up his youthful nose.

'Anybody would think it was a Gutenberg Bible you were talking about.'

'A real first edition of *Venus and Adonis* is worth more than a Gutenberg Bible, if you are speaking of money value.' Herenden gave Sherry a glance of reprimand.

'But I happen to know that the first and second editions of the book you are talking about are exactly alike, except for the date. Now, how can it matter which one you possess?'

'You know very well that, to a collector, age is the pre-eminent point of value. Age in a book is much the same as youth in a woman.'

'Such a fuss about books!'

'But where is your book, Leigh?' asked Garrett Sheldon. 'Seeing is believing.'

'Sorry, but I can't show it today. It isn't yet tuned to the atmosphere of my collection. Come back Sunday night and see "the first heir of my invention". You'll covet it, I know.'

'Hardly that! As I have one of my own. A real one.'

'You have a first *Venus and Adonis*! I never knew that!'

'A fine copy, too.'

'Bring it with you to the party tomorrow night. We'll show off together.'

After the guests had gone, Herenden said to Gorman, his book-buyer and librarian, with a perplexed air, 'Did you hear Sheldon say he had a first?'

'I did, Mr Herenden, but it can't be possible.'

'No, I suppose not. Of course, people in England are glad to sell their books over here just now. But another first *Venus*! It can't be.'

'Unless somebody found a nest—'

'Don't be silly, Gorman. They didn't have nests in those days.'

'No, sir. But Mr Sheldon must have something. Could it be a faked copy?'

'Oh, no. That book is too well known to be faked. There were thirteen or more editions, and every copy is located. We know where each one is, though, of course, the later editions are of far less value. Keep the secret, Gorman—don't let anybody know where our book came from. Some day, perhaps I may tell.'

'I've told no one, sir. Not even Rand knows where it came from.'

'It is a wonderful find. Sheldon couldn't have got one the same way, could he?'

'Not likely. Such things don't happen often.'

'And the lad is all right? He won't tell?'

'Oh, no! He won't even remember it.'

'If ever the proper time comes, I shall tell the whole story, and give up the book. But you won't suffer, I promise you. All I've given you, you may keep, and I shall give you more if all goes well. I suppose I'm an accessory before the fact. Even so, I assume all responsibility, and if we are found out, no blame shall attach to you. You have confidence in Baines?'

'Oh, yes, sir. He has no idea it is a valuable book. He is more than satisfied with what you paid him.'

'Am I interrupting a private confab?' Rand's cheery voice was followed by his appearance.

'Not at all,' Herenden replied, a trifle coldly. 'Come in. What is it?'

'Only this, Mr Herenden. May I have the afternoon off? I've got the desk cleared and I'd like to go to the golf tournament; a friend of mine is playing today.'

'Certainly, Rand. You are a wizard at finishing your work, I must say. By the way, Rand, can you be here tomorrow evening? I'm going to show my new *Venus* to some admiring friends, and you know where everything is.'

'So does Gorman. But just as you say, Mr Herenden.'

Rand left them, and Gorman said, 'Do you suppose he heard

what we were saying? He's a quick fellow, and we were talking pretty plainly.'

'Don't worry about it. And now I'm off to the golf tournament myself. Put the time lock on the safe, if you go out.'

After Herenden had gone, Gorman went to the safe, where he could have found any book in the dark, had it been necessary. He took down the *Venus and Adonis*.

Back again in the library, he sat down to gloat over the acquisition—a small volume, measuring a bit over seven inches one way, and a trifle over five the other. Its cover was of old calf, worn and rubbed, a little soiled, and showing no title or legend of any kind.

Ralph Gorman was a practical man He opened the book with intense interest but with no feeling of reverence, and read the title-page. *Venus and Adonis*. Then some lines in Latin, which he did not understand. Then the information that the book was printed by Richard Field—in 1593.

Just those four figures gave the tiny volume its worth. A fourth edition of the *Venus* had once sold at auction for $75,000. Rare books had gone up in price since then. And what would a first sell for? His eyes widened. He knew of several men in these United States who would gladly pay more—a great deal more—than $100,000 for this plain little book!

He put the precious volume back in the case which Herbert Rand had made for it. Rand was clever with books. He did any necessary repairing—Herenden knew better than to have any unnecessary repairing done—and he could collate with neatness and dispatch.

Gorman pored over Herenden's reference works on rare books. Yes, the second edition of the *Venus* was exactly the same as this first, save for the date, 1594, on the title page. The first edition was 'printed with remarkable accuracy, doubtless from the author's manuscript'. The only known copy was in the Bodleian Library at Oxford, and many facsimiles had been made from it.

Aha! thought Gorman, that's it! Mr Sheldon has a facsimile and he thinks he can put it over on us! We'll see about that!

On Sunday evening the party came. Most of Leigh Herenden's friends were interested in books, for one reason or another, and many of the guests were collectors. Others were writers or playwrights or actors. They all knew enough of the situation to be eager to see the two books that were to be shown.

Garrett Sheldon came in, bringing a stranger, whom he introduced to Herenden. 'Malcolm Osborne,' he said, 'and I warn you, Leigh, he knows his first editions from the ground up. He can decide which of us has the real first.'

'Very kind of Mr Osborne,' Leigh said, politely. 'You have your book with you, Sheldon? Gorman will bring mine.'

As the librarian returned from the safe room with Herenden's copy, Sheldon produced his volume.

'After you,' Herenden said.

Sheldon opened a dark-red morocco case and took out his book.

It was impossible to misinterpret the murmur of surprised disappointment that rippled through the room. Two or three young people even laughed, but Garrett Sheldon winked at Herenden and said, 'I assure you that this little book makes up in worth what it lacks in size.'

As the crowd surged toward him, he handed the book to Leigh Herenden. And it certainly looked like the real first edition of *Venus and Adonis*. Gorman, standing by him, looked at it too, and they were both startled by the verity of it, or the perfection of imitation, whichever it might be.

'And now,' said Sheldon, smiling, 'where's yours, Leigh?'

Gorman, feeling queer, as he said afterward, passed Herenden's book to him. Removing the case, the host offered the volume to his guest.

Sheldon took it smilingly, looked it over rather carelessly, and placed it on the table beside the one he had brought.

'They look alike,' he said slowly.

They did look alike—almost exactly. Two small, seemingly insignificant books, both bound in old calf, both dark brown and worn at the edges and corners. Nondescript affairs, with no physical charm or beauty.

'May I open this?' Herenden smiled.

'Indeed, yes. I'll look into yours, then we'll turn them over to Osborne, and ask his opinion.'

Gorman stayed beside Herenden as they looked at the title-page. Both were amazed at its perfectness. Surely those figures were neither facsimiles nor fakes. Sheldon must have achieved the miracle of getting another first at the same time Herenden acquired his.

Sheldon and Osborne had their heads together over the other book.

'This is yours, Mr Herenden?' and Osborne tapped the old brown binding.

'Yes, Mr Osborne.'

'You don't care to tell where you got it?'

'I'd rather not. You find no flaw in it?'

'Sorry, but I most decidedly do. It has an entire new title-page for one thing, there is a fly-leaf missing, and it has been rebound. That's all I can see without a magnifying glass, but it is enough to prove to my mind that you were badly hoaxed. Have you had any other expert examine it?'

'No, but I have absolute confidence in it.'

'Absolute confidence, Mr Herenden, is a fine thing. I wish you had it in me, for what I tell you is true. While I hate to displease you, I think you should know the facts, whether you like them or not.'

'You are quite right, Mr Osborne, and I thank you. But I am sure this is boring our other guests. Shall we go to the living room?'

After the guests had departed, Herenden turned to his librarian with a face of utter wonder.

'What does it mean, Gorman?' he said.

'I'd like to think there's been some jiggery-pokery and the books were switched—but that's impossible, Mr Herenden.'

'Yes; mine has been in the safe room ever since I have had it. It *is* my book, isn't it, Gorman?'

'No doubt about it, sir. Here's your bookplate, that I put in myself. And here's that old inkspot on the back cover. It's faint, but we decided it was ink, didn't we?'

'Oh, yes, I remember. We decided that anything used to remove it would make a worse stain.'

'Yes, sir. And Mr Osborne says this whole title-page is new. It doesn't look so to me. But you must remember, sir, that when you—er—bought the book, you were given no guarantee of its genuineness—'

'That is quite true.' Herenden smiled now. 'All the same, I shall not rest until I am certain about the matter. I want to have another expert pass on it. Osborne may be all right, but there's no one in the world with the knowledge of old books that Kent has.'

'Kent?'

'Yes. The English statesman. He's in this country now on diplomatic affairs, but if anything would interest him, this matter will. I'll set about getting him.'

Herenden did set about it, and secured Godfrey Kent's promise to visit him and stay overnight. Herenden was so elated that he invited Sheldon to come and hear the final decision from the great man.

Sheldon came, and Herenden sent his car to meet Kent at train after train. He telephoned to New York and found that Godfrey Kent had left his hotel about five o'clock, intending to visit him. But the last train passed, and the Herenden chauffeur brought back an empty car.

'Some official business turned up, I suppose.' Leigh Herenden hid his disappointment as Sheldon smiled and told him good night.

The next morning a visitor arrived early. Herenden hurried into his clothes and went down to meet him.

'I'm Pierson,' the stranger announced, 'of the New York Police. Do you know Godfrey Kent? He was found dead in the woods along the Palisades. Brutally murdered. He had your address in his pocket.'

'What a terrible thing! It seems incredible.' Herenden told how Kent had intended to visit him. 'Gorman,' he called, 'Mr Kent has been murdered.'

'On account of the book?' Gorman said impulsively.

'What book?' the detective asked quickly. 'The notes with your address seemed to refer to some play by Shakespeare.'

'A poem.' Herenden nodded, and told the story of his *Venus* with the doubtful title-page.

'May I see it?' Pierson compared the book with Kent's type-written notes which were headed *Re V. and A.* 'This says the true book must have two fly-leaves in front, and two in back. I find only one in the back of your copy, Mr Herenden.'

'I fear my book is not a real first after all.'

'When you got that book, Mr Herenden,' Gorman said, firmly, 'it had two fly-leaves in the back. Somebody must have torn one out!'

'Easy now, Mr Gorman,' Pierson said, in his common-sense way. 'Someone has done more than damage a fly-leaf. Now, if you will give me the name of Mr Kent's New York hotel, it will help the Homicide Bureau. Confidentially, we think the murderer was a hired thug.'

He left Herenden shuddering.

'I hope,' Gorman said grimly, 'that they get the fellow.'

When Pierson came back to the Herenden house, he was greeted like a long-lost brother.

'Any luck?' Herenden asked, after the detective had been made comfortable in the library.

'The answer is yes. First of all, we have the hired gunman who murdered Mr Kent. We haven't found out yet who is back of the crime, but we will. I have a pretty definite notion myself.'

'What did you learn about the book?' Herenden could hold off no longer.

'I went to the Public Library and to several other libraries, and I can face the examiners as to Shakespeare's earliest printed work. I hate to hold out, Mr Herenden, but I have suspicion of a crime against you. Let me get my bearings.' Pierson rose. 'This is your library. There is your safe room. Here is your office. Now we make our real start. Which desk is whose? I must look into them all. Much may be learned from a desk.'

Gorman became their usher, and Pierson worked methodically. He went through the desks quickly, yet seemed to see all their contents. He smiled at the stenographer's, which held a complete beautifying outfit and an old copy of *The Adventures of Sherlock Holmes*. Then he passed on to Rand's desk.

'Meticulous chap here, and a good book-keeper. Not a blot nor erasure in his work. And his handwriting tells his character. See, not a flourish or unnecessary stroke. You trust him completely?'

'I'd trust Rand and Gorman with my life, liberty, and pursuit of happiness, and I'd come out on top.'

'All right. Now, Mr Herenden, I want to go over to see Mr Sheldon.'

As he left, Muriel Jewell, the stenographer, came into the library.

'Mr Herenden,' she began, 'I didn't mean any harm, I only meant—'

'Miss Jewell, if you have a confession to make, and it sounds like that, please tell us frankly what it is all about.'

'I didn't think it was wrong—'

Just then Sherry Biggs came in. He was a privileged visitor, and he helped himself to a chair and a cigarette.

But Muriel had lost courage for the confession she wanted to make. 'Oh,' she said, 'Mr Herenden, please let him stay long enough to tell me something. It's this, Mr Biggs,' she went on, as Herenden nodded permission. 'You were talking about our slang phrases being in Shakespeare. Did he really write, "I'll tell the world"?'

'*Measure for Measure*, Two, four, one fifty-four.'

'And did he really make up "Not so hot"?'

'Sure thing: *King Lear*, Five, three, sixty-seven.'

'And—'

'That's enough. You can find all these things in a Shakespeare Concordance. Hello, here comes the policeman. Want me to go away, Mr Herenden? Why don't you have some arras in this room—they're so nice to hide behind.'

'Arras are not plural, Sherry. Arras is the name of a place in France, famous for its tapestries.'

'Must I go, Mr Herenden?'

'Sorry. Run along now, Sherry.'

Young Biggs went off, and Muriel was sent out of the office as they heard Pierson returning. She spoke to him in the hall.

'Tell me that again!' he said.

She told him, and he grinned.

'We've got 'em!' he cried. 'Sure you can remember?'

'Oh, sure. Five, nineteen, thirty-three, forty-seven.'

'Marvellous, Holmes, marvellous! How do you do it?'

'Just add fourteen each time. See?'

'Faintly. Whoever would have believed you could do a thing like that?'

'Do you think Mr Herenden will be mad at me?'

'Mad! He'll give you a medal!'

Two red spots burned in Muriel's cheeks as Pierson insisted that she set forth with him on the great quest of the *Venus*. The entire library staff was drafted for a short and pleasant march over to the Sheldon house. Pierson led off, escorting Miss Jewell; they were followed by Herenden and Herbert Rand; Gorman brought up the rear.

When they reached the house, Pierson rang the bell. The door opened, and he saw to it that all the others were inside the house before he went in himself. Sheldon greeted them in some surprise.

Without preamble, Pierson said, 'Mr Sheldon, I am here to charge you with taking a book that belongs to Mr Herenden, and claiming it as your own; also, with putting in its place a book of similar character, but of far less value.'

'That is a strange charge to make, Mr Pierson, and I deny it!'

'Will you produce the copy of *Venus and Adonis* which is now on your shelf?'

Sheldon brought the volume.

'I will first,' Pierson said, 'show you that this copy is changed and amended to make it look like the other, and then I will tell you what happened to the books. This,' he picked up the one that Sheldon had given him, 'is a real 1593 edition of *Venus and Adonis*. Except for this, there is only one copy known, and that is in the Bodleian Library at Oxford. But all present know the details of this first edition. You know that the second or 1594 edition is exactly like this except for the date on the title-page. As you see these two books now, they both appear to be dated 1593. But while this one is a true 1593, the other is a 1594, which has been supplied with a new title-page, dated 1593. This title-page, in order that it should be of the right paper, was made of one of the fly-leaves, taken from the back of the book. This in itself gives away the fake, for often the fly-leaves of old books were of a trifle thicker paper than the rest of the book, as is the case in this instance. The volume was taken apart, the new title-page put in place and the old one discarded, the book rebound—in its own binding, of course, and that part was done so neatly that it is almost unnoticeable. I accuse Mr Sheldon of doing this work, or having it done, for the purpose of exchanging his own made-over book for the honest-to-goodness 1593 of Mr Herenden's. The switch was made on Sunday afternoon, before Mr Herenden's party.'

'You have heard a tissue of lies,' Sheldon began, but it is not wise to call a detective a liar. Also, though Sheldon did not know it, two other men had entered the room, behind him. They were the Assistant District Attorney and another police official.

'You still insist that this 1593 copy is your book, Mr Sheldon?'

'I certainly do!'

'There are some peculiar designating marks on the pages here and there. Suppose you tell me what and where they are?'

'That's a trap, and I do not intend to fall into it. I put no marks in my most valuable books.'

'No? Well, Miss Jewell put marks in Mr Herenden's copy, before you appropriated it for your own. They are tiny marks, which, if they are still present, prove positively that this is Mr Herenden's book. What pages did you mark, Miss Jewell?'

'I can tell you the pages, but the marks are so small I doubt if you can see them. I used a very sharp penknife to scratch the tails off certain commas on certain pages. This turned them into full stops, you see.'

'Why did you do this?'

'Only that there might be a positive identification if anything happened to Mr Herenden's book. The defects of those comma-tails are scarcely noticeable.'

'Can you tell me on what pages you made these erasures?'

'Oh, yes—five, nineteen, thirty-three, forty-seven.'

'I can't look them up as fast as that. How do you remember them?'

'I added fourteen each time.'

'I see. Now, I am looking on page five, but I can't find a tailless comma.'

'Haven't you a lens? A document lens? Here is one.'

She handed over the lens, and the tailless commas showed up.

Pierson then drew attention to the bookplates. 'You rather

slipped up here, too, Mr Sheldon. Mr Gorman is too particular to use glue on a bookplate. He uses paste.'

'That is a special gum I use on my own bookplates. I know nothing of what Mr Herenden has on his.'

'Well, then, note this. With this document lens I can see clearly the gum at the edges of the bookplate in both volumes. Moreover, this glass shows me that you used a blotter to press down the bookplate. This made the gum ooze out a bit, and it caught a little purple fuzz from the blotter.'

'What's all this nonsense?' Rand suddenly looked angry. 'Who used blotters to mount a bookplate? I never heard of such a thing!'

'You hear of it now,' Pierson told him. 'Take this glass. Look at the gum and the specks of purple blotter on the edges of these two bookplates.'

'He knows all about it,' Sheldon said, suddenly. 'He put in those bookplates, both of them. He was over here helping me one day, and he put in a lot of bookplates for me. I hate to do it myself. And I assume he may put in bookplates for Mr Herenden.'

'Do you know, Rand,' said Pierson, 'I believe you can't do better than to spill the whole business.'

Rand looked frightened. 'How can you ever pay me or pay for your book, Mr Sheldon?' he almost groaned. 'The second, you know.'

'Squeal on me, will you, you young thief! Then I'll beat you to it. That is your book, Mr Herenden—Rand thought it would be a fine thing to do what he calls a switch. He—'

'That will do, Sheldon.' Herenden assumed charge. 'Herbert, tell the whole story, briefly and truly.'

'Yes, Mr Herenden. Mr Sheldon said he knew where he could get a second edition of *Venus and Adonis*—just like the first, except for the date. He said if I would fix that, he would pay me a thousand dollars to have a new title-page printed, using one of the fly-leaves. And he made me make a sort of stain on the back cover, like the ink stain on your book. He got me in deeper and deeper. He said if I didn't obey him, he'd tell you and make it all seem my doing. And he made me switch the books on Sunday afternoon, before the guests came.'

'Where did Mr Sheldon get his second edition?' Herenden asked.

'I bought it.' Sheldon was now trembling. 'I intended to pay for it from the proceeds of the one which I took from you.'

'And now you have spoiled that second edition, which you still owe for, and you have nothing to pay with.'

'That's about the size of it.'

'Hand over Mr Herenden's property to him,' Pierson said, sternly.

'Let him take it himself,' Sheldon screamed, as Herenden did so. 'You can't prove it's your property. You're afraid to tell where you got it.'

One of the men at the back of the room interrupted him.

'Mr Sheldon, it's for you to tell us what you had to do with the murder of Godfrey Kent.'

Sheldon collapsed as he recognized the Assistant District Attorney, who took him in custody and kept Herbert Rand for further questioning.

Sherry Biggs was passing as the others left that stricken house. He took Muriel off for a drive, to teach her more Shakespearean slang. Herenden took the path home, with his true first *Venus*, flanked by faithful Gorman and Pierson.

'I want to tell you about my book,' Leigh told the man who had helped them, 'though it's really Gorman's story. What was your English cousin's name, Gorman?'

'Baines. He's my second cousin. One night there was an unusually heavy air raid over London, and many homes fell to the ground. The next day, when Baines was walking around the ruins, he saw a chap sitting on a bit of fallen timber, reading an old book. The boy offered to sell it to him.'

'Baines knew nothing about old books, but he knew Gorman

did. So he sent it to America, saying that if we liked such silly old things, to sell it and send him half of whatever it brought.'

'How did he get the book over here?' Pierson was deeply interested.

'Baines wrapped it up in newspaper and gave it to a lad who was coming over—a refugee. He sent word to Gorman what ship the boy was on. Gorman met the boy, took the book, and brought it to me. Here it is. Now, let me hear your opinion as to the ethics of all this. We don't know in whose ruined library the book was found, and we've no way of finding that out. So, what can I do but keep it?'

'Until the war is over and we can trace the real owner, it is your book, Mr Herenden. The precious little volume is also a refugee, and a refugee is ever a sacred trust.'

THE END